STEPHANIE HUDSON

Wrath's Siren
Lost Siren Series #3

Published by Hudson Indie Ink
www.hudsonindieink.com

Wrath's Siren/Stephanie Hudson – 1st ed.
ISBN-13 - 978-1-913904-22-7

As a huge animal lover myself, I dedicate this book to all the animal shelters and charities out there that tirelessly take care of abused, mistreated or abandoned pets and work so hard at trying to find them a new home. I was the kind of kid that brought every injured animal home to try and nurse back to health and the reason my parents came back to find two baby ducks in the bath. So, when I talk about Roger in this book, I can assure you, no cats were harmed when researching this book...

I love cats.

Roger loves no one.

PROLOGUE
DEATH OF A DREAM

"T*his can't... be possible,"* I muttered, like some mindless idiot as the elevator doors closed after I finally made it to my floor and stepped from what felt like one of my many dreams of... *Him.*

My Enforcer.

Alright, so he wasn't exactly mine, he was Raina's Enforcer and until right at that moment, then both of them had been fictional.

My hero and heroine, the characters of my epic love story.

Both of them total fabrications, thanks to my overactive mind that had been dreaming of their story for the last six years. A dream that had been my obsession and become the core of my existence.

But now here I was, after just witnessing my hero in

the flesh, making me now question everything! Because if he was who I thought he was, something I felt down to my very soul, then there was only one thing left to do and that was…

Run for my life.

Because he may have been the hero in my books, but in real life he was, without a single shred of doubt, one scary son of a bitch! A powerful Demon ruler who lived on Earth, known as one of the Enforcers, who was ready to kill any mortal that stood in his way. Say, like a human girl who foolishly wrote a book about him and his world, had it published and now could have quite possibly become the most hunted girl on the planet should any of his people find out!

Oh yeah, *I was so screwed!*

Because this wasn't the happy ever after story of two lovers united.

This was no longer the story of Kaiden Wrath and his Siren, Raina Ashton.

No this was now about my own story and in it…

I was the foolish Author hunted by…

The Enforcer I was obsessed with.

The Demon Lord I secretly loved.

CHAPTER I
MUCH MORE THAN AN AUTHOR
EMMELINE

"Yes, yes, just stop beeping at me!" I snapped at the inanimate object that was my alarm, and its hopeless endeavors at trying to warn me that I needed to be up for something important. But after hitting snooze about five times, it finally started to sink in what that something was, and it was at this point I bolted upright and started the day swearing like a sailor!

"Shit! Shit, shit, shitty, shit, shit!" Of course, this usual late morning mantra never really helped me as I scrambled to get dressed, grabbing the first things I could find.

"Damn it, jeans… No, knickers then jeans!" I told myself as I raided my drawers, trying to find anything that didn't come with a stretchy waist band. But then this was tricky as, admittedly, it made up for about sixty percent of my wardrobe… oh, who was I kiddin'? About seventy-five, maybe eighty. But then again, I worked from home and basically lived life like a hermit crab, just a single camping trip away from being a fully-fledged cave dweller.

Okay, so slight exaggeration with that one, as I lived in the busy town of Manchester, England. But working from home did have some advantages, like only needing makeup about once a week when my best friend made me leave my flat to partake in the art of social interaction. It was for my own good, she would say, just in case I ever felt the need to join the rest of them in the joys of living. Of course, I would laugh this off, secretly cringing and wishing I was back at home and immersed in my own world.

One of fiction.

One where he ruled.

My not-so-secret obsession. Not now that I actually got up the guts to publish my first book just over a year ago. Unfortunately, it didn't do well enough to pay all my bills, but it was enough to give me a little nest egg, while my actual job as a freelance product writer paid for those pesky little things, like food and electric. A job that admittedly bored the shit out of me, hence why I wrote fiction the rest of the time. But according to my friend Natalie, this was most of my time, and it was the way I liked it. And if I were honest, then Nat wasn't wrong but then again, she wasn't wrong about most things… well, other than trying to set me up with her brother Mark.

Mark was an asshole.

No, not just an asshole, he was 'The Asshole'. Like if there was a place called Assholeville, it would have been named after him and he would have been mayor there. Yes, it was safe to assume asshole Mark had done a number on me. The type of number that made me believe that I meant something to him, only to find out that I didn't in the worst and most humiliating way.

Yay me, *today was going to be fun then*, I thought with a grimace, knowing he would be there. But of course he would, it was his sister's wedding after all.

"Fuck! What am I doing?!" I groaned, stopping mid-way through pulling up my jeans and realizing I was supposed to be getting ready for a wedding!

"Ah ha!" I shouted, grabbing the garment bag hung over my dressing gown from the back of my door. Then, as I stepped back, I felt something soft and squishy, falling sideways in order to save my cat. One that hissed at me and this time, I couldn't say I blamed him.

"Piss off, Roger!" I snapped, knowing the cat hated me.

"Get a cat, everyone said. It would make a great pet, everyone said," I muttered to myself as he hissed at me again, making me give him the finger. Although as usual, this had no effect. But then, also as usual, I felt guilty, so grabbed a packet of the stupid expensive cat food I had no idea why I bought... maybe at one time I'd thought I could buy the damn cat's affections. As for now, well I was just stuck buying the same brand because he goes on an eating strike if I don't. And though our relationship was one of love/hate, I didn't want the little bugger to starve. I was actually an animal lover, despite getting some demon cat that I swear sometimes looked more like it was plotting my death than cleaning its paws.

Well thankfully it hadn't clawed my bridesmaid's dress, one that was bright white, as the bride herself was wearing the unconventional red. It also kind of reminded me a little like a tonga style, with its swathes of floaty material tied to one side, pulled in at the waist with a gold band of silk and a starburst of crystals. It was floor-length with a slit up one leg, and I thankfully remembered to shave last night.

However, my not so saving grace was my hair, which was a riot of white-blonde, tight curls that didn't do as they were told… as in ever! And because of this, Nat and I had agreed it'd be best if I wore a wig, so that my hair, combined with my pale skin, wouldn't just make me look like a ghost in all the pictures. My image tended to get washed out in the daylight and this combined with wearing white, well we both knew it screamed disaster!

So, I twisted all my hair up as best I could, and donned the sleek honey blonde wig that was already styled into soft waves down my back. I continued to stuff little curls up into it as I looked around my pokey little flat, trying to find my much-needed shoes.

"Emme Raidne, you can do this," I told myself,

already feeling the nerves kick in about seeing Mayor Asshole again. I wondered how I had managed to go six years without seeing him, considering he was my best friend's older brother. But then again, I had thrown myself into my writing since then. Of course, Nat didn't know the full extent of our breakup, I didn't want to do that to her. I didn't want to break her heart that way, as I know she would never have forgiven him for what he did to me. Fuck, but she would have cut his balls off, family or not!

So, with this in mind, I took extra care with my makeup, being thankful that I had nice skin at least. Despite it most likely needing some Vitamin D as it was looking rather pale. Something that made my big brown eyes look even darker, but then again, this could have been thanks to the thick, dark lashes I had inherited from my mother, who had been half Greek. This had been according to my nanna, who had brought me up after my parents died in a boating accident when I was only a baby.

Naturally, I didn't remember them, but my nanna made sure I had memories of a different kind. She filled my head with stories of how they met and fell in love, declaring them as soul mates. That them dying together was a kindness as neither would have been able to live without the other, had I not been around of course. In all honestly, I think telling me this story gave her more comfort than it did for me. But then again, it was most likely why I wrote the love stories the way I did.

As for the rest of me, I was little like my nanna, being

only five feet tall, and relied heavily on heels so I didn't look like Gimli from Lord of the Rings next to his elf friend, Legolas. Nat, who was a whopping ten inches taller than me, could have used my head as an arm rest. She was also on the slim side of tall and looked more like a super model. As for me, I was her curvy little friend who was a few muffins away from needing stretchy granny knickers to make my belly flat. Thankfully, my waist went inwards, and the little pouch didn't yet overhang the waistband of my undies, but damn… *it was close.*

As for my breasts, well, they were a good D-cup handful, so not too big that I got backache from carrying them around all day. But unlike Nat, I could fill out a corset with the best of them, so I wasn't complaining. Now, as for my little legs and wide hips, then yeah, I could complain about them all day long, I thought as I stuffed my little feet into four-inch heels.

"Bag, bag, ba… ah, there you are!" I said, muttering to myself as I usually did because well, I lived alone and could get away with it. Plus, who was going to complain? Not Roger… he hated me anyway. I gave my flat one more look, and it resembled something a tornado had picked up and plonked down in the land of Oz. My clothes had spilled out of my bedroom, that admittedly only had enough space for a double bed, one bedside table and a built-in wardrobe that definitely wasn't big enough. It was also a horrible pink colour that I hadn't been allowed to paint because I would have lost my renter's deposit, because I didn't even own this craphole I called a home.

This also meant that I had to fight with my landlord every time something went wrong with the place, like when the taps leaked and left stale water around the top of the sink. Or the brown stains on the carpet when I first moved in, with the promise someone was going to come and replace it but never did. However, this was the price I had paid to live more cheaply so I could pursue my dream of becoming a full-time author.

Which meant take-outs were down to once every two weeks, no more gym membership, drinking wine was a luxury and reserved for birthdays, and a one-bedroom tiny flat with a living space I couldn't swing Roger in—although why would I as I would most likely get my face torn off? So I therefore ignored my little sofa, basic flatscreen, and corner desk which was admittedly where I spent most of my time.

I quickly grabbed my white wrap to match my dress, giving myself one last glance over, now standing at the long mirror attached to the back of my door. Dark eyes looked back at me, ones decorated with a shimmer of gold and a sharp line of black liner, and my lips were painted a matte red. I gave myself a nod of approval, before swiping my keys from my sideboard that was also near the door.

"It will have to do," I told myself before rushing out the door, already having a feeling as if something life changing was going to happen. Well, of course it would, I was losing my best friend since high school to the man of her dreams. Because as much as she said it wouldn't change things, I knew it would. First, those weekly girls' nights out would dwindle down to once a month, maybe two. Then the first baby would arrive and then the second, and before I knew it, my friend would have a family and hang out with friends that had families. Her friends would be other mums, and nights out would be dinner parties and chatting over wine about the colour of baby poo and the price of nappies.

I would forever be the spinster who refused to date, all because no one could possibly live up to the ideal of my perfect man.

Kaiden Wrath.

My Hero.

I sighed just thinking about him, half of me wishing he were real and the other half thanking the Gods that he wasn't. Because I knew if he had been, then simply put, I would have been a dead woman walking! I often dreamed about this, when I wasn't dreaming that I was in fact his lost Siren, not Raina.

I often wondered if that's why I wrote it first person style, because secretly I wanted to be her. And why wouldn't I? She was everything I wasn't and everything I wished I was. My alter ego I could lose myself in. She was brave, courageous and beautiful. Tall, graceful and stylish, with some traits of my own thrown in there for good measure. This was because I liked to think I could be funny and most people who knew me thought of me as a kind soul. Of course, they also called me a chatterbox that never shut up, as I was also a nervous talker that thought my reason on this earth was to fill the silent void in every situation.

So yeah, naturally, dates weren't my thing.

Speaking of which, after a quick drive into the city, I parked in the fancy hotel car park and walked inside. Lucky for Nat, her husband was also rich, thanks to some new social site he owned, and therefore could afford to give her the wedding of her dreams in utter luxury.

I knew which floor Nat was getting ready on as she had stayed the night, something I had offered to do with her. But she had told everyone in the wedding party that she wanted her last night alone. This I knew wasn't exactly to contemplate life or anything deep and meaningful like that. No, it was more like a last night to wear pjs, lay in bed and pig out on junk food while watching reruns of Paul Ru's Drag Race. A show which hadn't long been out and was all the rage. Oh and admittedly, *she was an addict.*

Something I suspected her husband-to-be didn't yet know.

I looked at my blackberry and saw how late I was, and knowing she would be freaking out, I ran for the elevators, just as it was about to close, calling out,

"Please hold the door!" I then watched as it started to

close, no doubt because it had looked nearly full. Damn it, I would have squeezed in, I didn't have time to wait!

"Oh come... *on*... oh thank you, I..." I ended this sentence the moment a large, strong looking hand had created a barrier between the two doors, giving it no choice but to open again.

And that's when my unbelievable, life changing day completely blew my once safe life apart. When my wishing for the crazy to happen had bitten me on the arse, naming it a bite from fate.

This was because that hand belonged to someone I knew and for once, *I wasn't dreaming.* Even though I knew it would have been a lot safer had I been. Which was why my words, along with my thoughts, totally left me the moment I looked up and up, and up some more, and straight into the dark green eyes of my Demon Enforcer.

The utterly ruthless ruler and lord of all Supernatural life in his sector of Northeast America.

One totally terrifying...

Kaiden Wrath.

CHAPTER 2
LIFTING THE REALMS OF REALITY

"Miss?" This startled me, making me jerk back a little when one of the other men spoke, and I quickly averted my eyes away from the very real sight of my obsession. One who was now living and breathing as if he had been real all this time! No, but it wasn't fucking possible!

It just couldn't be!

He must just be someone who looked like him, yes, that was it. It couldn't be anything else. I mean, there must have been thousands of men that looked like Viking Gods… *right?*

Although I don't know how he looked exactly like the man who had haunted my every dream for the last six years. The man who dominated every space he occupied, as he was usually the biggest by far, just like he was now. Gods, but he looked every inch of the six foot five I had written him as. He also looked to be built like some axe swinging Viking King, there was more muscle on this guy to fill out two male bodies!

The guy looked like he ate a freaking rugby player for breakfast! Although, if he was the real deal then perhaps, I should say American football player, as that was where he ruled. As for the rest of him, he was dressed in dark jeans and a leather biker style jacket, as was his usual attire. I knew it didn't just hide all that muscle, but also honey toned skin covered in an array of badass tattoos. And to go with this badass persona, his dark brown hair was shaved to his skull at the sides of his head. His much longer hair on top was tied back in an unusual man bun style, tied with leather string, and pieces of the twist of hair were made thicker thanks to the few dreads I could see wrapped up there.

But it was his devastatingly handsome face that I could barely take my eyes off. His full beard was trimmed closer to his square jaw and tapered down longer at his chin, with it closely trimmed around his lips. Lips I just wanted to feel kissing and biting along my skin, they were so full and perfectly shaped. I also knew that if he had actually smiled at me, I would have been awarded with a blinding sight, because in my dreams his grin was killer. A row of white teeth, with the slight hint of fangs I knew would lengthen dangerously should the need arise for his Demon self to come out to play.

But above all of this, it was his eyes that were my

favourite part. The rare dark-green depths that always looked like they knew too much and saw all. Deep set and framed by a dark slash of brows that gave him a frightening, intimidating stare, powerful enough to make even the bravest of men cower.

And cower I did.

Okay, better get your ass in there, Emme, I told myself. All I wanted to do was turn around and run, but that would have looked even worse. Plus, I swear he was now frowning down at me, no doubt wondering why I was acting this way. Although, looking the way he did, then I could imagine it was a regular occurrence. Hell, but even without knowing who he was, I thought I was going to faint and needed to start fanning myself.

So, without saying anything, I made a point of giving him as wide a berth as possible and after pressing the floor number I wanted, quickly made my way to the back of the lift. I swear I had never had to ask my legs to work before, or ask my heart not to beat so fast, despite this last one being in vain as it was pounding!

He's not real. He's not real. He's not real. I told myself over and over again, but then I heard him speak, and what he said had my breathing stop instantly.

"Make sure the plane is fuelled and ready to go, Hel."

Hel! Hel…! Oh Gods, Helmer was real!

"So soon?" the man asked in return, and I gasped the second I heard his brother's name being spoken. Naturally, the handsome man turned to look down at me in question. So, I purposely dropped my wrap, so I could have the excuse not to look back at him. However, this backfired as he bent down and retrieved it for me, meaning I had no choice but to take in the startling beauty I had spent a long time writing about.

Because if Kaiden was all hard, handsome lines, his brother was the beautiful one who could have fooled you into believing he was an Angel. Not the cunning, yet deadly Demon he was, as both of them were sons to a King in Hell…

Wrath.

Hence their last name.

Hel was clean cut and wearing a suit, with his dark blonde hair styled perfectly, cut short at the sides and longer on top. He had startling turquoise eyes, framed by long lashes that had no business being on a man, just like his bigger brother did.

He also had a jaw line that would have made a sculptor weep and an easy-going grin that was bordering on bad boy cocky. I swear if he had winked at me, I would have dropped my purse to the floor again, just for a second showing. However, he just smirked, which was bad enough and had my childish lady flower fluttering like it was flirting with a damn bee!

But of course, as handsome as Hel was, in my eyes, he was nothing compared to his brother, who I admit would have held all my attention, had I not in that moment been terrified of doing so. Gods, how badly I wanted to look, but other than the quick glance at the back of his head, I kept my eyes averted.

He was huge and I mean that as in, he looked like some damn wrestler! His brother Hel was muscular to be sure and had a fine body, but as for Kaiden, he was at least four inches taller and a whole lot of muscles bigger! He was so wide, it was no wonder no one was standing next to him as he faced the doors. Meaning that I tried not to stare at all those muscles straining against his leather jacket, one I knew was his favourite. Dark grey, with rough piping around the edges, which was thicker and ran in lines at the elbows. Gods, but I could even smell its delicious masculine scent from here and would have given anything in that moment to hear it creak as his arms wrapped around me.

His hard features that had only glanced at me once had the power to strike the fear of God into any of his men that were also standing with us in the lift. Some of these I recognized as being on his council. Those dark brows looked formidable as he glanced back at me over his shoulder, with his dark green eyes that seemed permanently narrowed in distrust and distaste.

But he was also a lot scarier, and this wasn't just down to knowing what he was capable of, if he was in fact who half of me feared he was. Because the other half was still trying to convince myself it was crazy, and this couldn't possibly be true. No, it was just some twisted and fucked up coincidence.

It had to be!

However, going back to the half that thought this could be real, then I knew he had been picked for the job of Enforcer because he was the most powerful of his kind. Therefore, was leader of his own race of Demons, The Wrath Dealers. He was also a freaking Prince destined for his father's throne in Hell should Sathanas, the King of Wrath, ever fall in battle. Something that if my books were correct, was a position he didn't want, hence him now being on Earth's plane and working for the King of Kings.

Dominic Draven.

Of course, I knew the name, along with the club where he held his supernatural business in, one called Afterlife. But as of yet, I had not written about the place, as most of my stories were based on my dreams and well, if I didn't dream it, I didn't write it. However, I knew enough of their world to know that Dominic Draven was like the Overlord. One that ruled all Supernatural life that lived among mortals in the shadows of the unknown. But he was only one being after all, so he had sectioned out the world and appointed the most powerful beings of both Heaven and Hell, to help him rule and keep the balance of peace.

These were known as his Enforcers.

But again, there was no proof of this, only the story that I had in my head and had been writing about for the last six years. Of course, I had more than one book written but so far only had the courage to self-publish one of them… *something I was already quickly regretting!*

But as for this story, well that featured and focused all my attention on the Enforcer known to most as Wrath. However, to me as the author of his story, he was always known to me as Kaiden, just as he was to his Siren. And here he was! Right in front of me! I would have known every inch of him, which was why I couldn't stop my heart from trying to beat its way out of my chest!

Because I knew… I fucking knew… with every fibre of my being that this was him! Oh, I could try and convince myself for as long as I lived that he wasn't real. That I was mistaken or like I said, this was just some fucked up coincidence but deep down, I knew the truth and honestly…

It fucking terrified me!

Because I knew then, right in that moment, the sheer gravity of what I had done! I had written a damn book about this secret world that lived among us, and that offence was punishable by death, mortal or not! Which meant I needed to think about my options here and what I had to do next.

Thankfully, for me at least, my fan base was small and the number of books I had sold wasn't going to make me a best seller any time soon. So despite my once aspiring dreams of making it in the big leagues, my lack of achievements could only be classed now as a good thing.

But still, it was out there!

Fuck!

I almost jumped out of my skin when I heard a phone ringing, and didn't avert my eyes this time when his brother answered a call.

"Warden Za'afiel, to what do I owe the pleasure?" Hel answered in that smooth way of his, sounding more American than his pissed off brother. But at this, Wrath still reacted, glancing back at him and therefore catching me staring at him. I quickly averted my gaze back to my feet, like some little subservient bystander. I also twisted my hands around and around the handle of my bag in a nervous attempt to stop my mouth from opening and spewing out the truth.

"Now that is as interesting as it is unfortunate," Hel replied, making me wish I knew what it was they were talking about. I felt as if I were being cheated in some way. As though I was the writer of some TV soap opera, and now I was getting kicked off the show and being made to watch at home just like everyone else!

"One moment," Hel said, before informing his brother,

"It seems as if you were right, we will be needing that plane sooner than I thought." Then he held out the phone to Kaiden, who took it and said only one name,

"Ward." Then after a few minutes of listening, he replied with,

"We will have a team with you by nightfall." Then he ended the call and handed the phone back to his brother, being that he was a man of few words, I wasn't surprised by his reaction.

"Did you hear what he said, about finding his…?" A deep rumbling sound ended what he was about to say as Kaiden warned,

"Not here, Hel." At this he looked back at me, making the meaning loud and clear. *Not in front of the human.* I don't know why but that statement felt like a lash against my heart, which was totally irrational, I know.

"Call the men, I want them ready within the hour," Kaiden ordered, just before the doors opened and I found myself glued to the spot. My mind now going a million miles an hour and strangely enough, none of it was to do with saving my own skin. No, now it was all to do with wanting to know what this new situation was they were dealing with? Hell, but did I really know anything at all?

"Miss?" The sound of Hel's voice brought me back to the fact that the doors were open on my floor. I shook myself out of my own headspace and forced myself to move, mumbling a quick,

"Oh yeah." I ignored his knowing and handsome grin, instead shifting around him and walking to the front, feeling the fear mounting the closer to Kaiden I got. But then, as the doors started to close, his hand shot out again like it had done the first time. So, I stepped through, trying to leave as much space as was possible between us, and instead of just walking away without a word, I said a quick,

"Erm… thank you." But as I was about to take a step away from him, suddenly, that same hand shot out and gripped the top of my arm to prevent me from moving. I looked down at his meaty grasp circling my entire arm, thinking irrational thoughts once more that his hands were definitely much bigger than I'd described in my book. In fact, I didn't think that I had given them justice or fully explained just how beautifully manly and sexy they were. Gods, oh but what it would have been like to have them all over my body, holding me prisoner to his embrace.

"What did you say?" he asked in that deep timbre of his, making me shiver in his hold. This was when I finally braved looking up at him and into those incredible eyes of his, and in that single moment, I swear…

Time stood still.

"Brother?" Hel's voice must have broken whatever spell he had been lured under as he instantly let go of me. Then, without taking his eyes from me, I took a step back, meaning that seconds later the only thing to break our eye contact was the gold doors that slid across. Then finally, I was staring back at my own reflection, and I was once more…

All alone in my world.

CHAPTER 3
VOWS

"Seriously, will this day ever end?" I muttered as I made my way back up to the floor Nat had been getting ready on. The ceremony was over, and the wedding breakfast had been underway for the last hour. However, my friend had forgotten her white wedding Converse, a pair she told me she desperately needed as she didn't want to look too tall for her new husband during their first dance together. I had naturally come to the rescue, being just so happy to get out of there and away from Asshole, who had been trying to create opportunities to speak with me. Thankfully, I had successfully been avoiding these as they happened but knew my luck on this would only last so long.

Besides, I most definitely had bigger problems than ex asshole boyfriends following me around like some wounded puppy in need of care. No, I had fucking

Demonic Rottweilers that would have torn me to pieces if they had only known of the fresh mortal meat they had been standing next to in that elevator.

Gods, but for the last few hours I had been on a sort of auto pilot, just going through the motions of bridesmaid's duty until I was able to say my goodbyes and get the Hell out of this place! But the big question was where? Where could I ever hope to hide where they wouldn't find me? That was if they even thought to look, but really…

Could I take that chance?

Well, wherever it was going to be, I had better figure it out and quick, because I had until the end of this wedding to make my decision. One thing was for sure, Roger was going to be pissed. I just hoped this didn't mean another month of having him shit in my shoes. But then this thought soon became the very least of my potential problems as a real one was waiting for me around the corner. One in the form of a cocky arrogant wanker I had once thought to be the most handsome man I'd ever known. It was true I had been crushing on him since high school, which was why I felt like all my dreams had come true the second he finally asked me out. I had just been about to turn twenty-one when Nat and her brother came to visit me at College.

But then, I had grown up at lot since the last time he had seen me, by both filling out in curves and discovering my love of high-heeled shoes. Hence why he finally took notice. Besides, at a party he saw how much attention I received from other guys and well, this to an asshole like Dean, was like waving a red flag in front of a bull. I became the action doll he wanted to play with after first snatching it off the other boys.

And clearly, there was no other fuckable options at this wedding for him to toy with, so here he was, adding to my torment. Only this time, he wasn't the centre of my universe… no, there was only one man who now held that claim.

Kaiden Wrath.

Fictional Demonic character no more.

"What do you want, Dean?" I snapped, walking straight past him and unfortunately for me, knowing he would follow.

"Aw come on, don't be like that, babe." I tensed my shoulders, hating that I had once loved him calling me that. However, now it just grated on me like finger nails scraped along a brick wall.

"Look, let's make this easier for both of us, I am not interested," I said, only stopping when I reached the lifts, at least thankful that Kaiden said for his men to be ready to leave within the hour, so there would be no chance of bumping into them again.

"So, you can really say that you haven't thought about us in the last six years?" he asked, making me laugh without humour, turning fully to face him as I heard the elevator doors open behind me.

"Oh, I don't know, I guess whenever I see a toad in the

park, I think of you, or say, if I step in shit and need a place to wipe it off." I heard a chuckle behind me but before I could look, Dean scowled at them and then turned his nasty eyes on me,

"You always had a way with words, babe."

"Yeah, well here's some more for you, *babe*… if all that was left on this Earth was you and slimy tentacled aliens with wrinkled skin, monobrows and an overbite, I would still take the alien. Now leave me alone!" I said, and turned on my heel to walk into the lift, feeling great for all of about two seconds. This was because for the second time that day, the top of my arm was grabbed and soon restraining me back. However, this was when history started to repeat itself as the one who saved me the first time, was here again to do it a second. Although this time he wasn't facing his brother but a mortal asshole.

"I think the lady made her feelings perfectly known, don't you agree, lads?" Hel said, referring to what looked to be most of Wrath's council members who were standing in the same lift, making me suck in a quick breath. Each one of them as frightening as the next and all thankfully in my favour, for they clearly agreed with their leader.

However, Dean, in his fear, squeezed me tighter instead of letting me go, making me wince and boy, didn't Hel take notice. Now narrowing his eyes at the way his fingers bit into my arm.

"Just say the word, boss," one of the men said, who I knew was named Boaz, which meant Strength in Hebrew. He was as tall as Hel with slightly less bulk than Kaiden, but I knew he was also the Enforcer's second in command. This basically meant that he was in charge of most of the men and security at their private club, situated in the heart of New York city. He was like most of them, gorgeous in his own right, being of the tall, dark and exotically handsome category. He also looked like a mean son of a bitch.

Hel raised a hand, telling him no before stepping closer to Dean and telling him in a deadly, threatening tone,

"Now this is where you take your hand off her before you give me the great joy and pleasure of removing it for you." At this he suddenly let go and took a tumbled step back, making Hel chuckle and comment just as the doors closed,

"Pity… I was looking forward to breaking something." After this the lift started taking us down and I closed my eyes, facing away from all of them, before they could see me as I started to tremble.

"I apologize, Miss." I frowned and before I could stop myself, I said,

"For what, you're not my asshole ex who I would pick an alien over." At this he chuckled.

"No, but I am brother to the first asshole who thought he could manhandle you today," he said, surprising me enough that I didn't think before I turned to look at him, and snapped back,

"He's not an asshole." At this I quickly lowered my eyes when I saw him raise his own in shock. Then, in my shame and panic, I quickly reached out and pressed one of the numbers that I knew the lift would stop at sooner. While doing this I saw the way Hel looked back at his men in a questioning way, nodding as if he was trying to silently communicate something with one of them. I think his name was Tristan if the descriptions in my book were correct, as he was what you would have classed as having those boy next door good looks. With his sandy blonde hair, all tussled as I knew his habit was always running his hands through it. He was also dressed as if he lived for music, wearing ripped jeans, and some worn Metallica T-shirt that had grey snakes over black cotton.

"Excuse me and thanks… for your erm… help," I said, knowing it would have looked odd had I not.

"Are you sure this is your floor, are you not part of the wedding taking place on the first floor?" Hel said, being far too perceptive for his own good, but then that was his brother… *he never missed anything.*

"No, yes, I mean I am… but… but I just need something from my room. Good day, gentlemen," I said, quickly nodding to them all before rushing off down the corridor and trying to get away from the potentially deadly situation. Then I darted around the corner and only felt as if I could breathe again when I looked back and found that no one had followed. It looked as though they were all ready to leave and something must have delayed them, making me wonder where Kaiden was?

After about ten minutes of being unable to move from my shitty hiding place, I used the staircase to make my way back down to the first floor, deciding it was a good idea to keep away from all lifts from now on. I then made my way back to the top table and did my duty as a friend, giving Nat her shoes. And like a good friend not wanting to spoil her day, I waited until it was her first dance, watching from afar with a tear in my eye. This while silently saying goodbye as I honestly didn't know when it would be that I would see her again.

If at all.

So, I made a secret vow to myself that I would do whatever it took to save myself from my potentially deadly fate. Because surely the Fates had something better planned for me if they had wanted me to write Kaiden's story the way I had. And if he was as real as I now knew him to be, then it stood to good reason that the Fates were real too. Because in his world, the Fates were everything. They were the Gods over the Gods and ruled above all. Even Lucifer himself couldn't deny them. Which then meant that if I were somehow connected with Kaiden finding his Chosen One, then surely that had to account for something…

Right?

Gods, but why was that thought such a painful one.

Because you secretly want him for yourself, my inner bitch told me. And it was true. Despite knowing Raina's character, as well as my own, I could honestly say that there was no one who would love him as much or as deeply as I did. Which was precisely why I would try and find her for him, as he deserved to be happy.

He deserved to find his Siren.

Hence why I swiped at my tears and whereas others watching would have thought this would have been happy tears in sight of a friend's happiness, it was in fact more the feeling of loss. The broken heart I knew I would never mend, for I knew in that moment I had lost everything.

I had lost my friend, lost my home and my safe little life. And now I had lost the chance at the career I had always dreamed of having. But most of all, I had lost the one who brought me more love and comfort than all of those things put together…

I had lost my hero.

CHAPTER 4

THE HEATED FLAMES OF MY DREAMS

Who would have thought the hardest part of leaving would have been trying to get my damn cat in a fucking cat carrier? And now I had the scratches to prove it! Brutal fucking thing, I swear it was sent by Lucifer himself as a bloody joke to torment me!

Should have named it Damien!

Of course, the practical side of me leaving only really hit me while I was packing and the shampoo bottle slipped from my fingers. I had slumped on to the toilet, crying as I asked myself the most important question…

"Where am I going to go? I have no one!"

After this I wasted ten minutes on crying and another ten on cleaning up shampoo so I wouldn't slip and break my neck, making this runaway a moot point. Of course, there was still my crazy nanna. But then I didn't need to worry about her, as she was in an old people's home and was lost enough in her mind to believe I was still a little girl. One who liked to twirl in my skirts while she played Pearl's a Singer, by Elkie Brooks on her ancient record player.

"What a mess, Nanna," I said, looking down at my picture of the both of us, me hugging her tight, while she looked smug and I looked beyond happy, because well… *I was with my nanna.*

"You would know what to do, just like that time we were at your caravan and… but of course!" I suddenly shouted as I knew exactly where to go! I kissed her picture and said,

"Thank you, Nanna, you genius, you!" Then I stuffed the silver framed picture into my backpack as I couldn't leave her behind like that. After all, she deserved to be on this adventure with me. Now, as for Roger, well I wasn't so sure about him.

Yet despite this, it still meant that an hour later and he was on the front seat next to me as I took to the road. I glanced in my rear-view mirror to see what was pathetically most of my life all piled up there. My life in a suitcase and with food in a box, because hello, I wasn't made of money. Besides, no one had knocked on my door in the whole two hours it had taken me to pack, so I figured I had time. That was, if they were coming at all.

I was half tempted to leave Roger there but after asking all my neighbours to look after him and receiving a firm and resounding no from them all, then I had no choice. Which was a shame as this would have given me the excuse to ring and ask if anyone had been around looking for me. But as it turned out, there wasn't anyone left in my building that was brave enough to look after my little fluffy Hell spawn. Because oh yes, he was well known in the building and had made himself quite the reputation. He had even dragged my name down into the mud with him, as my trick or treaters had dwindled down into practically nothing last year as the kids were calling me the lady with the killer cat.

Jesus, it was a British shorthair, not a fucking panther, and this was over the lady in 3C who had a five-foot python named Derek. Stupid name for a snake if you asked me but then again, I couldn't say anything as I had a cat called Roger, a cat who I would bet all my money on that he could take Derek in a fight any day.

Hence why I packed all his food too, I was too afraid of tipping him over the edge after this journey. Besides, I would need to bribe him out of his carrier with something, or he was likely to just fly right out of there like some screaming banshee with claws… *just like last time!*

This was also why, the moment I pulled up outside my nanna's old caravan, in what was now a rough and tired looking site near Blackpool, I tried not to wince at the state of it. No, instead I located her obvious hiding place for a key, under a plant pot that now only held soil and some dead twig in it. Then I opened the door and instantly wished that I hadn't.

"Holy Zeus, that's bad… here you go, enjoy kitty, go fucking wild," I muttered in reference to the stale smell of what could only be described as where 70's shag carpets went to die! Then without thinking twice, I slid Roger's carrier in, unhooked the front and ran out, pulling the door to as quickly as I could. Admittedly, it looked like I was releasing some wild beast back into the wild and other than throwing some dead carcass in there to calm his ass down, I thought it best to be a wimp. Meaning I sat down on the steps that led to the door and deflated back against the cold frosted glass door, asking myself for the millionth time…

What the fuck was I doing?

I had naturally already removed the e-book from every platform it was sold on and closed all social media accounts. However, I was unable to close down all the Facebook groups or at least if there had been a way then I didn't know how. But as for now, it would have to be good enough as I didn't know what else I could do. It had been brutal, especially when sending out a heartbroken message to all those who had supported me throughout my short career and bought my book. I had been so close to publishing book 2, that I just couldn't force myself to delete them from my laptop, bringing it with me like some way to torture myself.

Sweet perfect life had been so close.

Which meant that this time when I cried, I did so for longer than ten minutes and over much more than spilled shampoo.

⸙

How I managed to sleep on my nanna's old lumpy bed was beyond me, but somehow I had. Then again, after I had given it some time to tame the devil out of the cat, I had cleaned for hours, giving myself something else to focus on. Although I confess, I had felt like crying again when opening the fridge, a place where old food had clearly gone to die. A smell so bad it had made me want to puke up the fancy wedding meal I'd only half eaten. Things that smelled that bad needed to be condemned, that was for certain… that and packet meals were only ever going to be in my future!

Who really needed chilled goods anyway and milk was totally overrated! In fact, the smell of mould might have been what helped me sleep, as I wondered if spores in the air could knock you unconscious? Either way, I had slept and when I had, I soon found there was only one person waiting for me in them…

My hero was back.

However, this time it was all different, and no guesses needed as to why I found myself back at the hotel. Only this time when the doors to the elevator opened, there was only him.

"Kaiden," I said, letting his name escape me like a lover's kiss and speaking of kiss, he quickly reached out and grabbed me. Doing this by curling a muscular arm around me and reeling me in, making me gasp.

"My Siren," he growled down at me before lifting me enough that he could kiss me with ease, locking me in his arms as he possessed me in a way I had always dreamed he would… *this just after calling me his.* Of course, as Raina, I was the epitome of playing it sexy cool, meaning my kiss was just as addictive for him as his was for me.

After this he turned us both and I felt my back hit the elevator wall as he pinned me there between it and his intimidating frame that dwarfed me, even at my imaginary Raina's height.

"I've waited for you… fuck, *how I have waited, woman!"* he snarled down at me before kissing me again, stopping only once more when he accused,

"Why did you make me wait?" I closed my eyes wishing it was truly me he wanted, knowing that what he saw in me was not what I would have seen in myself when looking in the mirror. Because it was strange, like Raina and I were connected as one person. Yet I knew how in my mind she looked, and it wasn't like me.

Her hair was perfectly straight for one, and a golden blonde that shone like the sun on some exotic beach. She was tall, slim and every inch toned. Her face was compared to that of a Goddess, and most of all, she shied away from no man.

She was also kick ass and could even run in heels. She wasn't afraid to fight for those she loved, not like me. Not like when I even let myself get bullied into agreeing with them to put my nanna in a home, convincing me it was what was best for her.

I never forgave myself for that.

Now, I was just about to open my sexy smart mouth, ready with some sultry comeback when suddenly Kaiden did something out of character in my dreams…

He spoke the wrong name.

"Why did you make me wait, Emmeline?" I opened my mouth to say something when nothing would come out. My words had gone and with it my other persona. Because my dream world was being stripped down to its true form. It was ripped from its veil, one I had built up for the last six years. I even looked down at myself to see it was me in his arms held against the wall. It was plain little me. Naturally I freaked, making him growl back at me when I tried to fight my way free.

"Please… this isn't… this isn't the way it's supposed to go… I'm not…" At this he stopped me from speaking with another kiss and this time, it was more raw, more passionate, more… *everything*.

Then, when I was near breathless from it, he pulled back enough to place his forehead to mine, telling me on the same breathy whisper,

"You are my only... and I will find you... I'm coming for you, my Siren."

"NO!" I screamed and the second I did, my dream started to fade away, merging into something else. I had fallen from one dream straight into another, but this time it was like it normally was when Raina wasn't playing a part in them. Therefore, I was left watching on like a spectator hidden in the shadows as myself.

I took a good look around, seeing for myself I was in some sort of warehouse district, and could tell instantly this was most likely somewhere in the US. I focused on the name of things, mainly the building that the black heavy-duty SUVs were parked outside of, knowing that they belonged to Kaiden and his men.

It was some kind of factory, that looked to deal with food packaging, yet the name didn't ring any bells. Although, I am not sure why it would. Either way, the second I heard gun shots inside, I felt my heart plummet. I ran out from my hiding place toward a pair of roller doors that were opening. I knew no one could see me, I was like a ghost, having no say in this dream that this time felt like so much more.

It felt like the Fates were showing me something real, like the future.

I watched as Kaiden's men all came running out, dressed in black military gear, and each of them were carrying unconscious women as if they had been there to save them. But there, in the centre of all the chaos, was Kaiden carrying a woman, running towards another large man who had looked frantic.

"Ward! I found her!" Kaiden shouted to someone who seemed to be his friend, and it was a name I recognized as he had been the one on the phone. What did all of this mean exactly… was what I was witnessing now just a glimpse into his immediate future or had this already happened? Had this been the reason for his call, had he been looking for this woman and enlisted Kaiden's help?

I watched as he passed the unconscious woman over to the tall man, who looked as grateful as he did ruggedly handsome. In fact, he looked as though he had just been passed his very reason for living.

"Is there any more?" the man named Ward asked, making Kaiden shake his dirty head, as it looked as if he had just walked though fire to get her out. This made me squint my eyes to the building, where the flames could be seen from behind windows to what looked like a line of offices.

Just then we all heard a woman's scream and Kaiden hissed,

"Fuck!"

"Brother, we have to leave, the place is gonna fucking blow!" Hel said removing his tactical helmet as he approached, looking both frustrated and damp from sweat as it was clear he too had been in the thick of it.

"He's right, Kai, she is lost," Ward agreed, making Kaiden growl low, then he grabbed his brother's helmet and replied,

"Not if I can help it... now go, get back to the club and I will meet you there!"

"But I am not leaving you..." Hel tried looking pained at the idea of leaving his kin.

"You will do as I fucking order you to do, little brother, now go and get these women out of here!" Kaiden snapped, before turning to his friend and telling him,

"Take your Siren, while I make sure there are none left in there so no other Enforcer feels the same pain of losing one as you might have this night... GO!" he roared, before putting on his helmet and running back into the burning building. This made me scream out as the second his brother and friend were free of the building, the whole thing exploded with my Enforcer left inside.

"NOOOO!" I screamed again, falling to my non-existent knees as it felt like my world was being ripped apart. Of course, this same call was echoed by his own brother who looked to be trying to fight his way back in there, only to be held back by Tristan and Boaz.

"Don't be foolish, Hel, he would have survived that, now come on, we need to get out of here and get the girls to safety before more humans come. Trust in your brother's rule... come on, my friend," Boaz said, and through the fog of my tears, I too tried to hold on to the same hope that his brother had survived.

Kaiden had to be okay... *he just had to be.*

So, after Hel admitted defeat, he got in his car and

drove away with his men, and I watched as the one named Ward did the same, now with who I knew was his Siren nestled safely in his arms.

Which meant only one thing…

The first Siren had been found.

drove away with his meds, and I watched as the one that had Ward did the same, now with who I knew was his Siren nestled safely in his arms.

Which meant only one thing.

The first Siren had been found.

CHAPTER 5
DON'T SAY IT, ROGER

The first Siren.

This I knew would mark the beginning for the others, and Kaiden knew that too. It was why he had run inside, no doubt intent on saving them all just in case. But then one look at the burning building, one that now looked totally consumed by Hellish flames as if it had been set alight by the Devil himself, I knew that Kaiden may have the power to survive it, but the poor women left inside wouldn't.

It made me wonder if he thought it could have been his own Siren in there. Had he thought her call for help had been the famous Siren's call that was supposed to let a Fated know she was his?

It was written that way in my own story, that a Siren's voice had that power, becoming a sound that was only recognizable to their intended Enforcer. But until the first one was found, then they would forever be waiting, as the first one was supposed to kick start these fated events. Events that would eventually lead one lost Siren to her fated Enforcer, and that in turn would do the same for the next and the next and so forth. Because all Sirens needed to be found by the next Summer Solstice, which according to the Greeks, was in May. Well, seeing as we were already in September, that gave the ten remaining Enforcers only eight months to find them.

The mythology went that there were eleven Sirens in total, and according to my nanna's stories when I was a kid, it had to do with Zeus's daughter Persephone. She had been given Eleven Angels known as the Sirens to guard and protect her but seeing as they were also known for their incredible beauty, and enchanting voices, Zeus also took notice. He found they used their powers of persuasion as it was said they could bring a man to their knees at just a mere whispered word. Yet despite these gifts, they were each of pure soul and therefore naive to the ways of the Gods that wished to use them.

Therefore, Zeus made a deal with his brother Hades, who was another ruler in Hell and not to be mistaken with the Devil Lucifer himself. He bargained for his daughter, as it was said Hades fell in love with her instantly and offered up his loyalty to his brother. Hades, who was gaining more and more power over his domain in the Underworld, enough that Zeus was getting worried about being overthrown.

So, he gave him his daughter, something Hades wanted far more than the rule over Olympus. Of course, her mother had something else to say on the matter and forbade the union. Now this was where Zeus enlisted the help of the Sirens, and unbeknown to them, instead of protecting Persephone, like they were told, they were in fact luring her beyond the protection of Mount Olympus.

Zeus had told them to take her to a secret garden and hide her there from Hades. Yet the ruler of the dead was already waiting there for her, as was always planned between the brothers. Naturally she was kidnapped and taken back to his Kingdom to become his Queen.

As for the poor Sirens, they were quickly blamed for this and would receive no help from Zeus who cast them out at Demeter's request. She was then free to put a curse on each of them, stripping them of their powers and their wings, casting them down to the mortal realm to become human.

Which meant that eleven Sirens lived on and passed over the latent gene into any girls born. It was then prophesied that at some point, the first Siren would be found, calling out to her fated when he was near, and this would then awaken all other Sirens to the same fate. But each had to be found before the Summer Solstice, so they had a chance at gaining back their powers and becoming eternal once more. This was after they had claimed their Enforcers through a ritual called Klidonas, which was Greek and translated into Power of the Oracle.

Although it was also said that this claim had to be one of utter certainty. Especially seeing as it was totally against the rules set by the King of Kings for one of his Supernatural kind to claim a human as his own. This was unless it was fated, meaning, like I said, each had better be damn sure as this offence was punishable by death.

But as for me, well this was a story I had learned in detail through dreams and after doing my own research, being that my last name was the same as one of the lost Sirens. A reason my nanna used to tell me the tale as a kid, as her mother did for her and so on and so on, being passed down through the generations. I had just thought that it made for a cool story to be written but then that was before I had discovered Kaiden was real.

Which meant that if he was, then so was Raina, his Siren. Hence why it made sense that Kaiden would risk himself for the potential of her being inside a burning building. Of course, what he didn't know was what I did. That it wasn't her... *it wasn't his Raina.* Because they didn't meet this way and in fact, she was the one to save him. She had seen the danger to his life and simply acted.

Their story started similar to how I had met him, in the sense that he had been coming out of a hotel when his enemy, Dagon Weaver, who was Enforcer to the Southeast, had his men shoot at him and Raina sees the guns first as the car drives past. But without thinking, she runs into the danger, throwing herself against Kaiden, knocking him to the ground. She lands on top of him, pulls back and asks if he is alright. Which was when, the second he hears her voice, he knows she is his Siren. He wants to hear her speak again but unbeknown to herself, she has been shot in the shoulder and just when she is about to speak her name for the first time, she passes out.

The rest of the story is how Kaiden takes her back to his incredible mansion home where his people live, and she learns of his world after he heals her. Of course, they fall in love and butt heads along the way and with a few kidnapping attempts thrown in there for good measure, that was the start of their story. Which let's face it, had they just met and that be it, then it wouldn't have been much of a story if they just lived happily ever after from that point on, now would it?

But it did make me wonder if and when this would happen for him, especially after this dream, one I admit to never having before. So why now? Was it after meeting him in real life, that I had unknowingly unlocked some sort of connection with him? Had I tapped in to being able to tell his future or was this just my tender heartbroken mind trying to make sense of being forced to walk away from that part of my life? A way to make me see I had to let go of the obsession, once and for all?

Was this just my dark and desperate goodbye?

I didn't know, but I was left questioning it once more the second the dream started to change again. Only this time I was left even more baffled, as none of it made any sense!

I found myself playing witness again to what looked like a construction site and one look at all the skyscrapers around, I could say with confidence it was making way for another one. It looked as if they had been building a crude stadium down in the ground. Which I knew must have been how these colossal buildings were made, as they must have been getting ready for the foundations to be put in.

But then it was also clear that work had been long ago finished for the day as no one was around. Which was why when a van and chauffeur driven car turned up, I was surprised, as they made their way down the man-made ramp. One that was obviously put in for heavy duty vehicles to get down there as it was wide enough for much larger lorries. There were also massive pillars stacked and piles of metal bars the width of my arm spread around the large open space. Cranes left like dead giant spider's legs were dotted around, with larger ones above the colossal sized hole in the ground. These created creepy shadows that framed the space the second a load of floodlights were turned on, showcasing the spot the vehicles now stopped at.

But soon my cries of horror would add my own private sound to the scene as I watched men dragging a chained Kaiden from the van. He was bloody and clearly beaten, but he also looked formidable as he remained on his feet, even after they tried to beat him back to his knees.

I started running down the sides of the vast space, not even asking myself what I could do at this point, only that it had to be something! But then, the second I saw who emerged from the car, I stopped, hissing out his name,

"Dagon!"

The Enforcer had been trying to find ways to bring Kaiden down and therefore take over his territory but seeing as it was utterly forbidden to kill another Enforcer, then he had never achieved this. Because nothing was done in this world without the say so of their King and for that to happen, first a crime needed to be committed. Which I had to say from the looks of things, one was just about to.

"Ah, but the mighty Son of Wrath in all his glory, oh but how I do love to see the strong when they fall," Dagon sneered, making me want to gouge his eyes out! He was an older looking man, no doubt coming into possession of a mortal vessel who was already in his fifties. This meant he had salt and pepper hair, styled like a man who cared greatly what the world thought of him. His light grey suit and now dirt covered shoes mattered to him, as he looked down at them in disgust and disdain that he himself was being made to do some of the dirty work.

"I'm still on my feet, asshole," Kaiden muttered as if he were bored, making me wonder why he didn't just burst out of his chains and kill these dickheads. Because I knew what he was capable of. Meaning it would take a lot more than just some thick chains to keep his Demon form from erupting and wreaking havoc on these goons. After all, he would be allowed to kill them as they were fair game, even if Dagon wasn't. Gods, would I be made to witness their slaughter? I had written the way Raina had witnessed his brutality once, and even she had run from it, but question was…

Would I do the same?

Although, I had to admit I would prefer that than what the alternative could mean. Which was why I started to panic the longer he was in those chains, making me question why.

"You may still be on your feet for now, but even a big bastard like you has their limits, and I can see that those chains I had cast and forged were worth the price of over half my army in Hell to make, as they do subdue your Demon quite well, don't they?" Dagon said, making me gasp as I could see now that they weren't just regular chains like I first thought.

"Yes, indeed, as for once, rumours are true. The sorceress did well and is as powerful as they say she is," his enemy added, making Kaiden snarl back at him with a warning.

"Then why not fuck off and go praise the bitch, while you still can, for if you continue down this road with me any longer, you will force my hand in killing you."

"Ah, but even I know you are not permitted to kill another Enforcer, as is our law, and I would not be so foolish as to incur the wrath of our King of Kings," Dagon replied, making me frown in question, because if he didn't have killing him in mind, what exactly was his end game with all this?

"Then I fail to see what you hope to achieve here if it's not my death?" Kaiden asked as if our thoughts were in tune.

"Ah, but there are always other ways around death, for you should know this by now, as isn't twisting the laws of our King one of your favourite things to do?" Dagon sneered, making me start shaking my head as the snake of dread started to coil tighter around in my stomach.

"I told you, old man, the death of your daughter was no fault of mine!" Kaiden replied, making me suck in a quick breath, as even I had no idea this was what had started their age-old feud. It was like watching a bombshell being dropped in your favourite book, and had I been holding one in that moment, I would have likely dropped it.

But this enraged Dagon, making him snarl viciously before he nodded for his men to start beating on him again, trying in vain to get him to his knees. But Kaiden wouldn't have it, beating them back with his shoulders or head butting them when they got too close.

As for me, I felt fucking helpless, wishing there was something I could do! However, as for Kaiden, he started laughing like a madman, letting me see a terrifying glimpse of the sinister side of him that I knew he was famous for in his world. But as for his Demon, it may have not been allowed free thanks to the chains that contained him, but that didn't mean man and Demon weren't one and the same. I knew that the moment he bit into the neck of one of Dagon's men who got too close. He then ripped a chunk of flesh from his jugular, making blood spurt out in a sickening spray of crimson mist. This then made Kaiden spit out the blood pouring from his split lips, before he grinned down at the fallen man now bleeding out on the floor.

"Toss him in the box!" Dagon snapped, and I watched in horror as a carved coffin was dragged out of the van. It was covered every inch in Demonic looking symbols, just like the ones now glowing on his chains. It was as if they were reacting as his Demon fought even harder to be free, making the symbols pull forth more power from Hell just to hold him.

"This was what cost me the other half of that army and again, worth every soul, for I will rest easy this night and all nights to follow. Especially knowing you will soon be buried under fifty feet of foundations with hundreds of tons of my own tower built above you. Oh yes, how well I will sleep, Wrath." At this Kaiden actually looked a little panicked, as it was clear what fate held for him. I screamed out my own horror as I watched him try and fight them even harder this time. But in the end, it was useless as the chains prevented him from stopping the masses, and soon twenty of Dagon's men were dragging him into the box.

There were just too many of them!

"You had better kill me, Dagon, or so help me in my father's name I will hunt you down and kill you myself, wrath of the Kings of Kings be on my head or not! I WILL FUCKING KILL YOU!" Kaiden bellowed, just as the lid to his coffin was sliding home and being sealed shut. Then, as it was being put into place, I started running, doing so in vain as I was nothing but a ghost in Kaiden's fate.

"Are you sure about this plan?" one of Dagon's lackies asked, making him grin down at the coffin.

"But of course, after all, I am breaking no laws."

"And what of when his host perishes away, and his soul is forced back into Hell?" the man said as he followed his master back to his car.

"By that time, plans should already be underway to overthrow the King of Kings, for there are snakes in his den that he is unaware of." I gasped at this, as surely nothing had that type of power.

"You speak of the Vampire King, my lord?" Again I reacted to this, knowing of the one they called Lucius, who was a mortal enemy to the King of Kings, rumoured to be his only equal in power.

"Him and others… now go bury him in the hole you prepared and cover him. I want no one to find him until the foundations start being poured this coming Monday," Dagon told him, making him bow to his master. Then I watched hopelessly with tears running down my cheeks as the bellows of anger began to die down the lower the coffin went into the ground.

After this I watched until the bitter end, and long after the bad guys had left. I had watched as they had used dumper trucks to fill in the hole and cover the tracks they had made after. But I knew where he was, as I hadn't taken my eyes from the spot.

How could I, when the man I loved was buried alive?!

Then I thought about being there right above him and suddenly my ghost of a body was right there. Which was when I let myself fall to my knees once more, just like I had done outside that factory, a trap they must have had waiting for him inside. Had the girls' screams even been real?

I placed my shaky hand over where he lay below and made a vow.

"I swear to you, I will do all I can to stop this… I will help you. I will risk it all just to save you… I will find a way… *you have my word, Kaiden."* After this I let a single tear fall to the ground and a second later, I woke with a start.

"Fuck!" I shouted, suddenly scrambling to get out of the little lumpy bed and taking a moment to wonder why I wasn't where I thought I was. It was also bright daylight outside, making me realize I must have slept most of the day away, seeing as I only crawled into bed last night just before the sun was rising. It had taken me that long to clean and being a bit of a freak that way, I wouldn't have slept without doing it first. The fridge, however, had been a hard limit to this rule.

But now my plan at hiding was about to go completely to shit because if there was one thing that dream told me, it was that Kaiden was in trouble. He was real and he was in trouble. Which meant that he needed me, because I was the only one who knew where he was. Which also meant that I was the only one who could save him!

Now all I had to figure out was a way to do that without getting myself killed or imprisoned, as the characters in my books were all very nice to Raina, but I wasn't her.

I wasn't his Siren.

I was just a mortal.

Which meant I was expendable in all this. But worst still, I was a mortal that had unknowingly committed one of their biggest crimes... *the threat to expose their world.*

So, even though I might have been on the way to save their Lord and leader, if my true identity was ever discovered, then I knew that this would only end one way... *it would be a suicide mission.*

Because I knew they would kill me in a heartbeat!

Which was why I looked to my angry cat and said one thing before making the craziest decision of my entire life.

"Don't say it, Roger..."

"... 'Cause, I already know our fate if I fail."

CHAPTER 6
'O FORTUNA'

Okay, so when I vowed I would do all that was in my power to save Kaiden, that meant using practically all of my savings so I could buy a flight to New York. A place I had naturally never been to before. In fact, I had never flown further than Europe, which included a few cheap holidays to Tenerife and the odd one to mainland Spain with Nat. But other than that, I was pretty clueless when it came to travelling, which was why until I had grabbed my passport in my haste to run from my life, it had previously been gathering dust on the top shelf in my room.

Well, now it was still in my hand as I made my way through the busy arrivals at JFK, wandering around like some lost sheep asking myself how the other sheep knew what to do. In fact, for once it made me miss Roger, who I, once again, had to brave getting in his carrier, enduring even more injury as I drove to the nearest cattery. Then, pretending that the little Snuckems was my whole world and my dear old aunt who didn't exist was dying in a country I had never been to, I paid a bucket load to drop off the little bastard.

After this I googled the weather, and dressed for the occasion, thankful I had left most of my things in my car. So, I added to my skinny indigo jeans, a pair of heeled combat style boots that I think looked kick ass with their many straps and buckles. Then I added a gothic looking sweater dress in dark burgundy. It was one that was ribbed at the arms, had long sleeves I could put my thumbs in like gloves and had cool slashes on one side near my hip. It also had a wide neck that rolled off one shoulder if left without a jacket but acted as a scarf with one. As for my jacket, this was black, thick and had a huge hood in case I needed to hide in the crowd. It also had lots of inside pockets that might come in handy if I had to ditch my bag.

After this quick outfit change outside of the cattery, I drove to Manchester airport and left my car at a long stay carpark. The I got on the next flight to New York. Hence why I now looked around hopelessly for a way out in hopes of getting a taxi into the city. But then, just before I walked out of there with every kind of ID on me in the single backpack I had decided to bring and what felt like my whole life inside it, I took pause. I couldn't just go walking in there with all this on me, not when half of this plan relied on them not discovering my real name.

So, I ran to an information desk and asked the lady there if they had storage lockers, something I was grateful to discover they did. So, I took all the things I would need, which in the end was only about five hundred dollars and a small can of mint fresh breath spray.

Then I left my phone, wallet, passport and everything else behind, which included my bank cards as they obviously had my name written all over them. Thankfully, I had already taken out some cash and had it transferred to dollars while waiting for my flight at the other end. As for the lockers, they were fancy new code ones that you picked yourself, so I didn't need to carry a key around with me.

So, this meant that by the time I walked out of the airport, I was feeling pretty good with myself, knowing my name couldn't be traced. That was as long as I could be relied on to keep my big mouth shut, then I would be just peachy.

Which was why I made my way outside and got in the first yellow taxi cab that was waiting. I already felt myself trying to reach for my phone so I could take a picture of the iconic moment like the rest of the tourists would. However, I had to remind myself I didn't have my phone on me for a reason, and that was because I was on a mission to save the man of my dreams… in the most literal sense there was!

"Where to?" the driver asked in that typical American

New York accent I would have expected. Which was when I cleared my throat and asked him,

"Do you know 731 Lexington Avenue?" At this he laughed and replied,

"You mean the 55-story building... yeah, it's kind of hard to miss, and I wouldn't be a very good cabbie if I didn't know where one of the biggest builds was, now would I?" I shrugged my shoulders and told him,

"I guess not." Then I sat back and thought about the address I had just given him. It was a building that had come to me in my dreams, knowing that this was his city base and where he had his secret nightclub, 53 Sins. This was of course, named such as it was found on the 53rd floor and well, owned by a pair of Demon brothers known to most as the Brothers Wrath. Which was why I also knew this was most likely where I would find Helmer, his brother, as he would no doubt still be waiting for him.

It had also been one of the places Raina had run from in my book, after being taken there one night so she may experience for herself first-hand the true nature of who and what Kaiden really was in his world. I like to think I would have dealt with it a lot better but then again, I had been the author and knew more about him at this point than my lead female character did. After all...

I understood him like no other.

Gods, but I still couldn't believe he was real and here I was, in New York, running toward the danger I had cowered away from my whole life. But then, what was the point of spending endless hours writing about the power of love and all the incredibly brave things it made you do, if I was going to run away from it the first chance I got? And there was no denying how much I loved Kaiden, no matter how crazy that might have made me sound.

He had become my life.

And now, well if I had the chance at saving his, then into the belly of the beast I must go. And speaking of that belly, 731 Lexington Avenue was an eight-hundred-and-six-foot monster made from glass and concrete, which was also one of the tallest buildings in New York City. A fifty-five-floor skyscraper on Lexington Avenue, on the East Side of Midtown Manhattan. It had first opened in 2004, and also housed businesses, retail outlets, restaurants and 105 luxury condominiums. The residence section of the building was known as One Beacon Court and it had its own separate entrance, one I knew led up to both Kaiden's nightclub and private penthouse suites.

A seemingly impossible belly to get in to so I knew I had my job cut out for me, as the place was heavily guarded for a reason. This was on purpose, as he had the nightclub built only a floor below his own accommodation and was a place he found himself spending most of his time. His country mansion was one he rarely spent any time at, even though it wasn't far from the city, being in Greenburgh, New York.

Well, that was until his Siren came into his life, as

Raina, like me, preferred the country, seeing as she too was from England.

In fact, in my stories of him, the only time he laughed or smiled was once his Siren had come into his life, and it made me wonder if he would be the same in this regard. Raina, his fated Chosen One, who I couldn't help but now wonder, where in the world was she? Shouldn't she have been here now, doing what was no doubt the impossible?

For starters, I didn't even know how I was going to make it up to the top floors. It wasn't like you could just walk right in there and ask for the big man himself. Or in this case, his brother, as he was the only one who could help me now.

But then I also had to remember, that like the mansion, I knew the ins and outs of this place, as I had walked them in my dreams enough times. And after all... hadn't I written down everything in that first book? No, all I needed to do was actually make it inside one of the elevators and it would be easy, as I knew the passcode to get up to the club and even beyond it, if I needed to. Which was why, instead of making my way through to the front entrance, all I needed to do was make my way into the garage as there was an elevator I could use.

So, I had the cab driver drop me off there and walked down to the guard that I knew would be there, making sure everyone who had the right to park in the garage showed their card. His name was Toby, even though he didn't have a badge, which I used to my advantage, walking straight up to him now, with I had my story already planned out in my head.

"Oh thank God, someone is still here. Look, can you let me in real quick, my boss left some papers in his car and if I don't get them for this meeting he's having, I am gonna be soooo fired!" I said dramatically, throwing my hands up and fluffing out my hair for no particular reason. People seemed fixated on my hair as it was… well, unusual to say the least. It also seemed to throw a lot of people off their game, which right now I was totally going to use to my advantage.

"Erm, I'm sorry, lady, but unless you got a card I can't let you in there." He nodded to the barrier people usually swiped their cards against to allow them access.

"Toby, isn't it?" I asked in a sweet tone, making him frown before answering with,

"How did you know that?"

"Like I said, my boss kind of owns the building."

"You know Mr West?" Ah so that's what he was telling the mortals his name was… I suppose Wrath was a little… *Hellish.*

"I do and well, you know his utterly gorgeous, all black, Bugatti Veyron you have hidden away in the back, well that is the beauty that could save my bacon on this fine day," I said, making him chuckle.

"Mr West hasn't driven that in a while," he admitted with a smile.

"Nope, and precisely why those files got left in there

and forgotten about until today," I said, thinking on my feet and hoping for once here was a guy who would do his job badly and let me pass. So, I laid it on thick, put my hands together like I was praying and said,

"Pretty please." Then just as he was about to say no, I took a leaf out of Raina's book, literally, and put on a different type of voice, one I was actually surprised to hear coming out of me like some sexual purr.

"Now, just what does a girl have to say to get you to trust her, hmm?" At this, he sort of glazed over for a moment, just like the men in my book do when Raina speaks in that Siren way of hers. Making me now wonder how the hell I just learned that, as seconds later and he nodded for me to go through without another word.

"Haha," I blurted out once inside, before covering my mouth in a fit of nervous giggles as I rushed inside, ignoring the gorgeous million-dollar Veyron in sight of the private elevator. Then, once inside, I made the rash decision to go up one floor above the club and to where I knew the VIP was located, knowing that I only had one shot at this and if I was caught, then I may not get another chance.

So, I typed in the code I knew would take me up there and waited while my nerves played havoc with my fidgety nature, making me tap a foot on the floor as it counted down the levels. Of course, there certainly was enough of them, landing on 54, seeing as the club on the floor below was called Club 53 Sins, it made sense. Of course, what also made sense was the armed guards that faced me the second the door opened.

As there, plain as day, was Tristan, a gorgeous Demon who had been with Hel in that lift when asshole Dean had been hassling me. Which meant that I was really left hoping that thanks to my wig that day, I wouldn't be recognized.

"Fuck!" I muttered under my breath, making another guy smirk before Tristan turned my way and said,

"Hey darlin', you lost little girl?" I swear I wanted to roll my eyes at being called little, but of course he would, seeing as with my hair I had been compared to everything from a doll to Shirley Temple. But then I knew this would have been even worse without that added four inches my heels gave me.

"No, but if you want to get lost, then that's fine with me," I replied and, to his shock, I walked right past him. However, I made it about two feet when I was apprehended and held against the wall with a knife now pointed at my neck.

"What, you can't take a joke, doll face?" I asked, making him look at me like I was nuts, and maybe I was.

"Well, it has to be said, you got balls, lady," he replied, and damn him his handsome face.

"Yeah, that or a death wish," I muttered, making him grin.

"You said it, which would be a shame 'cause you're

fucking beautiful," he told me, making my mouth drop open in shock because wow, that was nice of him.

"Aww shucks, that's sweet… kind of wish I hadn't told you to get lost now," I told him, making his grin get even bigger.

"Along with other things," I added, trying to turn his knife away from me, making him tut down at me,

"Yeah, nice try, sweet cheeks, but it ain't moving until you tell me who you are and why you're here."

"Oh, little ole me? I'm just Hel's new squeeze," I said, making him narrow his gaze down at me in question.

"Now that is surprising," he commented as if he knew the reasons why this wouldn't ever be.

"Why, not his type?" I asked, because I kind of really wanted to know.

"That depends, are you here for him to fuck or eat?" he replied, making the other men snigger behind him. Which was when I added a bit of spunk to my reply by getting up on tip toes and whispering,

"What if I like both?" Then I winked at him, making him throw his head back laughing before saying to himself,

"Oh, I like this one, and if Hel wasn't in such a fucked up foul mood, then he may do too, but as it is now, he will kill you where you stand just for asking for him and truth is, I kinda like you for myself." I released a sigh and told him,

"It's a shame, you had pretty eyes too," I said, making

him frown before I sprayed him in the face with my mint spray and causing him to bellow like a beast. But since he let me go and had twisted his body around, I snuck under his arm and ran straight for the doors I knew led into the club. Oh, and now with the sound of them all after me combined with the sound of that heavy base line rock music the second I was inside.

A sea of dark waves was the floor below, as bodies all flowed to the same song, throwing themselves around in the crowd, their moves only showcased by the lines of strobe lights illuminating them. It was therefore hard to make out much of the main club below, as there was a heavy band playing at one end and a packed-out bar at the other. But then again, I knew enough from my dreams that the theme of this place was raw industrial beams meets brushed steel table tops and seats and black marble flooring.

Now, as for the VIP level, that I was currently invading, this was slightly more plush looking. The whole place occupied the level above, with enough cut out of the floor to allow all to be seen below it. Directly opposite was a staircase that allowed those fortunate enough entrance to the VIP, and they would first have to walk around the raised walkway, one that hung from cables from above. This was so they could make it to this side of the club that I was now standing in, the VIP. But for this they would first have to be allowed through by the army of guards below, something I knew now, I would have no chance at doing.

Now once up here, they would then find themselves in far more luxury, as it was all plush scalloped shaped booths of black velvet and black and white pictures on the walls of all seven deadly sins. They were everywhere, with the whole of one wall dedicated just to Wrath alone.

The highly polished black marble floor made it look as though you were walking upon some lagoon and would fall into its dark oblivion at any point. Just then the band started up with a new song that was a dark metal version of 'O Fortuna'. It was a haunting song and was one I knew played regularly at the club due to its origins. It was written in the 13th century as a medieval Latin poem, which was part of a collection known as the Carmina Burana. It literally meant 'Oh Fate', and it is about the inescapable power of fate.

This meant it became the perfect background theme to what I was trying to do now, which was attempting to save the man I loved by first throwing my mortal self at the mercy of Wrath…

Helmer Wrath.

CHAPTER 7
BROKEN WORDS

It didn't take me long to find the private seating Hel would be sitting in as it was front and centre, overlooking the club below. It was also directly across from the grand sweeping staircase that was heavily guarded, only letting the ultimate Supernatural elite up it. Where once through, they would find themselves on a balcony that would lead them all the way around the edge of the club before getting to the VIP area that was situated on this side. Which meant that the council members and their ruler could watch both the club below and anyone coming their way.

As for me, well I was pretty sure they weren't going to expect me, and if I didn't want to get caught before saying my piece, then the only way for me to get through was basically jumping over booths which was the seating behind them. This was because they were surrounded by guards which made it nearly impossible to get through unless well… you were welcome. Something I wasn't ever going to be.

"Yep, I'm a dead woman," I said, putting my hands to the rails and telling myself,

"Good talk, now jump!" And I did just that before landing right in front of Hel and his men, barely staying on my feet. Then the guards came running around, and I quickly held a hand out to them and said on a rush of words,

"I know where…" This was all I got out before I was thrown to the floor, knocking all the air from me before being hauled back up.

"What the fuck, Tristan?!" Hel bellowed in clear rage, getting to his feet at the same time I was held before him.

"Sorry Hel, this cunning little hell cat fought her way in." I wanted to roll my eyes as they didn't know what a fucking hell cat was unless they had met Roger!

"And just how did she get up here, ever think to ask her that?" Boaz, Kaiden's second in command asked, making me wince knowing what a ruthless bastard he could be, especially playing with that fucking bowie knife of his like it was his favourite toy… which yeah, basically it was.

"It doesn't fucking matter how, she obviously overheard someone speaking the code," another man snapped, and I knew his name to be Alessandro, which literally meant 'Man's defender and warrior' in Greek.

Because these guys were big on names that meant something to represent their personalities. He was like most, big, broody men and had the face of a living God, one that would take most of the female population's breath away. I also knew him to be an Angel, but not ever to be fooled as the good kind… he was as ruthless as the rest of them on Kaiden's council.

"Silence! Go wipe her fucking memories and get her the fuck out of here before I change my mind and just kill the bitch!" Hel snapped, sitting back down and making me suck in a quick breath, because well, shit just got real… *real!* Meaning this was my last chance as I coughed through my brief winding and quickly warned,

"I wouldn't do that if I were you!"

"Yeah, and why the fuck not, little…?"

"…Girl, yeah, yeah, I get it. I'm short and have all the hair… Look, if you kick me out now then you will never see your brother again!" I shouted this last part as I was being dragged away and oh boy, if there was one sure way of getting me killed quick, then that had been it!

"Wait!" Hel ordered, now with his voice like thunder and his face just as frightening. Then he rose to his full height and stormed over to us, nodding for his men to let me go. But if I thought this was in my favour, I was oh so very wrong. I knew this as he gripped me brutally by the chin and started walking me backwards. This was something he did until my body was being bent backwards over the railings, ones that were all that separated me from living and breathing on the VIP and becoming splat and dying on the club floor below.

"Now, why would you be so foolish as to say something like that to me, huh?" he asked me in a deadly tone, and well I knew he had it in him, but he had always been so nice to Raina. Damn it, Emme, but when will you fucking learn, you are not fucking Raina!

"If you kill me, you will never know where to find him," I reminded him the closer to the edge he pushed me, making me reach out and try in vain to hold onto the railings. Then he grabbed my throat and barked,

"I swear to the fucking Gods, that if you have hurt my brother…"

"What! No, I would never hurt Kaiden!" I snapped back, shocking him enough to pull me back over to the safety of the VIP, just enough that it felt as if I was no longer seconds away from being tipped up with barely a push.

"You speak his name as if you know him?" he asked, after letting go of my throat and making me scoff. If only he knew just how true that was.

"Look, I am not the enemy here," I told him.

"And you are what exactly?"

"Well, that I can't tell you, but one name I can give and that's Dagon." At this his hissed a curse and said,

"Fuck! I knew that fucker had to be involved!"

"Yeah, but then when is he not?" I muttered, making

him frown at me and I therefore I quickly tried to cover my tracks.

"I mean, what a twat, eh?" At this he narrowed his beautiful blue eyes at me and said,

"And how exactly can I trust you?" I looked around and released a sigh before asking,

"First, is there somewhere slightly less, killing mob vibe where we can talk? Because I feel like any second I am going to get maimed… perhaps your office or Kaiden's?" I nodded behind him where I knew the raised glass window that looked like a huge, mirrored wall was actually Kaiden's office. He cocked a brow at me as if I had surprised him and I gathered, I shouldn't have known this. However, if he thought this, he didn't say it. No, instead he held out an arm telling me to go before him, which was when I knew what this was… *a test.* He wanted to know if I knew the way.

Fine, so be it. Because I had already hung myself by giving him all he needed to know. 'Cause I couldn't exactly play dumb here. So I walked back towards the way I came and into the lobby area, but instead of going for the lifts, I walked in the opposite way and around the corner to a small staircase that would take us up to his brother's office.

Of course, it was exactly the way I remembered it from my dreams, and I even found myself looking towards the sofa, where I knew that him and Raina had made love once in my book. As for the rest of the room, and not just the black leather sofa that was arched and situated in front of the window, there was a whole wall of what I knew was Kaiden's whiskey collection, all made up of frosted glass shelves and lit up from below. It was housed in dark wood, that panelled the rest of the space and matched the massive desk that was situated in the middle of the room.

"Nice view," I commented, after Hel walked over to the bar in front of the wall of whiskey and pour himself a drink, not offering me one.

"This is the part where you start talking," he snapped, making me sigh.

"I have… erm, should we say… conditions."

"Ha yes, but of course you fucking do!" he all but snarled, making me flinch.

"And just what is that supposed to mean exactly?" I couldn't help but snap back, unable to think of all the shit I had put on the line to do this... namely my life!

"Just how much money is my brother's life worth these days?" At this my mouth dropped open in utter shock.

"Careful, sweetheart, or I may be tempted to punish you by putting something in there, you keep it open any longer." At this I snapped it shut but the shock only increased.

"I will pretend you didn't just say any of that."

"Which part, the money or when I force you to your knees to give me a blow job?" he brazenly replied.

"All of it! Gods be damned, I don't want any of your fucking money and I certainly don't want to give you anything, let alone a blow job!" I barked in an utterly insulted tone, and at this he actually smirked before asking me,

"Then what do you want if not money?"

"It's simple, I want your word." Now this did surprise him, and he pulled back a little as if I had struck him.

"My word on what exactly?"

"Two things," I replied, having already rehearsed this part in my mind.

"And those would be…" he paused, rolling a hand around as if to prompt me to continue. So, I took a deep breath and told him,

"That when you save him, you don't mention anything about me being here." Again, he looked shocked and after downing his drink, told me,

"Now you have me curious, and as for the second?"

"You let me leave the moment I tell you what it is you need to know," I replied with what I hoped looked like a casual shrug of my shoulders, even though, inside, I was anything but feeling casual.

"Which is?" he asked, making me release a sigh before telling him the painful truth.

"To tell you where your brother has been buried alive." At this I watched as his anger overtook his usual cool, and he threw the glass against the wall before coming at me like a madman, making me hold up my hands in surrender, getting out on a rush,

"I only want to save him!"

"If that were true, you wouldn't come here with your bargains to save your own skin!" he growled down at me, now backing me into the window that from the other side wouldn't have shown my panic but only a reflection of the club back in its mirror.

"Oh, so you're blaming me for trying to save my own life?" I asked, making what I hoped was a very good point.

"Yes, well let's see how long you can keep hold of that precious life for, because if you don't start talking and begin telling me what I want to know, then I swear to you, it will be seconds," he threatened, and Gods, but I believed him! Yet, despite this, I also knew he wouldn't kill me before I told him what he needed to know… as for after, then at this point, who the fuck knew!

"Not without your word," I tried again, making him snarl against my cheek and I yelped aloud.

"You have no idea who you are dealing with, little girl!" he warned, turning his back to me and walking away. This was when I decided to make my move, one that I hoped told him how serious I was. It was that or I was just giving him another reason to kill me.

"Maybe you're right, or maybe it's you who doesn't know who you're dealing with… *Demon.*" At this he paused and looked back at me, now knowing the truth. I was a mortal who knew of their world. At this he grinned knowingly.

"So, it really is death you're looking for then, is that it?"

"I told you once what I want, I don't need to say it again for you to know that's not what I am looking for… quite the opposite in fact," I answered with another shrug of my shoulders. However, when he didn't give me that, I continued,

"Look, this is simple, you want to save your brother and I want your brother saved… we want the same thing, Hel."

"And now you speak my own name like you know it," he commented, making me sigh and shake my head before telling him,

"You are wasting time."

"Time you do not have, is that it?" I swallowed hard and told him,

"Time neither of us have, but most of all, time Kaiden doesn't have… Please, all I want is the chance to do the right thing and still be able to walk away from this," I told him honestly, making him frown as if he was trying to understand it himself.

"Are you known to my brother? Is that why you run, have you done him wrong?" At this I looked to the floor and was about to deny it when Hel got there first,

"That's it, isn't it? That's why you want to run." I shook my head and told him genuinely,

"Your brother doesn't know me… no one… *no one here does,"* I added in what I knew was a sad, regretful tone. Suddenly my face was lifted, and a handsome narrowing pair of turquoise eyes was staring down into my own.

"You're not lying," he stated.

"I have no reason to seeing as I only came here to speak the truth," I replied, making his hold on me gentle.

"Then if it is the truth you speak, give me your name."

"And yet to do so would make me lie," I answered, making him growl in frustration.

"And yet you say you truly aren't an enemy to my brother?"

"No, not at all. I only want to see him safe," I replied, making him frown.

"You speak as if you care for… ah, that is it. You're a former forbidden lover trying to protect his…" At this I held up a hand and told him,

"No! Gods, that's not it either… bloody hell… sorry, no pun intended it's just, I am not, nor have I ever been, well you know… shaking that monkey's tree." At this he actually laughed at me.

"I must say, I am starting to understand why Tristan didn't just kill you on the spot when intruding here… there is something strangely appealing about you, and I speak not only of your obvious beauty," he replied.

"I am not… I mean you think I am… I know I am not beautiful, Hel, and you don't have to flatter me to get the information you need, just your word that you will let me go, will do," I said, making him smirk at me as if I had amused him yet again. Well, I guess that was better than pissing him off.

"Yes, well, I usually need a name to give such a vow of protection to." I swear, at this, I would have rolled my eyes.

"Fine, call me Doris." At this he chuckled and said,

"You don't look like a Doris."

"Thanks, unless you say I look like a Betty." He kept his grin in place and shook his head telling me no, I did not.

"So do we have a deal?" I asked, getting impatient now, especially when I knew where Kaiden was.

"Alright, you have my word, Doris, now tell me what I need to know… where is my brother?" After this I took a deep breath and told him everything in my vision, making him say 'fuck' a lot and hiss other things through his teeth. Then he walked over to a phone and called someone, snarling down the line,

"Get the team ready… we go to get my brother. Bring Teko, for we will need a spell weaver, and send Tristan in here!"

"Oh great, pick the one who hates me to escort me out of here," I muttered, making him walk up to me and take hold of my chin, doing so this time in a gentle hold.

"And who mentioned anything about escorting you out of here?" At his words, my whole body froze dead on the spot, as if I had been plunged into an icy lake surrounding the Vampire King's castle.

"But… but you, you…" I never got any more out as Tristan walked through the door, now with his red eyes gone but no less angry.

"I am tasking you with the new role of jailor. I want her taken to the Greenburgh and held in the cells there." I gasped at this and tried to step away from them, only to be grabbed by Tristan and pulled back in front of Hel.

"With pleasure," my new jailor rumbled, making Hel warn at the same time running the backs of his fingers down my cheek,

"She is to be unharmed, am I understood?" Tristan must have nodded behind me, as he didn't speak. But when pressure was felt under my chin, I was forced to show my tear-filled eyes up to him, making me point out,

"You gave me your word." This was when he grinned down at me before leaning in close and whispering in my ear,

"Not wise to make deals with Demons, beautiful… we have a habit of getting what we want regardless of the lies that comes out of our mouths." Then he pulled back and winked at me, making me scowl back at him.

"Oh and Tristan… don't let her get the slip on you again," Hel warned, making him growl,

"That won't happen."

"Oh good, because it won't be me you will be dealing with the next time you fuck up, but that of my brother, and something tells me he is going to be very interested in meeting this new prisoner of his…" He paused as I sucked back a fearful breath, making him grin before adding a sadistic…

"Very interested indeed."

CHAPTER 8

UNLIKELY SAVIOUR

WRATH

I must have fallen asleep for the second I heard her voice, I knew I had to have been dreaming. Although how I had managed to calm my rage enough to do so was beyond me. Yet there was no mistaking it, for there, above the ground, she was speaking to me in some sort of joint void. This being the space in one's mind that was free to dream, free to escape and free to invite those that you would wish to be there. And right now…

My Siren was speaking to me.

'I swear to you, I will do all I can to stop this… I will help you. I will risk it all just to save you… I will find a way… *you have my word, Kaiden.'* Her sweet vow made me place a hand above me, to what was now my coffin and the place my vessel may very well die and perish in. That would happen should no one find me in time. I opened my eyes the moment her sweet alluring voice faded away, telling me that my time was over. My gift of her was gone, and I couldn't help but mourn it, having never really mourned anything before in my life. But then, other than my brother, who was my only connection to life and the closest thing I came to caring for, then what else was there for me to mourn when it was all gone?

I was thousands of years old, older even than the King of Kings himself, having spent most my life in Hell alongside my father until I was asked to take this position. Of course, I would not accept without my brother, for I went nowhere without him. As for Dominic Draven, who back then was known as something far different, well he had been only too happy to get two powerful Demons for the price of one. And I can honestly say that even after all this time, the man still held my loyalty like no other, for he was a fair and brutally just King, two things I respected in a ruler.

Fair until you had to become brutal. That was the rule for successful Kings in my opinion. And speaking of brutal, well that fucker Dagon was going to die a slow fucking death, for what he didn't know was that Dominic Draven also owed me a life debt. And well, I would most definitely be collecting it in the form of an exception to the rules being broken when I was breaking his fucking neck!

Well, if there was one thing this imprisonment was doing, that was forcing me to fucking rest, for it felt as if I had not stopped these last few hundred years. As my mortal persona, I was simply busy getting richer by the day, but then this was often the way with elders like us, as we had to do something with our mounting wealth. Which also meant that if it took decades to make back a profit on our investments then that was the one thing we had in spades… *time.* Money bred even more money and money in this mortal world meant power, it was as simple as that.

Because you no longer had to be a king with armies of men at your back to gain position in this world, you just needed the largest bank account. In truth, I was fucking tired of it all and could quite easily go back to simpler days before board meetings and staring at fucking figures on a screen. It was why most of the time I had mortals deal with a lot of my business, allowing me time to deal with what I had been entrusted to do. The reason for my being here topside, and not sometimes where I thought I belonged. For I was too brutal for this world and too hard for its laughter and soft mortal hearts. It was why I preferred the city. Full of dark crime and cutthroat ways, both down in the streets and up in its skies, among its towering city buildings.

It gave me purpose and something to do.

It fed my Demon's Wrath.

So, when I had been given this Northeast sector, I had created my empire and naturally settled in the heart of the city. And now it seemed my body was to die here also. Oh, but Dagon had been one crafty fucker! For he was not actually breaking the rules but still managing to keep me contained and out of the way. As he knew that my brother would stop at nothing to try and find me. That it would keep him busy whilst Dagon himself would be busy making the claim to the King of Kings that I had neglected my sector. He would then make a bid for it to be added to his own, which was what he'd wanted all along. He wanted what was mine.

He wanted New York.

But then it also worried me, for even through the layers and layers of earth they were piling above me, I could hear them speaking of a traitor within my King's home, and that was something I needed to fight for. However, no matter how I had tried, I couldn't break free of these chains, and I couldn't get out of this damned fucking box!

In the end, I don't know how long it had been before I heard heavy machinery over me once more. But surely it was too soon for the work to be continued, for it couldn't have been days that had passed already. I had to say it was a clever method of torture, to be sure, for a weak mind could have quite easily lost it when wondering of their fate.

Of course, I also wasn't surprised when the box finally did open to find my brother's hand reaching inside and ripping away the chains that had kept me bound. This was with Teko's help, first making the Demonic incantations burn away like a dying Demon's body turning to ash.

"What took you so long, my brother?" I asked when my feet were finally on the ground once more, making him grin before I pulled him in for an embrace. A rare sight, for he was the only being alive that ever received this compassionate side of me.

"Oh, but do I have a story to tell you," he said, making me raise a brow, as I was truly intrigued, especially after dreaming of my own Siren speaking with me.

"Please tell me it started with the death of that fucker, Dagon," I growled.

"No, but you will like it all the same, I promise you that… oh, and I hope you have a thing for brazen little blondes." Now hearing this managed to stop me in my tracks, making him look back at me and burst out laughing.

"Now that is the reaction I was hoping for," he admitted, confusing the fuck out of me.

"You jest with me?"

"Any chance I can get, now come on and you will discover what I mean for yourself," he told me, motioning for me to follow him to the cars that were waiting and the rest of my men who had been here to aid him in recovering me. I looked back and realized they must have been led here and told the exact spot, as mine was the only hole made.

"You knew where to look, tell me, who did you torture to get this information from?" I asked after jerking my head, telling the one named Jericho that I would be driving without the need for words. I fucking hated being driven around by anyone! Hel smirked as he got in the passenger side, knowing himself what I was like. I then looked back at my men and after a quick glance of disdain for the fucking box I had been put in, I thundered,

"Leave the site like you found it, as I want not a word of my release to reach enemy ears, do you understand?" I said, giving my orders, knowing they would be carried out down to each word spoken. My men were some of the most loyal and had been with me and my brother for centuries, starting with my second in command, Boaz.

"My lord Wrath, it will be done," he replied with a bow of respect, before I was folding my large frame into the SUV.

"Now it's time to explain, just how did you find me?" I asked the moment we were on the road, but instead of answering me, Hel, informed me,

"You're going the wrong way." I shot him a questioning look before he told me,

"The answer is waiting for you at Greenburgh." I cocked my head a little telling him I was surprised, something that rarely happened, and oh wasn't this just my night for them. They just kept coming.

"Please tell me it comes in the form of someone I get to beat to death?" I replied, making him chuckle, answering,

"You could do that, only I have a feeling it will be the very last thing on your mind when you see who it is that I have in a cell waiting for you." I frowned in question and snapped,

"Stop fucking around, Hel!"

"But it's so much fun, and besides, it's about time I exchanged being the one pissed off and murderous, for this game." I snarled at him in warning, making him laugh before he finally gave me something,

"It's a woman." Now this did surprise me.

"Explain… *now.*" At this he released a sigh, and I knew it was because the game was done.

"She turned up at the fucking club and stood there bold as fucking brass and gave me a choice," he told me, surprising me, which I would soon discover would be the first of many.

"Which was?" I asked, already on the way to my secluded mansion home.

"Throw her from the club or allow her to speak so she could tell me where you were being held." At this I would have crashed the fucking car, had it not been the middle of the night and no fucker was around to crash into as I swerved into the wrong lane.

"She did what!?" I bit out in shock.

"And stranger still, I was unable to read her mind."

"That's not possible, she is mortal, yes?" I asked, wondering what new trickery this was.

"Oh trust me, she is very mortal and her fear smells fucking delicious!" I frowned at that, wondering why it pissed me off. But then again, it was understandable to feel protective over someone who had clearly saved my life, despite remaining cautious.

"Has she ever been seen in the club before?" I asked, making him shake his head.

"I confess to feeling as though I know her from somewhere, but I doubt someone would be foolish enough to bring their mortal pet into Sins," he replied, and I shrugged, telling him,

"But it is not unheard of all the same."

"True, and there is the matter of how she came to be there in the first place." I shot him a look.

"What do you mean?"

"She knew the code to get her up to the VIP." Now this did shock me, and he knew it as my look must have said it all, which in turn made him laugh again.

"Intrigued enough, brother?"

"And eager to speak to this little blonde intruder," I admitted, making him grin.

"Oh, but she wasn't without her demands." I rolled my eyes at this.

"Money?" I surmised.

"That's what I thought too at first but no, she wanted something else." I frowned in question before asking the obvious.

"And the price for my life, was what exactly?"

"You know I said the very same thing," my brother recalled, making my patience wane thin.

"Hel, just fucking tell me what it was that she wanted?"

"Oh, but you're not going to believe this," he replied in an excited tone that was starting to piss me off.

"Hel!" I warned.

"But this is the best part."

"Helmer!" I said, this time in a dangerous tone using his full name.

"She wanted nothing more than to be allowed to walk away after informing me of this life saving information and more importantly, without letting you know she had ever been there." I hissed in a breath at this.

"What!?"

"I shit you not, brother, those were her only stipulations, as she made me give her my word."

"You'd better not have fucking let her leave!" I snapped in some irrational panic, and I had no idea why.

"Of course not, I told her she shouldn't have trusted a Demon, hence why I am breaking my non-existent word and telling you all of this." I released a calmer breath now that I knew this mystery girl was safely imprisoned within my home. But this was when I froze and quickly asked,

"And is she unharmed?"

"What… you mean the girl who clearly just aided me in saving your life?" Hel asked, pushing my buttons, making me snap,

"What, can you fucking blame me? The least I can do

is concern myself with her own life." I said all of this after my brother gave me a knowing look.

"Please tell me being in that box for near two days hasn't made you soft."

"No, it made me fucking angry but even I have to admit, the thought of interrogating a pretty girl makes me less so," I admitted, making him grin.

"And who said anything about her being pretty?" Hel teased, making me fall for it.

"So, she is not then?"

"No, she isn't but lucky for you, she is fucking beautiful." At this I released a sigh and agreed.

"Then in that case, I am losing even more of my anger."

"There is something else, Kai," my brother admitted, making me tense my hand on the steering wheel.

"What?" I asked knowing this was about to get even more complicated.

"She knows of our kind," he admitted, making me hiss again,

"Fuck… and how the fuck did that…?!"

"Hey, don't blame me, she was there with me for all of five fucking minutes before she was calling me a Demon to my face, so it wasn't me or our men," my brother said, quickly interrupting my fury, and I raked a frustrated hand across the back of my neck, feeling the knot there from being in that fucking box so long. I would be needing one of the girls at the club to work it out before the night was over, I was sure. But then I remembered we weren't on our way back to the club, and instead we were on our way to our home far from the city. Oh, and not forgetting but on our way toward this mystery mortal who clearly knew too much of our world.

"Then beautiful or not, it is of little matter as her mind will have to be wiped if she is to survive," I said, at the very least feeling bad about it enough considering for all intents and purposes, she had saved my life.

"You mean if you deem her guilt-free and not our enemy, then she will survive?" Hel reminded me, making me sigh.

"You think she may be working with Dagon?"

"I had thought of that, yes… but to be honest, I can't see the point of it if she were, as she was the only one who knew where you were and how to free you," Hel admitted, making me gauge his tone and ask,

"But yet you still don't trust her?"

"She is clearly hiding something if she is too afraid to give me her name and then added to that, even more afraid of you coming back to find her there… it's like…"

"It's like, what?" I prompted.

"It's like she knows you, Kai." I frowned at this and shook my head a little.

"Well, I think we both know how doubtful that is… for I'd hardly be spending my time around mortal woman, no matter how beautiful," I said, even if I hadn't needed to, as no one knew me like my brother did.

"Well, she speaks your name as though she does and besides, what would force her to do something so reckless as risk her own life by trying to save yours, if she didn't know you…? She was clearly terrified enough of you, that her only request was you not knowing and her not be there when you return… so if that doesn't tell us something, then…"

"Yeah, I get it!" I interrupted, with a frustrated slash of my hand telling him to stop. Because now this did make me scowl, as what could she fear from me, the man she'd just saved?

"It makes little sense," I added after a moment of silence.

"My thoughts exactly, hence again why I didn't keep my word to little Doris."

"Doris? I thought she never gave you her name?" I asked with my scowl still firmly in place.

"Well, it certainly isn't fucking Doris, that's for sure. No, it turns out your new prisoner has quite the sense of humour… that or she is bat shit crazy, which could be the case considering what she faced to get inside and find me about to throw her ass over the balcony." At this my head whipped around so fast it would have hurt and snapped the neck of a mere mortal body.

"You fucking hurt her?!" I accused, outraged.

"No, I fucking scared her, there is a difference," he replied, and I tried to relax wondering why I was getting worked up over someone I didn't even know. Was it because I knew she had saved me…? Was it because of the voice I had heard in my dreams? Did she have something to do with it?

Could it be her?

"Where the fuck did she come from, and can she be trusted?" I asked my inner thoughts aloud.

"Well, these are the things left for you to find out, as I didn't think you would want anyone else interrogating her," my brother admitted.

"No!" I shouted out my objections suddenly, making the cocky bastard smirk. Which was also why I took a breath and tried again, this time in a calmer tone so as not to give him the reactions he wanted.

"No, you did right. I am the only one who gets to speak with her. Speaking of which, we aren't far away, who did you leave in charge of her?"

"Tristan."

"Oh fucking great," I grumbled.

"What?"

"He fucking loves mortals and will be trying to get into her fucking pants within minutes, especially if she is as beautiful as you say."

"One, I don't recall being that specific on her beauty and second, I told him not to hurt the girl," Hel replied with a knowing smirk.

"So she will be unharmed but that doesn't mean that Tristan's charms aren't painful," I pointed out, making him chuckle.

"Then it will just make her all the more susceptible when talking to you, wont it, Casanova?" I rolled my eyes at this and snapped,

"Get him on the phone, wise ass."

"And the order I am to give?" he asked in that cocky ass tone I didn't care for.

"Tell him to take her to the integration room. I want her in chains by the time I get there," I replied without looking at him.

"Oh, I just bet you do," he remarked, making me growl,

"Just fucking do it!"

"Anything else?" I thought on this and despite knowing it would only give my brother more fuel to tease me, I said it anyway…

"Yeah, tell him to…"

"Fucking keep it in his pants."

CHAPTER 9
BACKFIRED
EMMELINE

Well, so far this plan of mine had truly gone to shit!

Which was why I let my head hang down in defeat, staring at the floor of my cell and asking myself what I could have done differently. What I could have done to change my fate. But every single answer was the same as my new reality…

Kaiden was coming for me.

I honestly couldn't say that I had ever felt terror like it before, as all I had left to hope for now, was that he held some shred of pity for me. I had saved his life after all, surely that counted for something. But then if that were the case, why was I being treated like a prisoner?

Durr, Emme, that's because you are one.

I had been blindfolded when brought here, despite already knowing what the address was and what the mansion looked like. After all, I had been here in my dreams enough times. But they didn't know that. I was just sorry that I missed the sight of it, because to see if before I died would have been something. Okay, so I didn't know they were going to kill me for sure. I guess that was going to be Kaiden's call. I had however, been searched as I knew I would, and after only finding my money, a hair tie and a used can of mint spray on me, they had promptly put me in a cell. Of course, Tristan gave me back my cash and hair tie, which I stuffed in my jeans pocket, but he had scoffed at the mint spray before crushing it in his hand, making my eyes go wide. This seemed to please him at least, as he was still chuckling when he was locking the cell door.

A little time later and here I was, thinking how screwed I was, making me groan aloud and naturally, because of this I let my head smack into my palm. A second after, I heard a chuckle off to the side making me glance at Tristan, my happy jailor, who was now standing at the open door.

"I bet after what I did, you're just loving this," I commented dryly, making him shrug his shoulders and tell me,

"I will admit to wanting to strangle that pretty neck of yours after you sprayed all that shit in my eyes." I shrugged my own shoulders at this and admitted,

"If it helps, I have been wanting to kick my own ass for the last few hours." He scoffed at this and told me,

"Don't sweat it, kid, you did a good thing." I laughed and said,

"Your vessel looks about thirty," I told him, making him grin.

"Yes, well clearly, I am older than I look."

"Yeah, I know but so am I," I informed him, and he scoffed.

"Well, you look about sixteen, doll face." I sighed at this and told him,

"It's the hair, isn't it?" To which he laughed, making me tell him,

"I'm actually twenty-seven." Then I pulled my hair tie out of my pocket and started trying to contain the curls back into a ponytail that I knew would still look like a riot of spirals.

"No shit?" he replied, shocked by my age and I replied,

"No shit, chuckles." He grinned big at this and then told me,

"Well Miss twenty-seven, I have been instructed to feed you and seeing as the cook has gone for the night, cheese toasties were the extent of my culinary skills."

"You had me at cheese," I replied, making him laugh again, saying to himself,

"Funny and cute, poor bastard has no hope." He shook his head making me wonder if he was referring to Kaiden, which made me ask,

"Any news if he has been found yet?"

"Who do you think ordered me to bring you this," he said holding up a plate for emphasis, but it was totally lost on me the second he mentioned him.

"He's been freed?!" I shouted, getting to my feet and surprising Tristan.

"Whoa there, easy girl, or people are gonna think you're sweet on the big bastard or something," he said with a cheeky wink, making me blush scarlet as he looked as if he knew my secret already. But of course, he didn't... I was just being paranoid.

"I... I just meant that I'm glad and hopefully this means I will be released." Tristan granted me a look while putting down the plate next to the bench I had been sitting on. As far as cells go, this must have been one of the nicer ones. It reminded me of something you would have found in a police station. It was clean, had four brick walls, a small table against one wall, a bench seat and even a toilet and sink. There was also had a very thick metal door that had been standing between me and my freedom.

Tristan walked to the metal table and poured me a glass of water from the jug he had brought in about an hour before.

"I wouldn't count your chickens before they hatch, sweetpea," he told me, making me deflate back down onto the bench.

"But why not? If they freed him then that means I wasn't lying!" I argued as he brought me the cup,

"Drink!" he ordered, making me sigh before doing as I

was told, wondering if my scratchy, croaky throat was why he brought me a drink. Was he concerned? Perhaps I could use that to my advantage.

"Look, you have to help me get out of here, I did nothing wrong… in fact, I did the opposite of wrong and yet I am here being punished." At this he released a sigh and got down on one knee in front of me, so we were at eye level. Damn all these tall men!

"I get that you're scared, little doll, I really do, but until we know who you are for sure, then I am afraid you won't be going anywhere. Now, if you were to give me your name, then I might be able…" I turned my head away and told him,

"Thanks for the food." I heard him release a regretful sigh before he was back on his feet.

"Very well, doll, but word of warning, the next person to ask you these questions won't be as nice as me, you might want to think on that. Wrath is on his way back here and well, he's called that for a reason." After this, the sound of my cell door closing made me flinch along with the echoing sound of the lock sliding home. This was when I slumped to the floor and couldn't keep the tears at bay any longer. My only solace was that they had found him.

Kaiden had been saved.

"Then it has all been worth it," I told myself on a whisper, because it didn't matter what happened to me after this point. I could at least say that I had aided the

Fates by keeping him alive. Now all that was needed was for him to find his Siren and the rest was their own history.

I tried to find comfort in this, I really did, but no matter how much I tried, there was still a small piece of me that was heartbroken. That selfish part that wanted him for myself, despite knowing it would ruin everything for him. Because I wasn't his Siren, I was just the author of his story and no amount of wishing would make it any different.

I was the one who got to tell his story, not feature in it. But if that was completely true, then what was I doing here now? I shook my head, trying to clear it of the fog that was named Kaiden Wrath. A Demon warrior that was on his way here to question me and in all honesty, for the first time, I had no idea how this story was going to end.

But one thing was for sure.

I doubted this was my happy ending.

I knew that about twenty minutes later, long after my food had been consumed and Tristan walked back inside my cell looking grim. But then I knew why after glancing down at what he now held in his hands, making me get up and run to the other end of the cell.

"No, no, no please! You don't have to do this!" I shouted, making him release a frustrated sigh.

"It's just orders, doll face, nothing personal, yeah." I started shaking my head telling him no, knowing now my time was up. Kaiden was here and I was to be dragged into an interrogation room with him!

"Please, Tristan... I am begging you here," I told him, making him wince as if he got no pleasure from being the one to do this to me.

"Look, play nice and come with me and I will let you walk in there without the use of these," he said, nodding down to the thick manacles in his hand. So, I nodded, thinking this would be my very last chance to escape this fate.

"Good girl, now this way," he told me looking pleased, and I half felt bad for him, knowing that I was planning on running for my life the first chance I got. But for now, I did as he asked and walked out of the door, seeing what I had the first time. I was in the basement that had been converted into a full-on prison, as it was just cell door after cell door. Some were as you would have expected, but others looked a little more reinforced, with the similar symbols and incantations I had seen in my dream of when Kaiden had been buried.

Then the closer we got to the end of the corridor, I saw my opportunity as a door was opening. So, I suddenly started running for it, making Tristan swear behind me. But I cared of little else than escaping, running for my life and just as the door opened all the way, I threw myself through it, trying to barge past the person in my way.

However, the second I saw it was Hel, I skidded to a stop, falling backwards on my ass, now resembling a little crab trying to scurry away. His cunning bad boy grin was the only response I received as he looked to Tristan behind me and said something truly chilling, making me scream…

"Hence my brother's request for chains."

CHAPTER 10

CAPTIVATING CAPTIVE

WRATH

"Report!" I ordered the second I made my way down to the cells that were situated in the basement. The property was one I'd had built about ten years ago and from the outside, looked every bit of the 15,000 square foot of pure luxury it was. However, it also held in its lower levels the real reason for it being built, as it was a heavily fortified prison. It was also less than a forty-minute drive out of the city and unless I had prisoners to deal with, then it was often only a place I came to if I was forced to entertain the King and his council. Needless to say, he preferred it to the city, seeing as it was definitely more private but seeing as he too had his own preferred place of business in the country, it wasn't surprising when he suggested that I have it built.

As for now, I had showered since arriving and rid

myself of the days' stink and the smell of dirt being in that box had awarded me.

My brother smirked at my question, making me wonder what curve ball this little saviour of mine had thrown their way now.

"Apart from your little rabbit trying to run right out of here, nothing much," Hel replied, making Tristan cower slightly under my harsh gaze.

"She bested you?" I almost snarled the words, angry that she could have escaped before I even had chance to see her. At least Tristan had the good grace to look sheepish.

"She's cute and unsuspecting," was his excuse, making me scoff.

"Then you are weak if you let the sight of a pretty face overrule your better judgement… who recaptured her?" I asked, making my brother grin.

"It wasn't so much a recapture as it was just showing up and frightening her until she fell on her ass." I sighed in such a way that it ended with a rumbled growl.

"Anything else I should know?"

"Well, other than now knowing her age, which is a lot older than she fucking looks, I can tell you that!" Tristan replied.

"Which is?"

"She looks like I wouldn't sell her fucking alcohol that's for sure, but according to her she is actually twenty-seven." Hmm, I was starting to question just how unsuspecting this little mortal looked, for it seemed to be her only advantage at this point.

"And that's all we know?" I asked in a sceptical tone.

"We searched her and found nothing."

"Nothing at all?" I asked, finding this odd.

"Well, just a few hundred dollars and a mint spray, one I became well acquainted with," Tristan complained dryly, making me look to my brother for answers.

"That's how she got into the VIP, she sprayed him in the face and then ran for it," Hel added, making me scoff.

"Then it looks like she bested you twice, Tristan, and let the hit to your ego be your punishment," I replied, knowing that it would as his sneer of anger was easy to see. In all honestly, I would have laughed under different circumstances. Besides, my men would have thought I was under some Hellish substance, like Devil's rum had I laughed now, seeing as the sound was rarely ever heard coming from my lips. After all, I was known as a ruthless bastard for a reason, not an easy going, amused one.

"As for the girl, did we discover a name at least?" Tristan shook his head, and Hel continued to smirk like this was the most fun he'd had in an age.

"It would seem that the honour is all yours to discover," Hel told me, making me scowl, knowing now that after all my talk, I was going to look bad should I come up empty handed. But then again, I couldn't see this happening as I was well known for my interrogation skills. Although, I had to admit, even for me this was a new one. Not only for it being a mortal woman but one that had for intents and purposes, saved my life.

"Which shouldn't be too hard seeing as she is clearly fucking terrified of you," Tristan commented wryly, making me frown.

"But I have never met her until this day." I don't know why I made a point of saying this or felt the need to justify myself.

"Well, she certainly seems to know you, although stranger still, I couldn't tell which emotion took centre stage more, her fear of you or the obvious relief she displayed when I told her you had been saved," Tristan replied and well, this really did make me frown, as none of it made any sense. Although it was like Tristan had said, she certainly seemed to know me, regardless of being unable to claim the same in return.

"Other than being terrified, is there anything else I should know?" I asked, now eager to get in there and witness this all for myself.

"Like what?"

"Has the girl suffered any harm, has she eaten, drank anything, slept since being brought here!?" I snapped, making Hel smirk, whereas Tristan just looked blatantly shocked,

"You care?"

"Oh, for fuck sake, the girl did just save me from rotting away in a fucking box, so yes, I fucking care enough not to see the girl harmed!" I barked, making Hel snigger.

"And you can shut the fuck up!" I said, pointing a finger at my brother who held up his hands with a big fucking grin I wanted to punch off his face!

"Perhaps its best someone else were to interrogate her, Boaz maybe, as he always had a way…" Tristan suggested, making me roar in anger,

"NO!" This made him take a step back.

"No one is permitted near the girl without my say so, is that understood!?" I ordered on a growl, making Tristan answer me quickly.

"Of course, my Lord Wrath."

"Hey, I didn't fucking suggest it," Hel said as I turned my dark gaze to him, then when I turned my back ready to go in there, I heard him mutter,

"No, because I wouldn't miss this for the fucking world." I released a rumbled sigh and ignored it, choosing to take another calming breath before unlocking the door to the interrogation room. And the second I did, even I had to admit the room had never once before been graced by so much beauty.

My brother had been right when saying she wasn't just pretty, but he had also forgotten to use words like stunning and Goddess! Fuck me, but I was struck dumb at just the sight of her, for simply put, she was…

Blindingly beautiful.

But then the second she saw me entering the room, her

fear of me was something that thickened the air and was enough to make a fucking meal of. For I sucked it back and absorbed it like a fucking feast. However, for some reason, the feeling didn't leave me as satisfied as feeding from someone's fear of me, not like it usually did.

I knew I was intimidating as well, I had a fucking mirror and seeing as I had been buying my own clothes for a while now, I knew I was a big bastard. Fuck, but in my rage I had many a time split my clothes that had been pulled tight over muscles tensing in my anger. But right now, there wasn't an ounce of anger in sight of this fearful little Angel in front of me. No, in fact she seemed to calm me like no other and I felt urges kick in that made me want to get closer. Urges like protection and another that admittedly confused the shit out of me… it was *lust and need.*

However, I stopped the second I saw her bolt out of the seat, tipping it over in her haste to be further away from me. She then tugged on the long length of chain that connected her bound hands to the ring on the floor.

The sight vexed me, but instead of showing my anger, I simply raised a brow at her in question. In turn she tugged at the chains again, making me narrow my gaze on those heavy shackles at her delicate wrists. I don't know why but the sight struck me like a heavy blow from my brother in the ring. It was too many things to process at once, so I didn't give it time to manifest into a discovery.

No, instead I took the time to discover her. Gods, but I

had never seen hair like hers before, as I swear it seemed to glow under the fluorescent lights. A mass of tight little curls all attempted to be tamed back and contained in a tie that didn't look up to the task. This making me wonder if she knew that not all curls wanted to play her game.

I suddenly had the mad urge to touch them, almost needing to know if they were as soft and delicate as they looked. But then she tugged on the chain again in an attempt to be free, making me wonder what she would do if she were? Would I get the pleasure of chasing her down myself? Now that did invoke a thought that didn't need any time to process, for I knew it as pure, fuckable desire.

Yet, despite this I decided I couldn't give into her needs in leaving space between us and I couldn't give into my own, which of course was to plaster her fuckable little body up against the wall the way I wanted. So, I settled on somewhere in between, walking around to the side of the table she had been sitting in front of. This was so I could lean back against it, knowing it would hold my massive bulk seeing as it was metal and also bolted to the floor.

I had chosen this room as being one of our less intimidating rooms, being that it wasn't filled with torture devices and tools aimed at making grown Demons cry. No, it simply had a camera in the corner, four bare cinder block walls and a metal chair that matched the table I leaned against now. Then I folded my arms across my chest, feeling my black T-shirt tighten around my biceps and released a sigh.

"Come here, little one," I tested, seeing if she would comply, however she just shook her head, making a muscle in my jaw tick, which was a clear sign of mine, *I was displeased.* But then trying to keep my calm I told her,

"I believe it is you whom I owe my escape to?" Again, she refused to speak, and those beautiful big eyes of hers looked like swirls of dark melted chocolate.

"Now the question is why would you do something like that for someone you have never met until this day?" I asked despite even now, feeling as if we had met somewhere, as it was like my brother had said, she looked familiar. And I continued to question this, seeing as now she looked a little hurt by my comment.

"Why would you do something so reckless that would no doubt put you in danger, for me? Especially seeing as you are after all, *a very breakable human,*" I tested, after what Hel had told me about her knowing of our world. Oh, but this got me a response as I watched her, now being utterly transfixed as she swallowed hard, making me drink in the sight like the bastard I was. So, I continued to push for a reaction, knowing as of yet, I had still not heard her speak a word and something I confess finding myself impatient for.

"My brother foolishly thinks it is because you care for me, but I fear he has lost his mind to madness, for to care for such a ruthless being as myself is the definition of insanity." Again, I enjoyed watching as she swallowed down another lump of fear. Oh yes, this was going to be easy, for I would break her will soon enough and then she would give me what I wanted. The question was my own limitations on how much I would take, as right now... well quite honestly, *I wanted fucking everything!*

I was almost disappointed for I really liked it when my enemies fought back, wondering if she could be classed as such. I cracked my knuckles at the thought, something she shivered at, and no doubt took as a silent threat.

"Would you like to know what I believe?" I questioned, and smirked when she shook her head telling me no, she didn't. She was beautiful to be sure, but she was also a cute little thing, it had to be said. Even if she was trying to hide in the shadows of the room, something I wouldn't allow for long. As I had to confess, I wanted to see more of her. Something in itself, was also surprising. She reminded me of a little bisque doll, with a halo of tight blonde curls that looked completely unruly as they continued to escape whenever they could from the confines of the elastic in her hair.

Heart shaped lips I wanted to do wicked things to and again, the thought was shocking, as I had never even thought of another human in such a way before. Sure, many were beautiful but the ones at the top of that list often used it as a weapon against men. Or they wore their vanity like armour and held themselves in higher regard than most other things. Their thoughts were often for their own beauty that they would hold like a blade to the throats of Kings, morphing their ambition of power into orders spoken from the mouths of those in charge.

I would not fall or succumb to such foolishness.

But then, strangely, I didn't get that from this one, for she seemed only to concentrate on her flaws, accepting them as if there was little she could do about them. But this was the only part of her mind she would give me, making me question why none of my men, my brother included, could read her mind. I had foolishly believed with my own strength and gifts in this I would be easy granted this insight into her mind, but it was not the case. For it was only the insecurities she felt in herself and that of her obvious fear of me, that was being projected.

But by the Gods, from what I had seen of her so far, she held a beauty of the likes I had never seen before, and I questioned what it was about her that held me so captivated. Although, I professed that one of my strengths was not giving way to my thoughts, so she would have no idea how much she affected me. I was a man without weakness and worked hard to keep it that way. Which was why this would only aid me in getting the answers I desired.

"My guess would be that you were sent here for a reason," I said, testing this theory by reading her reactions and her mind screamed this was ridiculous, as why would she risk herself if she didn't care for my life.

"Why indeed?" I questioned, wondering now if she knew of my kind, would she know she was projecting her thoughts. But then why not just speak them? Why hadn't she yet said a word?

"Perhaps you were sent here to ensure I was freed to gain my trust, so that you may infiltrate my stronghold and council," I said, making her shake her head again, and I suppressed a grin when this freed even more curls. The endearing sight had me urging to take hold of them for myself in a tight fist as I plundered her pretty but silent mouth. I even found myself wondering just how many times it would take for her to shake them free completely… hmm, a private mission perhaps.

"I must say, the fact that you have little to say on the matter only condemns you further," I told her, making her open her mouth and fuck me, but the sight had me hard in seconds… oh, but what I would love to put in that mouth right now. I shook these sexual thoughts from my mind, questioning their origins and asking myself now if she were in fact human, or a sorceress.

At this I decided to turn up the intimidation a notch and took off my jacket, knowing the sight of my larger frame tensing would make me more threatening to her, as she was tiny compared to me. Gods, but the difference in us was almost laughable, along with her reaction as her large eyes widened in a comical way. Then I rolled my shoulders which admittedly, was one of my habits when frustrated. My body hummed with power that sometimes felt as if my vessel wasn't big enough to contain my Demon. Someone, who was most definitely pushing at me, wanting a taste out of this little sweet morsel of a thing.

Surprisingly, though, the second thought my demon growled at me, was... *mine.* He wanted to keep her, and I had to say I was inclined to agree with him, wondering for just how long I could get away with it. But first, I would need to know all about her for that to happen, as I couldn't very well steal her away from her world without drawing attention to such. No, it would need planning, for she most likely had family and friends who would notice her disappearance. Which brought me to my next question, noting that again, she still hadn't said anything yet.

"What is your name, my little Halo?" I asked, granting her this nickname as it felt right, especially with the way her light blonde hair seemed to glow around her head. At this she looked unnerved and shook her head more forcefully this time, and I knew she was only a few shakes left in her before that golden Halo I named her for, would be free. Gods, but would it blind me again when it came?

Fuck!

What was wrong with me?!

"My men told me you were searched, yet nothing was found on you. Although, now I question the thoroughness of their job." At this she looked completely panicked and tugged hard on the chain in reaction. Hmm, now that was interesting. She looked utterly terrified at what my words might mean, which was when I tested such by adding,

"What is the human saying, if you want a job doing

right, you are best doing it yourself." The moment I said this her fear cranked up again, where she tugged even harder and shook her head, before finally whispering 'no' and a distinct little 'please'. But it wasn't loud enough for me, as it was barely even a whisper. I found myself frustrated that she was so fearful of me, annoyed even when usually this would have pleased me. I liked to be feared.

But now… *my Demon and I very nearly loathed it!*

It had soon turned sour and now tasted like fucking acid on my tongue, and I couldn't fucking think of why! It was no doubt the reason why I scowled at her, a harsh and brutal face of a killer that was only terrifying her more.

Fuck!

Her fear tasted bitter, a feeling that churned in my gut like poison.

"Enough!" I snapped, making her stop her struggles and after a moment of seeing her like a doe caught in headlights, I released a heavy sigh of frustration and said,

"It is time to give me what I want. Your time is running out, little human."

And it was, in more ways than one, as my Demon growled at me once more.

This time with only one demand…

Claim her.

CHAPTER 11

THE POWER OF A NAME

EMMELINE

Gods, but he was a beast!

Something I had expected to find, as much as I hadn't.

It was insane to feel this way, but I had been so used to writing him as something different. But then, that had been writing him as a lover and someone who cared for little more than his Siren and his brother. And right now, I seemed a million miles away from being someone he would ever care for.

I had to remember that.

Because right now I was his enemy, and as someone who had seen that other side of him, well I knew how dangerous he could be. Fuck me, but just the sight of him now had me shaking, rattling the chains which only seemed to anger him further.

Bloody Hell, but I had even been too afraid to speak,

knowing that when I did, my runaway mouth could give me away. I had always been too chatty, never knowing when to shut up and an utter freight train of words. As for now, well ha, even Nat would have laughed at me, as around this man I couldn't even form one word! In fact, to those who knew me, then I doubted they would have believed me.

People even joked that if I was ever to be interrogated by the cops, I would be the first one singing like a damn canary! But not now. No, now it felt as if this guy had stolen my voice and taken it prisoner. Unsurprising really, when faced with such a being, as I took note of every muscle I already felt as if I knew intimately. After all, I had spent hours writing each line of his incredible body and describing this mountain of a man as the Viking God he looked to be. Despite him being more like the Devil, as I knew he was the son of Sathanas, the King of Wrath, and a powerful son of a bitch at that!

But of course, I knew it all.

I knew everything about him and yet it felt like right now, I knew nothing! That's why I was so terrified, because I knew if I opened my mouth then I could reveal everything, as words would come crashing out of me like a tsunami of truth. Then I would be signing my own death sentence as I knew humans weren't supposed to know about his kind. I knew because I had bloody written it!

Damn it, but I had most likely broken fifty of their laws in that one book alone. And if he googled my name, then I was a gonner! Okay, so my little fan base wasn't exactly known all over the world but still, up until two days ago, you could buy the damn thing on Amazon! Which meant that was game over the second he discovered who I was.

Damn it!

Fuckity fuck fuck!

I was screwed and so not in a good, finally losing my virginity, mind blowing Demon sex kind of way, because yep, those had been some hot scenes and not going to lie, but a big selling point for my books! Oh great, just great, now that was all I needed, to be blushing like a nun in a peep show! But then could I really be blamed when knowing what those hands were capable of?!

"Mmm, now that added colour to your cheeks does intrigue me, for what would warrant such a reaction when your fear still lingers?" he asked, and I raised my hands up to try and brush back my crazy hair when the chain stopped me. So, I gave into the impulse and blew the curl from my lips, making him smirk. Gods, he was handsome! In that totally raw, bad ass way that made me realise my writing hadn't done him justice.

No words ever could.

Suddenly, his slow movements brought me back to my insane situation as he leaned down to one side in that predatory way, not taking his eyes off me. But then when I saw him take hold of the chain, I felt as if I couldn't breathe! Which was why I let out a surprised and frightened yelp when he tugged it and snapped the links as if they had been made from plasticene.

The action also made me stumble a step towards him and I instinctively pulled back quickly. But then he started to wrap the end of the chain around his massive fist, and I gulped at the muscles that bulged, stretching the material of his T-shirt. His extensive tattoos seemed to vibrate from his skin as if the Demon beneath was getting some high or a kick with what his actions were doing to me. Tattoos that I knew signified the many lifetimes he had lived through already. I also knew they would cover most of his skin, like some history book of living, breathing art.

Which meant that if he removed his clothes now, I knew what I would find. I knew every blood-stained painting upon his flesh there was to show. I knew everything other than the reasons for them. The ink sleeves were the only ones he ever spoke of to Raina in my dreams.

Which was why I knew they were the wars he had fought through, shown by black ink on his arms, with shades of grey as phantoms that seemed like souls trying to escape his skin. I knew of the Demonic hands in reds, oranges and yellows that rose up from the flaming rivers of Hell that rippled across his shoulder muscles. I knew of the single twisted dead tree that rose up his spine, one that seemed to evaporate into ash before turning to red leaves that added to the fire above.

There were still so many stories left untold between us

and painfully, I knew I wasn't entitled to ever hear a single one. Which was why I couldn't seem to take my eyes off those tortured painted souls on his arms, that seemed as if they were now silently screaming out the same fear I was.

Fuck, but it felt as if my heart was going to pound right out of my chest! Especially when he slowly started to reel me in as if I was a wild pet of his. One he was trying to tame, and make come to heel. But with my hands now out directly in front of me, I was being reined in and I tried in vain to fight him, pulling and putting all my weight back. But it was as if it meant nothing to him as he continued to calmly pull me closer. Gods, but the strength of him! I was near panting now with exertion in this one-sided game of tug of war, as it was not even challenging for him.

"Please." I let this slip out, and he paused for a moment as if shocked he had finally heard me speak. Then he frowned as if questioning himself before shaking his head a little. This was before he started again, and another step was quickly lost between us. I then shook my own head and felt the rest of my hair come loose as the tie flung off somewhere in the room. My hair rained down just past my shoulders, bouncing around me like coiled springs been released from a can. Something that once again made him grin. But then I knew only a few more steps remained, and I tried once more with my shaky voice.

"Please... just stop." At this he did stop, narrowing his gaze again, and looking sterner this time. It was as if he was angered by my plea not to be close to him. This was when his face hardened further and he now tugged on the chain firmly, sending me falling forward, stumbling on my feet. This caused me to land into his hard chest. My head only coming up to the height of his pecs, he was that much taller than me, even in my high heeled boots.

My hair was all around him and I slowly lifted my head up, so I was able to look up at him with what I knew was wide eyes. Eyes that I knew were silently pleading with him not to hurt me. Begging for him not to just snap my neck like a twig because he wanted to be cruel.

But then he would need information first, wouldn't he? However, this was a when a curious thing happened as he grinned down at me and spoke in a teasing tone.

"Hello, little Halo." I had to say, I liked that he gave me this nickname as it felt personal... Like a piece of me had been claimed by him.

I swallowed hard and his eyes flashed a deeper shade of green. I then blew more hair from my face again, and said a small, embarrassed,

"I'm sorry." This made him first look surprised before it made him chuckle. In turn, I took a step back from being plastered against his chest. But his fist snapped up and tightened the chain so I couldn't go too far.

"You're a fearful little thing, aren't you?" he commented, making me frown and forget myself by looking pissed off, something I tried to mask just as quickly so as not to anger him. However, he didn't miss it. Evidently, him thinking I was a fearful little thing was due to my obvious terror of him. But then really, who could blame me? Seeing as I knew he prided himself on that very fear he had the power to extract from others.

"Tell me, Angel, have I given you any need to fear me so, or is it as I suspect it is, and you know a lot more about me than a mortal ever should?" he asked, and the second I reacted with a flinch, I knew I had given him my answer. His thoughtful gaze said it all before his lips did.

"Ah, so that is it… clearly, I have myself a beautiful stalker, do I?" he asked as if amused at the idea, and I blushed at both being called beautiful and being called his stalker.

"Albeit a silent one," he commented, and my mouth opened before I had chance to stop it this time.

"Well, I gather loud ones don't fare as well." Then I slapped a shackled hand over my mouth and surprise made his features change, lightening his eyes before he erupted into laughter and the sound… Gods alive, it was beautiful!

After this the door opened quickly and two shocked faces stood there, looking ready for action. His brother and Tristan then saw that it was just their Lord laughing, and it looked as if it had shocked them enough to believe something was wrong.

After this he held up a hand and spoke in a different

language to them, obviously telling them all was well and to leave.

"Well, that's fucking new," Tristan commented dryly.

"Didn't even know the asshole knew how to laugh," Hel replied with a grin as he left, and I would have thought this comment would have angered him, but he seemed too busy being amused by me. Then I froze in place as he raised a hand to my face, doing so slowly, as if he feared he would scare me further. But when I remained still, he took one of my curls in between his thick fingers and rubbed the strands between the callous pads, before his gaze shifted to my eyes.

"*Captivating*… and silky soft, just as I thought it would be," he murmured to himself and again I blushed because of it.

"Now for your name." This question managed to break the spell and I took a quick step back, making his hand snap up and prevent me going too far, as he still commanded my chains.

"Oh no you don't," he commented as he jerked his arm down and a little further back behind him, doing so enough that I was yanked forward again. This put me just as close as it did the first time, which meant that I needed to put my hands up against him, just to save my face from planting in his chest again.

"You go nowhere, little one, for you belong to me now and be warned, *for I will know you, and soon.*" I gulped at this and spoke before I could think better on it.

"Please, Kaiden, don't do this," I said, and at the first mention of his name his eyes warmed, glowing brighter this time.

"You speak my name like you know me," he told me on a rumble of words, and I couldn't tell if he was angry or not that I had said his name.

Whichever it was, it clearly affected him in some way, as he took hold of my chin and forced my head up, so he could then growl down at me what sounded like…

The most dangerous question of all…

"What are you, Halo?"

CHAPTER 12
BITTEN BY A SONG

The moment he asked me this, I felt my body tense all over.

"I…I…" I couldn't answer him as the intensity of everything that was him was too much to speak through. He was too consuming, too intense, *too powerful to fight against.*

"Say it again!" he demanded suddenly and I didn't really know what he wanted, so I answered him in a questioning way,

"Please?" At this his lips quirked, and he said in a soft, luring way,

"My name, beautiful… say my name once more." I sucked in a quick breath before giving him what he wanted,

"Kaiden," I said, and for some reason, it came from my lips like a sexual purr and in a way my voice had

never sounded before. Even when I was trying to talk my way into his building, it still didn't sound this way. This was when suddenly his hand collared my throat, making me cry out in fear.

"Easy now, for I will not hurt you," he told me as I clearly started to panic but then he was right, he wasn't hurting me.

"Now, once again," he demanded, and my look must have asked him why.

"Because this time I want to feel for the spell you clearly cast over me." I frowned in confusion and was allowed enough slack on my neck to speak freely, so I told him,

"Spell… you think… I… no, no, there is no spell," I said, and again those who knew me would have laughed at my inability to speak.

"We shall see, for I will feel it if it's there. Now once again, speak my name, little sorceress." I bit my lip first, fearing he might feel something that wasn't meant to be there. And now questioning why he even thought this in the first place, it made no sense. Had something happened to my voice? Was I somehow putting him under a spell without even knowing what I was doing?

But more importantly… *was this just another thing that could get me killed?*

"I am waiting, little Halo," he informed me as though this was some great crime I was committing, and I guess I knew it was, as it had to be said, the guy had zero patience and had only ever shown any to his Siren… well, and I guess now me, as I wasn't dead… *yet.*

Or so I thought.

He squeezed his hand around my throat to get my attention back and my eyes widened in fear once more before giving in to his demands.

"Kaiden." Again, it came out like I was sexually seducing him, and I didn't know why or that I even had it in me to begin with. I mean, I had always been good at talking myself out of trouble but with Kaiden, well first I would have needed to be given back the ability to speak. And well, unless he was commanding it of me, then it didn't really help me now. However, the moment I said his name, it seemed to do something to him, as this time he even closed his eyes and groaned a little, as if I really was a sorceress. Naturally, this made me say quickly,

"I swear, I am not a witch." In response, his fingers tightened again, and I panicked thinking this was it! He had obviously felt me putting a spell on him that I didn't know I was capable of, and he was going to kill me because of it!

"Oh, but you are most certainly bewitching me," he admitted, making me blush again because it sounded nice when he said it in that husky way. However, I didn't want that compliment to mean my death, so quickly added,

"Please… I don't mean to if I am… I can't even convince my cat to come in at night or let me stroke him and if I was a witch, well then don't they command cats or at least have some power over them? Because really, Roger hates me and only puts up with me because I have food and a bed with a fluffy throw at the end… Oh, Gods, please make me stop by squeezing my throat or something!" I said in some kind of verbal onslaught of words, which clearly shocked him as he jerked his head back a little as he took it all in.

Then once he had processed what just happened, for the second time in minutes, he threw his head back and bellowed with laughter. But seeing as this was even more so than the first time, it wasn't surprising when the door opened again. However, he held up a hand without looking, telling them he was fine once more.

"Gods, twice in one day."

"Must be a fucking witch." They both muttered as they left once more, leaving me dumbfounded. Was his laughter really the cause for concern?

"You named your cat Roger?" he asked, and I found it strange that he wanted to know.

"They were out of rabbits at the shelter," I commented, and this he clearly didn't get, as he raised a brow in question and Gods but that was hot.

"It's my favourite movie," I told him, and again he frowned as if he had no idea what I was talking about. But because the cage had been opened, letting loose the beast that was my chatty nature, I therefore started again, feeling the need to explain.

"He's a cartoon rabbit that gets framed for murder and

has to help solve it with Bob Hoskins, who plays a detective, but he's not a rabbit or a cartoon for that matter. His wife is a cartoon person though and she is this smoking hot, redhead who sings at a jazz club and has huge… erm…" I paused and motioned with my hands at my own breasts, making him look stunned for a moment before I continued like a crazy person.

"But hey, lucky for him right…?" I paused when his lips twitched as he was clearly amused. I also noticed how his hand had now left my throat and was instead stroking up and down my cheek and neck. It was as if I was now the cat named Roger, although I didn't dare swat out at him with my claws like Roger would if he was pissed off… I often wondered how my life would have turned out had I got that bunny instead.

"The detective is no doubt lucky to possess such bountiful beauty," he replied as if teasing me and wanting to keep me talking. Something I really wished he hadn't wanted, as it was clearly dangerous. But it was as if he knew this was my weakness and his hands touching me had the power to coax secrets from me. Or just pointless conversations about cartoon rabbits that would mean nothing to him.

"Roger is married to her, not the detective… she erm… loves the rabbit." At this his grin got even bigger.

"Umm… I am starting to see the appeal in the cute myself," he commented, as if musing this thought to himself and making me wonder if he was talking about me. Well, I blushed because of it, something he noted as he ran the backs of his thick fingers down my heated cheek.

"Am I… erm… ever going to see Roger again?" I asked in a tentative way, trying to gauge if and when he was going to stop being gentle with me and start terrifying me again. This question managed to keep his grin in place, only this time it was most definitely on the bad boy side of things.

"That depends on you and what you continue to keep from me," he told me, and I knew I was still in trouble here as I doubted I would continue to amuse him for much longer. This was because my mouth usually started to piss people off after a time of never shutting up. And well, his Siren had been a quiet, elegant beauty to be fair.

Nothing like me.

She was my alter ego and person I would have aspired to be, all grace and gentle pose. Me, well I was a hot mess of curls and random words.

"Roger won't be happy," I said softly, making him smirk before leaning forward a little and reminding me in a teasing tone,

"I thought you said he didn't like you."

"He doesn't, but he likes being hungry even less," I added, making his lips twitch again as if trying to fight the grin. Then suddenly he tugged me forward until I had no choice but to take a step even closer, so he could freely whisper in my ear,

"Then I suggest not keeping Roger from his dinner." At this I shuddered, and he felt it. I swear the way he said this, was as if he had just told me he wanted to strip me bare and fuck me on the table, not feed my damn cat!

"Well, he is… erm…"

"Yes?" he whispered against my skin sexually as he ran his nose up the length of my neck, taking in the scent of me.

"…Fat," I muttered, making him chuckle against my neck this time.

"He can afford to lose a few kitty pounds." He grinned again and hummed,

"Cute." Then he surprised me as his gentle handling turned in a heartbeat, as his free hand fisted my hair and yanked my head to the side, making me cry out a little. Then he pressed his nose in and inhaled a deeper breath this time, before a rumbled purr escaped. He finished this by licking up the length of my neck, against my trembling flesh, totally shocking me speechless.

"Mmm, delicious… I am going to enjoy interrogating you further." At this I shivered harder, and his grin grew bigger against my skin before he whispered,

"Your name?" I sucked in a deep breath and shook my head, but then his fist tightened in my hair, and I was forced to stop the movement.

"Very well, time for your first lesson in negotiations."

"And uh… what is that?" I asked, not liking the sound of excitement in his voice.

"It is simple, little one, first I ask you a question and if you do not answer, I will do something you do not like, and keep doing it until you give me what I want." I swallowed hard and force my words out,

"Erm… I am no Politian here, but I am pretty sure that's what you call getting screwed over." At this he grinned and pulled back to wink at me before dipping his head back to where it had been, saying,

"Let's begin, should we?" I tried to pull back when his hand snapped behind him, making my tied hands travel with them as there was barely any chain left between the two. His lips were back to my skin and he was running his nose up the length of my neck before reaching my ear.

"What is your name, pretty girl?" he asked in that smouldering hot voice of his.

"I can't tell you that," I whispered, and he clicked his tongue to the roof of his mouth in reprimand before telling me,

"Wrong answer." Then he opened his mouth and took my sensitive flesh in his, before applying the strength of his teeth, doing so until it became painful.

"Aah…aha…hhh!" I cried out, but then something strange started to happen, as it became strangely erotic. This was when I began squirming in his hold as he tightened his fist in my hair. Then, when he knew I could take no more, he let go and licked and kissed the place he had bitten, gently soothing the hurt.

"Now again, your name?" he asked, and again I knew

I couldn't give him what he wanted, as pain was better than death. Especially by the hands of the man I had been in love with for the last six years! Okay, so I had believed him to be just a figment of my imagination but still, the love had been real.

"I can't," I said again, and he chuckled before his hand tightened and yanked my head once more to the side, before his bite was back and I was crying out. And like last time, he only did this briefly until he was soothing the spot with his tongue and lips, before whispering,

"Make no mistake, girl, I am enjoying this, so it will matter not if you continue to force my lips upon you for more." I swallowed hard and said,

"Then it looks like Roger is *definitely* going to go hungry." At this he laughed and shook his head a little before telling me,

"Fuck me, but you are a delight, little one." Then he went back to his torture, and I swear it became more erotic than punishment, as I found myself near grinding myself against his thigh.

"Aahh oohhh yeah…" I moaned this time, and he growled against my neck. But I wasn't sure if it was in frustration or something else.

"Give me your name!" he snarled, breaking far quicker than I did and I smiled, feeling the shift in power. But then when I shook my head this time, he bit me in a new place and I cried out louder.

"AHHH!" This was when it felt as though he was

making a meal out of me but thankfully never breaking the skin. Although I didn't know how long I had left until he did. However, that's when I knew he didn't want to hurt me or even continue, as he was hitting his limit far sooner than I was. I knew that the moment he growled again,

"Name, girl!" But him snapping this only made me shout out,

"It's Angela. no, it's Pamela… I mean Sandra… wait, perhaps Rita." Like I thought it would, me saying this only made him groan before going back to my torture and focusing on a new spot. But then that catchy song just wouldn't leave me, which was why I let my head fall to the side and started singing each new name after he demanded,

"Tell me now!"

"A little bit of Monica in your life, a little bit of Erica by your side… oh ahhh!"

"I am not playing, little girl!" he warned, making me smile before I squirmed and said,

"I honestly can't remember." He then nipped at my cheek, making me cry out in surprise before he told me,

"Then I am not done with you!" Gods, I was almost glad… oh the Hell with it, I knew I was glad!

"Now give me your fucking name!" He snarled against the pain he caused in a new mark, making me wonder what it would look like when he was finished. Would I look like a Dalmatian? Then again, I couldn't

chance the truth so continued with my new 'dodging the name' game.

"A little bit of Rita is all I need, a little bit of Aahhh… Tina, is all you see… ohhh Gods!" I ended this in a cry as he bit harder and it hurt more, before he soothed it straight after.

"You test my patience, little one," he admitted, as if I was the one winning, despite my tender neck saying otherwise.

"Don't you mean a little bit of Sandra in the sun?" I tested, making him close his eyes like most people did when they didn't know how to deal with me.

"I have no fucking idea the game you play but you will not win against me, now… *Give. Me. Your. Name!"* I couldn't help but flinch in fear at his Demonic growl of words. Yet I had started this journey knowing that the only way I might survive it was by not letting anyone know who I was. So, despite being afraid of him, I still shook my head, tell him no.

This time when he bit me it was the hardest yet, and I cried out when I felt the pinch of his fangs pierce the skin, making me reach out to him and grab his T-shirt. Which was strange, as shouldn't I be trying to get away from the bastard hurting me? But then it was like he was a man lost as the second he got a taste of my blood, he sucked harder and I swear I thought I would come undone.

"Ahhh… little bit of Mary… *all night long... owww,"* I whispered in a breathless way, now feeling limp as he released my hair along with the chain, so I was now being held in his arms. Then he snarled down at me, as I was barely remaining conscious and feeling like jelly in his hold.

"Fuck!" he hissed in annoyance.

"Does this mean Jessica won our game and makes me your girl?" I asked in a soft voice that felt far away, and he swore again before I felt myself being picked up by the waist. He then turned me so he could sit me down on the table.

"Damn you, you stubborn woman!" he snapped, making me reach out to grip on to him to stop myself from falling. Then I heard a chain snap before landing on the floor, which finally freed my arms of the weight. Then, once this happened, he reached around me and picked me up fully in his arms before shouting out,

"Open the fucking door!" This order made me flinch in his strong hold and I watched as Tristan and his brother came from a side door I knew they must have been watching from.

"Don't fucking say a word!" he ordered the second his brother looked to open his mouth, seeing the amusement that was desperate to come out. Then he stormed past them and down the hallway I had been dragged down the first time. Doing so to the sound of Tristan commenting dryly,

"Never thought I would see the day he was bested by a cheeky little mortal." To which two things happened, the first being Kaiden growling another curse under his breath and the second was from me, as I waved a hand up over his shoulder at them and said,

"I guess he wasn't a Mambo No.5 fan." To which they both burst out laughing. Now as for me, Kaiden gave me a warning that had me squirming once more…

"There are other places for me to bite you, little captive, so don't tempt me into round two." My shiver was the only reply he got and finally, it was one that put a knowing grin back on his handsome face.

One that promised oh so much more...

Delicious torture.

CHAPTER 13

ANOTHER SIREN FOUND

WRATH

F*uck!*

She was my fucking Siren!

My Gods be damned Siren, here and now! She had saved my life. And what had I done but tortured her and covered in her in my bites! I had thought for just a moment that she could be when I heard her speak my name. But to know that she was mine was only something I was certain of when I tasted her blood. A fact that screamed out to my Demon as he roared…

She was ours!

Fuck! Fuck, fuck, fuck!

I had been gifted with one of the Lost Sirens! I was fucking astounded! Shocked beyond all reason and fucking ecstatic, happy, excited and thankful all at the same time. But I had fucked up as I had taken her as my prisoner and tried to force her name from her in a cruel way that now sickened me!

She was my fated one, for fuck sake, and what had I done? Of course, it helped a little that I could scent her arousal because of it. But this did little to quell the loathing at myself!

However, then when she had started speaking, by the Gods I didn't know whether I wanted to keep her going in some sort of addiction or to kiss her into silence! I had never wanted another like her and now of course, I knew why.

She was mine.

She had been destined to be owned and mastered by me and my Demon. And I was to be a slave to her protection, care and heart, for she had me halfway there already! I wanted to worship the girl and spank her ass red raw at the same time. I wanted her in so many ways it was fucked up!

She was the most beautiful girl I had ever seen, and funny. By the Gods but I didn't ever think I had laughed as hard or as much as I had ever before that moment. Hence why my brother no doubt believed she had put a spell on me. Well, she certainly had but unbeknown to her, as she was utterly clueless what she had done to me.

My Siren, my little saviour, and now my captivating captive. But did she know? And if she did, then was that what she feared? Did she think her life now completely changed by showing herself to me? In truth, then yes it fucking would, for I would make every aspect of it mine! But was this why she wouldn't give me her name, for surely, she should know I couldn't hurt her, despite what I had done.

I had known the first Siren had been found and knew that marked the beginning for all to be found by their fated mates. It had caused a chain reaction for the Enforcers and most powerful of my kind to find what was rightfully theirs. But I had not believed the Gods would have ever graced me with such a gift. One I had secretly hoped for and yet had already abused!

"How is your neck?" I asked, and she laughed nervously.

"It feels a little like a chew toy," she teased, and yet despite the humour and joke she made, I growled in annoyance, but done more at myself. Something she didn't yet know.

"I was too rough," I admitted, not knowing how to apologise as I had to confess, I had never done it before, having no reason to as ruler of my sector.

"It's… I was… am stubborn, so technically I'm half to blame," she said, and I could barely believe she wanted to ease my guilt. A new emotion for sure, and one I was admittedly struggling with.

"Don't do that, little Halo, for I do not deserve your kindness," I told her and when she looked to open her mouth and disagree, I silenced her with a stern look that stopped her from speaking. I then continued to concentrate on getting her to where I wanted her, which was of course, my bedchamber. However, a curious thing happened as the moment I started to approach the door she started panicking.

"No, oh no… we can't, I mean, I can't…"

"What is it, beauty?" I asked, now concerned for an entirely different reason and feeling her distress for myself.

"Please, oh please… I can't go in there. It is not…" she started to say, stopping herself quickly, so I pressed for more.

"It is not?" She released a heavy sigh and admitted almost shamefully,

"It's not my place." But as soon as she said this, it completely rocked me to my core, and to the point that I just stopped dead. Making me ask in a cautious tone,

"Just what do you think is behind that door?" She shook her head as if she had slipped up by giving something away, and I frowned in question. Something was going on with her and it was rooted deeper and far beyond this day.

"It is nothing to fear, for trust me, Halo, there is nothing of a threat to you inside these walls. I am master here and will let no harm come to you," I told her, hoping she would hear the truth in my words. But then she took a deep breath and asked,

"Is there another bedroom I can go in?" she asked, slipping up yet again as I knew now that she knew that it was my bedroom. Which only added more questions to consider, for what would she fear in there? Unless it was me and the carnal acts I wanted to do to her… did she fear my touch? Not that I would have blamed her after what I had done, yet she had still seemed playful with me. Even during the times I had bitten her, she had clung onto me as if anchoring herself to me. I had even believed that she enjoyed it, making me wonder of her sexual inclinations.

Was she into kink?

She was most definitely submissive, yet this wasn't surprising seeing as she was a Siren and they were said to be naturally this way. It made sense considering most Enforcers were dominant assholes who ruled with the iron fist of our King of Kings. As much as it pained me to do, I eased my hold on her, now testing just how far she would go for that 'other room'. One I confess there was no way I would give her, as there was only one place this little Siren was to remain, and that was by my side and in my bed.

Yet despite this, I knew I had to take things slow with her as she obviously didn't trust me yet, and one look at her neck and I knew the painted in bruises were the reasons for it… what was the mortal term…?

Love bites.

Well, she had certainly seemed to 'love' certain aspects of it, for I couldn't get the memory of her grinding herself against my thigh from my mind. Yet regardless of this noticeable attraction she had for me, it was also obvious she had no idea who she was to me. Or walking through those doors at her back would be the first place she would want to be, not the last. However, the biggest question to remain was how did she know it was my private bedchamber, for she most certainly had never been here before?

It wasn't as though I would have ever forgotten the experience.

No, something wasn't right here, and I was determined to discover what it was. But first, it was like I said to myself, I needed to test how far she would take this. So, I let her feet find the floor and her legs take her weight. I then held onto her slim waist, one of my large hands easily spanned the width of, making her feel tiny in my grasp. I heard her inhale a sharp breath at my touch and knew then that it wasn't without its power over her. Clearly, I affected her, even if it was nowhere near the same power that she held over me. But then I wanted to see if my intimidation would still work over her as it had in the beginning when I first entered the interrogation room.

Which was why, when I was assured she was steady enough on her own feet, I used my hands on her to walk her backward until she had nowhere to go but the door itself. I tilted my head to catch sight of that hard, nervous swallow and smirked because of it, knowing that she was struggling with this.

Good, *for I wanted that fucking name!*

"You do not wish to go in my bedchamber?" I asked, easing my voice to one of coaxing. She shook her head telling me no, and her beautiful hair went wild around her. Gods, but I couldn't wait to tame it in my fist as I claimed her, thrusting into her sweet little body and capturing her cries of rapture with my mouth, tasting them for myself. I took a deep breath that had nothing to do with her reply and more to do with the sinful thoughts my actions enticed.

"Then I will make you a deal, grant me your name and I will grant you your wish by situating you in your own room," I told her, making her eyes go wide. Then, as she opened her mouth, I knew the next name she gave me would not be one of her own. I could read it in her expression, which was why I placed a finger over her deliciously looking full lips and warned,

"No more games, little one." This came out as more of a growl than intended but it did the job in making her take me seriously. She released a sigh and shook her head again, giving me her silent answer.

She would give me nothing.

I released another sound of disappointment and while reining in my anger at being denied, I reached around her to open the door. This made her jump back from it as if it was the Gates to Hell I was about to push her into. Well, I was a Demon after all. But I was also her new jailor, so she wasn't far from that truth as I was about to make things far more difficult for her than simply walking into this room. For she would soon find herself locked to my side with no chance at a reprieve from her captor, for I would give her none.

"I... I... can't..." she started to say, and I almost felt sorry for her, but then the anger at being denied anything when it came to her was what overwhelmed any guilt I might have felt at causing her discomfort. After all, she would be spending a lot of time in this room regardless, so it was best to get it over with sooner rather than later.

Which was why I took her hand in mine, feeling how small it was being swallowed whole by my own. Then I squeezed it enough not to damage her but so that she knew she had no chance of pulling it away.

"That is a shame, for you will now find this your new prison cell," I told her in a stern tone, giving her one last chance to come clean.

She didn't.

So, I tugged her inside, ignoring her meagre weight offering some pointless resistance.

"No... please... please... I have no right, it's not for me..." she said making me frown, questioning what that even meant. I made sure she was through the threshold of her personal hell before I let her go and the second I did, she bolted for the door in panic. I threw up a hand, using my power to make it slam shut and lock, which was a sight that stopped her dead. Then, the moment her shoulders slumped I knew she had no choice but to admit defeat.

"What is and isn't right for you, is no longer your decision to make, little Halo," I told her.

"Then whose is it?" she snapped, and I turned side on to regard her before raising a brow, giving her a look to say 'isn't it obvious?'. But then in case it wasn't easily read, I answered her anyway,

"Mine." I watched her physically shudder at that and it was a curious reaction. Now where had that talkative little firecracker gone to and why had she left behind a shy shell of light, I wondered?

"Now you can explain why it is you do not think you belong here?" I asked, letting her know with my tone that I wasn't going to accept her being evasive.

"Because… well, this is where you and your… erm… girlfriend are to… you know," she said, and then she swung her hips a little, mimicking the act and suddenly I found myself booming with laughter for the third time that day. More than I had laughed this last decade, I was sure. Other than a slight grunt of amusement, then let's just say the sound was a rare one. But by the Gods, this little mortal was an utter delight, for she was just too damn cute, adorable and fucking sexy with it!

"For starters, I do not have a girlfriend, like you may suspect…"

"So, you haven't met her yet?" she muttered more to herself, and I found her response a curious one… *who was she speaking of...*

My Siren?

So, I was right, she didn't know who she was to me, making me cautious. Which was why I tested this further.

"And who I bring here to fuck is up to me and would never be classed as so, for there is only one being that would ever hold the claim as being my own, and that is one fated to me," I said, only to gauge her reaction and when her beautiful eyes widened, I saw only recognition in them before the depth of my words started to fully penetrate.

"And prisoners," she said, making me grin in a dark way as she tried to make the clear definition between the females I fucked, my fated and her. So, I decided to be vague, doing so to keep her intimidated, which would hopefully aid me further in getting what I wanted.

"We shall see, pretty girl," I said with a shrug of my shoulders, and I didn't miss the sharp inhale of her next breath. I turned from her and grinned to myself, knowing I was getting closer, as clearly she had her weaknesses and curiously, I seemed to be at the top of that list.

Hence why a plan quickly formed.

And oh yes…

I was a bastard.

CHAPTER 14

THE TEMPTATION GAME

EMMELINE

Oh Gods, but this wasn't going the way I expected it to!

Not that I was complaining as it was most certainly better than the alternative end of the Wrath spectrum. I would definitely prefer being someone who intrigues and amuses him, than the one who pisses him off. And I'd kind of had a taste of both and well, keeping him laughing was far safer.

Although, what it was doing to me both physically and mentally wasn't safe either. I could see myself crumbling before long. But then I also knew this was his main aim, as he was trying a different tactic now, knowing how much he had the power to affect me. Hell, but I almost welcomed the pain!

He was everything I had ever dreamed of and so much more, that I was now being given the opportunity to discover. I had never in my life been so jealous of what I now knew wasn't a fictional character, as Raina must be out there somewhere. Because I knew that if he was here, as real as I myself was standing here, then somewhere out there, so was she. Which as much as it pained me to admit, I think he had got it wrong, for he was acting now as if I meant something to him.

As if I was somehow his Siren.

Gods, but it was almost too cruel to bear! Oh, but how I would have loved to have said fuck it to the Fates and their rules, being only too happy to stake my own claim.

But I couldn't.

It was wrong.

As wrong as it was now by me even being in this room. A place that made me feel as if I knew intimately, seeing as it was the first place I wrote of he and his Siren making love for the first time. The first place he claimed her, in his bed after tying her to the gothic bedposts for what I had once believed was the most epic first love scene ever written. Gods, but everything about this room was exact and it pained me just being in here.

Like the wall of glass that showed the beautiful woodland views beyond, and the balcony that was picture perfect. This with its inviting sofas just waiting for the right couple to come along and make it every bit as romantic as it promised to be. But then the inside promised just as much romance if not more. This despite it obviously being a masculine space with its modern and minimalistic black, shades of grey and hints of navy blue, with natural stone being a running theme throughout.

The large room was also split into different sections and was divided by its clear glass walls. Like the living space, that was lower than where the colossal bed was situated, a piece of furniture that most definitely dominated the room. This, with its imposing gothic black posts that rose up like carved church spires and needed the extra height from the mansion's high ceilings. It looked as if it could have fit ten people and with one look at the size of Kaiden, then I wasn't surprised by this.

But in the raised level where his bed was, I also knew there would be two doors hidden in the walls by the panels of dark wood. Each would hold behind them a luxury bathroom and an extensive walk-in wardrobe, filled with everything from his usual jeans and T-shirts, to combat gear and even suits for the rare occasions he needed them. Most of this would have been in dark colours, as was his Demon's nature, hence the room I was standing in. Or should I say, freaking out in, as that was what I was only a few laboured breaths away from doing!

Because even without coming close to his bed, and still remaining firmly the six steps below, well, just seeing this place in the flesh was like being in the realms of pure fantasy. The large corner sofa in its soft greys faced the wall of windows, just like it had in my dreams. The long fireplace, that was inset into the raised floor and situated between his bedroom and the slightly lowered living space, created that warm glow I always knew it would.

Everything, from its dark bedsheets, its stone floors of black slate to its polished wooden coffee table and black and white pictures on the walls… everything was the same.

Everything was known to me.

And yet still, *it wasn't right.*

It was as though I'd entered some sacred place of worship, or some hidden temple where mere mortals like me should never be allowed to venture into. This was Raina's and Kaiden's world, and I was the intruder in it all. I needed to get out of here. I needed to leave before I freaked out enough that I passed out! It was then I started feeling dizzy, looking around as the pictures of forests on the walls blurred as I tried to find my escape.

"Little Halo?" His nickname for me cantered me for a time, enough that I was quickly reaching out for him.

"I… can't… breathe…" I wheezed out just as the door opened.

"We came to see if… wait, what the fuck did you do to her?!" I heard his brother's voice say.

"I don't fucking know, she just started breathing heavy and then her body started to sway," Kaiden snapped back in panic as I felt myself taken in his arms.

"She is having a panic attack." I frowned in question, as I wasn't sure who said this, as it sounded a bit like

Tristan. Perhaps it was because I hadn't heard him sound so serious before.

"What?!" Kaiden barked back furiously, making me wince in his hold.

"She can't breathe because she is having a fucking panic attack… now sit her down," Tristan shouted this time, and soon I found myself being led to the sitting area.

"Put your head down between your legs," he told me, making Kaiden roar,

"What the fuck?!"

"I am trying to fucking help her, so let me!" Tristan snapped in return.

"Just do as he says, brother," Hel encouraged.

"Alright, doll, just try and take deep, slow breaths for me… focus on my voice and breathe with me okay?" he said before taking deep breaths, stopping enough to tell Kaiden,

"Rub her back in gentle circles, it will help to keep her focused." Then he went back to breathing slowly, giving me something to follow, which started to work, well that and the soothing motion Kaiden was now making on my back.

"It's working," Kaiden said in relief, making Hel ask,

"How did this happen, what did you do to her?" Kaiden growled in response,

"Nothing other than she doesn't like being in this room."

"That's not exactly a good sign," Tristan commented dryly.

"Keep your comments to yourself, Wendigo!" Kaiden snarled angrily, mentioning the name of what I knew was Tristan's Demon. This made me act without thought, as I couldn't help but lean towards Kaiden as he was now sitting on the sofa with me. A move that I knew took him off guard before he acted by putting his heavy arm around me, tucking me close to his side. This was when I looked up at him and pleaded,

"Please, take me from this room, *I will do anything you ask.*" I heard him sigh in frustration before I felt him nod in agreement. A single second more was when he stood and simply picked me up in his arms, doing so as if I weighed nothing at all. Then he walked from the room and the second he did, I took my first full breath in relief, filling my lungs now the panic was over.

I had no idea where he was taking me, just as long as it was far from that room, then I was happy. It was also why I now clung onto him as if he was my saviour in all this and hadn't been the one not long ago that had forced me in there and caused the panic in the first place.

It didn't take long until he was placing me down on another seat, and I looked up this time to see a room I had never seen before. This was definitely softer in its decor, with its warm teal colours, light wooden floors and pale brick walls. It was also another room that looked more like some fancy hotel penthouse suite, having the same living sections his own room had.

Only this time instead of the darkness, there was nothing but light in this space, as even its furniture was carved oak wood, and two sofas faced each other, both in cream with lines of different tones of blue. Further back in the room was also a huge oak sleigh bed, which granted, wasn't as big as Kaiden's, but it would still fit him in it and with room to spare. This room also had plush cream rugs dotted around the place, making it seem even warmer than the cold, almost gothic décor of Kaiden's bedchamber.

Two doors on the opposite wall to where the bed was, had me wondering if this was a bathroom and yet another walk-in? I also couldn't help but wonder who this room belonged to, if anyone.

Once again, I felt like I could breathe freely and Kaiden took notice.

"Thank you," I told him, making him nod down at me, as if he was too annoyed to speak but wanted me to know he heard my thanks. Did my appreciation at least mean something to him, despite how angry he obviously was? But then my hopes were dashed at thinking it had all gone my way. I knew that when his brother and Tristan followed us inside and Kaiden ordered,

"Hel, have someone pack up some of my things…" he paused to look down at me after my head had snapped up.

"...As it looks like I will be moving in here for the time being."

"But I..."

"What, you didn't think that got you out of being my prisoner, did you?" he asked, making me swallow hard and ignore his brother's knowing chuckle.

"Tristan, you said our little troublemaker here was without a bag, yes?" Kaiden went on to ask.

"Yeah, she had nothing with her," he replied, making me wonder what new punishment he had planned.

"Then all she has on her is the clothes on her back... unless you have your things stashed somewhere you are willing to tell us about so we may retrieve it for you?" my new jailor asked, making me look away, giving him my answer and trying not to think about the locker full of my stuff.

"Very well, ask one of the girls to find her something suitable to wear tonight and remind them... *I want her neck on show,*" he added, making me shiver as my hand went to the tender area on its own accord. Something he grinned at.

"It will be done, my Lord Wrath." After this, Tristan made his way back to the door, obviously at the ready to do his master's bidding but before he could leave, Kaiden asked,

"But, before you go, I want to know, did she sleep at all?" Tristan looked back at me and then shook his head, telling him that I hadn't.

"Then it is time I get my prisoner settled. Brother, I will speak with you shortly." Hel scoffed a laugh and said,

"Yes, no doubt you have much to tell." I frowned at this and was still frowning after the door had closed behind them both. Of course, this meant I hadn't been focusing on what I should have, which of course was the predator still left in the room with me.

"AH!" I screamed the second I found myself grabbed and flung over his massive shoulder. Then, just before I had chance to shout for him to put me down, I was falling. Only this time, I did so landing with a bounce on the big mattress. I lay frozen still as he stood over me at the edge of the bed, now looking down with heat in his eyes as if the sight of me was one he wanted to burn to his eternal memory. But then he was suddenly tearing his T-shirt over his head, and it was in that moment my mouth went as dry as the Sahara desert!

Oh... My... Gods.

For surely he was one of them with a body like that! Because it was in that moment that I realized I was right, my words hadn't done him justice. The man had a freaking eight pack for Gods in Heaven sake! I had never written that! I swear I thought I was going to bloody drool, there was so much muscle on show that I didn't know what to do first, lick my lips or scramble back in fear!

He had the power to crush me with one sneeze.

Hence why I opted to scramble back, unable to take

my eyes off the sight of his naked torso. It was only when he chuckled a little that my eyes snapped to his, seeing now they were crinkled at the sides with his handsome cocky grin. Then he grabbed one of my boots and pulled hard enough that I slid back to where he had put me. My fearful gaze snapped back to my foot, to see him now yanking at the laces, before he was pulling it free of the leather boot.

I couldn't speak, I was in too much shock at the sight of him removing my shoes, letting my first leg drop to the bed the second it was as he wanted it to be. Then he reached for the other and did the same thing, only stopping when he took a moment to grin at my pizza socks.

Yep, I was a sucker for pizza!

But then with him half naked in front of me, I had definitely found something far tastier and more addictive than food. Holy Hell, the guy was hotter than anything in his birthplace, that was for damn sure. I shamefully couldn't take my eyes off him, making him smirk again.

"Like what you see, little Halo?" I couldn't do anything but bite my lip and shake my head, lying by telling him no. He laughed at this and said,

"I'm happy to see... *you're a shit liar.*" He whispered this last part after he had put a knee to the bed at the side of my legs, coming dangerously closer. This was before he grabbed my hips and slid me right under him, making me shriek in surprise.

"W-w-wh-what... what are you...?" I stuttered, struggling to talk once more.

"Is that why you refuse to tell me who you are, because you know you cannot lie and silence is the only game you have left to play?" he asked, ignoring my question as he caged me in with his huge body held above me.

"I...I..."

"*You* can speak to me," he told me, emphasizing the 'you' in that statement and this time lowering enough to run his nose up the side of my own. As for me, I held my breath after it first caught in my throat.

"Why are you doing this to me?" I asked on a whisper, making him grin down at me before his face turned serious. Then he asked in return,

"And what makes you think you're the only one being affected?" I sucked in a breath and for a moment he watched my lips so intently I thought he was going to kiss me. But instead, he pulled back and after snaking an arm under me, he started to shift my body. Now doing so in a way that it slid further to the top of the bed and on the pillows. After this he let his body fall to the side of me, before tucking my body into his so he could spoon me from behind.

"I... erm..."

"*You* have a big night ahead of you, so I suggest you get some sleep," he said, once more emphasizing the 'you' in this.

"What about you?" I asked, trying my luck and attempting to wiggle free, only feeling his arms tense around me when I did.

"I have slept quite enough these last few days," he said wryly, referring to the coffin he had been forced into.

"Then why are you… erm… in bed with me?" At this he rumbled the sweetest reply, and one I couldn't in my wildest dreams ever have imagined would be just for me…

"Because I am exactly where I want to be."

CHAPTER 15

HOW VILLAINS ARE MADE

I don't know how I managed to sleep with Kaiden's arms around me but somehow, I did. Or maybe that was the reason I did, because I had never felt safer in my whole life. I had never felt treasured before but then when awake I knew not to trust it. However, when I was asleep, then I was free to feel without doubt clouding the bliss I found in his arms.

I just wished it was all as real as it felt. Because at some point I was going to wake from my living dream and when I did, I knew my whole world would come undone. This amazing feeling was only going to last so long, especially when he discovered who I really was.

When he learned that the way he felt about me was a lie.

I didn't know, maybe this was a way for fate to intervene. Perhaps feeling something was a way to stop him from killing me outright. Maybe he had to care for me, as if he was compelled to or something equally as depressing.

Either way, this was the most painful experience of my whole life, as here I was, in the arms of a man I had been in love with and obsessed over for the last six years, and yet I knew I wasn't fated to be his. *He belonged to another.*

"I know you still do not sleep, little Halo." His rough voice hummed in my ear making me shiver.

"Why do you call me that?" I asked without looking at him but feeling his presence squeeze me from behind. Then I felt his hand come to my wild hair, before he started teasing the curls apart with his thick fingers.

"I have never seen anything like it," he confessed, making me chuckle.

"A wild mess, you mean."

"Wild indeed, but a mess? No, that is not a word I would use," he told me, and I allowed myself the moment of happiness to grin at the compliment.

"Unruly then." At this he scoffed and told me on a growl,

"Definitely unruly."

"Now I have a feeling we are no longer talking about my hair." At this he reached across me, cupping my shoulder and applying enough pressure that I had little option but to roll flat so he could look down at me. This was when I had to fight against what his luring voice had the power to do to me.

"What is your name?" His question took me off guard, despite it being one I had heard him ask enough times. I swallowed down the pain of denying him, before shaking my head, silently telling him no.

"I will discover it, but you must know this," he told me, as if this was fact and it was only ever going to be about 'when' and not 'if'.

"Then I will enjoy the feeling for as long as I can." At this he frowned and asked,

"And which feeling is that?" This was when I told him far more than I should.

"The feeling that I am not your enemy." At this he jerked back a little, and I regretted saying it the second it was out.

"Now that is a curious thing to say indeed."

"I shouldn't have said that… I'm sorry," I admitted quickly.

"Now apologizing for it is even more so," he said, making me wince. So, to change the subject, I looked to the window and saw that it was dark once more.

"I slept the day away again."

"Travelling long distances will do that to you," he replied, making me give him a coy look.

"I know what you are doing."

"And what is that, pretty girl?" I blushed at the compliment before telling him,

"You're trying to make me slip up by giving you clues as to where I have come from."

"Upon my word, you wound my honour!" he teased, faking hurt by putting a hand to his bare chest and I burst out laughing, something he seemed utterly captivated with. Which was why, the second I saw he was leaning down so he could kiss me, I acted quickly, turning my head to the side so his kiss ended as a chuckle against my neck.

"An enchanting sound," he hummed, making me sigh, as hearing things like this coming from his lips against my skin, well it was seriously the stuff of dreams. But with every minute I spent enjoying them, I spent ten times that feeling guilty about it. Which is why I told him,

"I shouldn't be in bed with you." I didn't expect him to laugh at this but that was what he did.

"You sound like some sacrificial virgin in bed with a villain," he said on another chuckle. However, I went as stiff as a board at the word virgin and fuck me, but he felt it! He too tensed and started growling the second I quickly rolled out of bed and put distance between us.

"Come back here, Halo," he ordered, making me drag my hands through my hair to try and tame it back. Although, as usual it just sprang up again, forcing me to ignore it. Then I found my boots and quickly stepped into them, as if trying to make a point that I needed to leave.

"I don't think that is a good idea," I muttered without looking at him, purposefully trying to ignore him now I knew with one look from me that he would know the embarrassing truth. However, I didn't hear him approach as, hell, I didn't even know he could move so fast or so quietly. Which meant I wasn't expecting it, as he was so big, I didn't think anyone would.

"Look at me, little one," he said softly, taking hold of my chin and forcing the action from me.

"Are you pure?" I frowned at this and spoke without thinking.

"Pure? What? No, I swear like a trooper." At this he smirked, like he was trying not to laugh before asking in a deep husky tone this time,

"Are you untried in the bedroom?" At this I sucked in a quick breath, feeling ashamed by the way he put it, as if I wouldn't know what I was doing or something.

"Answer me," he rumbled, making me snap,

"Yes, I am a fucking virgin, or not fucking anything, should I say! There, are you happy?!" At this he closed his eyes for a few seconds before blowing the wind from my sails and admitting,

"Immensely so."

"But why?" I asked, as I genuinely wanted to know.

"Why would I be happy that no other has claimed you with their cock, is that a serious question?" he asked in a hard yet surprised tone, and I shook my head a little as if this would help trying to make sense of what was going on right now.

"I…I don't understand what is happening here… just

who do you think I am to you?" I braved to ask, making him narrow his gaze down at me before speaking.

"I think you know exactly who you are to me, and I think it's what gives life to your fear of me, it's what makes you scared… is that why you hide yourself from me? Hide who you are, because I will take possession of you?" he asked, shocking me to my core. Because it was confirmed.

He did think I was his Siren.

Which was why I told him in a sad, devastated tone,

"I am not who you think I am, Kaiden." At this he rumbled a growl, and I knew by the heat in his eyes it was because I had spoken his name again. Which was confirmed when suddenly he had me in his arms, holding me captive against him so he could growl down at me a warning.

"Then if I were you, I would think twice about saying my name like that again, before I decide to claim you regardless!" Then he ended this by crushing his lips to mine, making me cry out before it ended in a moan of pure yearning. One he swallowed up and claimed just like he said he would. Because the second my mouth opened, he wasted not a single breath before he was in there, tasting my desire for himself.

Gods, but what a kiss!

I felt like it had the power to burn me, to wrap me in that perfect comforting heat in the middle of the sinful storm that seemed to be trying to consume us! This was so wrong, I knew it and yet, my heart wouldn't allow it to stop. Something inside me felt it sink into my core and bury itself there, making me wonder when this was all over…

Would I ever have the power to dig deep enough to get it out again?

A growl later and I was being lifted with one arm banded around my waist so he could access all of me easier, making me instantly put my arms around his neck. This was so I could continue to do the wrong thing, by holding him to me instead of trying to push him away.

I wanted him so badly, it was scorching me from the inside out. A feeling of something building that never had before and just from a kiss. Of course, I had touched myself down there and experienced orgasms by my own doing. But from a kiss… *never*.

I barely even understood how such a thing could happen without being touched, but yet here I was, my every sexual nerve-ending being overwhelmed. I felt completely consumed by it all, and this feeling came only from having his tongue in my mouth and his lips dominating my own.

Which was why seconds later it all came to its embarrassing head, as I tore my lips from his, threw my head back and cried out as I came, shuddering in his arms like some sex starved hussy.

I was so ashamed once it had stopped, and when I had

finally floated back to reality down from my high, I couldn't even look at him when I begged,

"Oh Gods, I am so sorry, that wasn't supposed to… I'm so embarrassed… I have never…" he suddenly growled, stopping me and suddenly, I found my back against a wall as he held me pinned there after forcing his legs between my own. He grabbed my ass in a rough hold and hoisted me up the length of him. This meant I had no choice but to spread myself wide for him, making me cry out in shock at the solid, hard length that now couldn't be missed.

Holy shit, had I really been able to do that to him?

"Don't you ever be ashamed of being the sexiest, Gods be damned woman I have ever known! The fucking hottest kiss of my life… fuck me, but don't you fucking dare apologize to me for that, girl!" he growled down at me before his hand was fisted in my hair and he was kissing me once more, making me cry out again at the raw intensity of it all. Good Gods, but the man knew how to kiss! I felt as though he was stripping me naked and laying me and my lies totally bare. All my secrets were going to come spilling from me, and I could no longer allow him to carry on.

I didn't deserve him.

"No wait… stop Kaiden… we need to… stop," I told him, panting through my painful words before he finally pulled back, placing his forehead to mine as we both fought for breath.

"You don't know me," I pleaded with him but then his eyes started to change, turning black as his Demon side came through. This was when he snarled and this time, it came out as two voices that merged as one.

"I don't fucking care who you are… *I know who you are to me!"* Then he slammed his lips over mine and this time, there was no stopping it. I felt as if the sins of our kiss had the power to erase all condemnation.

"Yes… Gods, yes!" I moaned, letting myself have the freedom to enjoy this in the moment, only the second the door opened, it was enough to catapult me out of this lustful daze he had me trapped under.

"Ah… bad timing, brother?" Hel said in a smug tone, making Kaiden snarl back at him dangerously. It was soon clear that Hel hadn't been expecting to be faced with his brother's Demon snarling as if he was about to take away his hunted prey or something.

"LEAVE!" he thundered, making Hel hold up his hands and say,

"Hey, easy big guy, I am just the messenger, the one you asked me to be when we found any footage of your little prize there." At this I sucked in a quick breath, making Kaiden fight for control as he panted like some wild beast. So, seeing as he was struggling, I put my hand to his cheek and whispered,

"Hey, it's okay, *come back to me, Kaiden."* The sound of my voice seemed to work as the next time he opened his eyes, they were back to their beautiful green without any black in sight. I looked to his brother who looked fucking astounded!

Then, without letting me go, he told his brother in a tense tone,

"I will be there shortly, *now leave!"* At this his brother left without another word, but the look he gave me now was more than just a little curious. He looked as though he was now seeing me for the first time and what he saw, well… *it concerned him.*

"I want you by my side tonight," Kaiden told me, and I knew what that meant. I had written him saying the exact same thing to Raina. I tore my gaze away and told him in a sad tone,

"I can't." But his reaction wasn't what I expected it to be, as he chuckled before letting me slide down him. Then he tipped my head back up with a hooked finger under my chin.

"What made you think that I was asking," he told me with a wink. Then he stepped away and told me,

"I will be sending a woman in here, she is to be trusted as she is a member of my council." Of course, I knew who this would be, and I had to confess, I was almost excited to see her. She was kick ass and funny as fuck… well, that was if she liked you and she was the same as she was in my books.

"She will help get you ready for tonight, as for myself, I will be back shortly to drive you to the club, one I believe you became acquainted with last night," he told me, making me nod, unable to speak in that moment, as after his kisses, well, I felt too raw. Too vulnerable. *Too open and exposed.*

"Hey, now… look at me, my little Halo," he said, now dressed in his T-shirt and standing by the door.

"Do not sit here with regret on your mind, or worry in your heart, all will be well in time… *I promise you this.*" I released a sigh and nodded, just because I knew this was what he wanted to see. But in reality, I knew it was the very reason I needed to escape him.

Because it was clear to me now the mistakes I made were the very last ones I ever expected to make.

I was his Siren's imposter and in this new story of his, it now made me only one thing to him...

The Villain.

CHAPTER 16
BAD ASS IN LOVE
WRATH

Gods in Heaven, how the Fates must favour me for granting me such a gift as my little Halo! Yes, I wished to know her name, but I also hadn't been lying when I told her I didn't fucking care who she was. Because all that I cared for was who she was to me, for nothing else mattered.

She had quickly become my everything!

But then I should not be surprised, seeing as this was always supposed to be the way when meeting your fated. It was an instant hit to your heart and an instantaneous reaction when connecting two souls. I knew of her fears and how deeply they were buried but it would not matter. For a few more kisses like that and she would be mine, regardless of her continued reluctance or her unknown fears. I didn't quite understand why she held back with me, but I knew it had something to do with who she was or perhaps, it was more like something to do with *who she thought she wasn't?*

Either way, the second she had come undone in my arms from just a kiss, I knew then that she wanted me enough that it didn't need to match my own intense need. The joy I felt at hearing how she was untouched, well I knew it made me a bastard, but I cared not, for she was fucking mine! But just knowing I was to be her first was the fucking innocent cherry on top… *literally.*

I would be the only one she would ever know in that sacred place of hers, and it honestly filled me with pride. For she would never truly know the gift she gave to me by unknowingly waiting for me. But then I never realized how jealous the thought of another with what I considered as mine could turn me into. I would lose my fucking mind should she ever mention another!

"Well, if I'd known that was going to be your interrogation technique, I would have bought you flowers to give to the girl," my brother said, not yet knowing who she was to me. But then he soon would as my Demon reacted quickly, pinning him to the wall with a Demonic hand to his throat.

"She is my Siren, asshole!" His gaze showed shock before it morphed to one of understanding.

"Ah, well that would make more sense than madness or sorcery," he replied calmly, making me drop him, but of course, the nimble bastard landed on his feet. I continued on down to the lower levels and to where the surveillance rooms were housed.

"Then I guess congratulations are in order," he added, making me calm enough to agree,

"I have been blessed by the Gods, indeed."

"Well, I saw for myself how well she tamed you, and now I no longer have to fear a witch being in our midst, I can claim it to be a match made in Hell, rather than Heaven, seeing as that's what she is getting herself into with an eternity with you," he joked. However, I couldn't help but grin as there was one word there that I focused on.

"Eternity indeed, and one I want to start experiencing with her as soon as possible."

"Yes, well for that to happen, you would first need to know who your fated is, as I gather she hasn't yet given up the named goods?" Hel asked, making me frown at the reminder of that one and only thorn in my side.

"She does not know who she is to me, but she will, as for her name, she still refuses me in knowing her," I told him as we entered the surveillance room.

"Well, this might help… show him," Hel said to Franklin, who was our resident tech genius and someone I had employed over thirty years ago.

"This was sent over from the Lexington," Franklin said, pushing up his glasses that I honestly didn't know why he still wore, as his eyesight would have been like the rest of ours was… *flawless.* Yet as a

Demon that had not long been turned and one whose vessel had struggled to accept its new claim, then I gathered this was done more out of habit and a way to cling onto his mortal past. He also looked every bit of the geeky tech he was, with his slight frame, made to look slimmer with his dress shirts and his bowties.

But getting back to my cunning little beauty…

"So, this was how she accessed the building?" I asked as I watched her sweet talk her way past the guard and I had to say, I couldn't help but grit my teeth in irrational jealously at the sight.

"Whoa, okay there, Kai, you might want to ease up a little on the chair or should I say, mangled piece of metal," Hel commented dryly, making me look down to see that I had indeed twisted the back of a metal chair into something that could no longer be used.

"Do we have audio?" I snapped, purposely ignoring my brother's comment.

"No, but he was already questioned," Franklin said.

"And what did the mortal piece of shit say before he was fired from his job?" I asked, making Franklin look to Hel as if to ask him silently if he should say.

"I am your Lord, Demon, you would do fucking well remembering it… now I asked you a question!" I barked out in anger, making him flinch.

"She told the guy she worked for you and that you needed some paperwork for a meeting that you left in your black Bugatti Veyron." I released a pent-up sigh at this.

"So, she knows which cars you own," Hel stated, making me grit my teeth again as it was not sounding good for my little Halo.

"Where did she go next… *show me,"* I said, ignoring this comment as well, and Franklin switched the screen to one inside the elevator. I then watched as she pressed in the code that she shouldn't have fucking known.

"So she did know the code." I was the one to state the obvious this time.

"I already assumed as much when she turned up at the club," Hel told me, making me drag a hand across the back of my neck. Then I snarled,

"It matters not!"

"Kai."

"No! I will not hear of it!" I told him before storming out of the room, making him catch up with me.

"Brother stop, just listen to reason, that's all I ask."

"Why, does it include how you believe she is here as a spy? How she is the enemy and that I should be rid of her!?" At this he jerked back as if I had struck him. Then he surprised me.

"Fuck no, not if she is your Siren."

"She is," I stated firmly.

"Then my happiness for you still stands. However, you cannot ignore this," he told me.

"Then what do you suggest?" I snapped.

"Only that we dig deeper and keep digging until we find the truth of who she is, for what other possible reason could she have for wanting to hide herself from you, if it is not for nefarious reasons?" Again I felt my jaw tense at the fucking good points he made. Hence why I admitted,

"You have a point there."

"Well, I am the smart one," he joked in return.

"Smart mouth maybe," I quipped.

"Alright, so what do you have planned?" I asked. My brother always did have a plan.

"She arrived at Lexington in a cab, so I have Franklin tracing it down to see where she was picked up from. Then we just work backward until we find the start." This was a sound plan.

"And until then, I suggest not taking your eyes off her for too long, for she may still be the snake in the nest, and you will have to decide what to do with her if this turns out to be the case." At this my grin turned deadly when I told him,

"Then I will have the perfect excuse to see her in chains once again, for I imagine taming my queen will be highly entertaining and gratifying."

"Spoken like a true bad ass in love!" he replied, making me grin.

"That I am, little brother, that I am."

A little time later, I was walking back to one of the spare suites ready to retrieve my girl. I had already made preparations with my council about tonight, telling each of them who the girl was to me. I also gave instructions as to the things they may ask her. The game tonight was simple; Who could make her slip up and expose herself first?

Because I may not have cared for her name, knowing without it that it changed nothing, but my council were right, just like my brother. I needed to know who she was for the sake of my people. But more so, for the fact she could also be a danger to herself, as someone could be putting her up to all of this.

Whatever it was, it was clear she was struggling with guilt when with me and in that, I most definitely cared to know why, for I would not allow my Siren to feel that way when with me. Our union was destined by the Fates for fuck sake, and she would learn this soon enough... *I was determined!*

So, with this new purpose in my life, I walked with quick, long strides back to where I hoped she was ready and waiting for me. I already had food sent to the room, for I knew enough about mortals to know they ate more often than we did. Three times a day, my brother had reminded me, making me realize with annoyance that I had missed some meals already, for she must have been famished.

As for myself, I had since showered and changed into a slightly less relaxed state of dress. Exchanging black combat trousers for dark jeans, and a black T-shirt for a black shirt. One that I rolled back the sleeves of, revealing my tattooed forearms, when I knocked on the door. I would have just walked straight in but knew if she was still dressing at this time, it would be just more of an intrusion of privacy. And well, if she did not yet trust me with her name, then I doubted she was ready to trust me with her body. One I couldn't fucking wait to see in all its beautiful glory, for I knew she would be spectacular.

And speaking of spectacular.

"Gods in Heaven." I hissed through gritted teeth for I was trying to hold back my Demon from growling and scaring her. This was down to the sight of her now, wearing a pretty black dress. One that Peri had no doubt picked for the reason as it was my shade of choice, for obvious reasons.

My Wrath liked the darkness.

"Erm… do you like it?" she asked in a shy and unsure way, and I swear for the first time in my fucking long life, I actually fucking bit my lip to stop myself from roaring out my approval and scaring the shit out of her!

Did I fucking like it!?

Was that really what she had just asked me? In the end I couldn't help my reaction as I snatched out with my hand and with a firm hold on her hip, stepped into her at the same time tugging her closer. Then I tipped her head back, burying my hand in her tight curls before kissing the stain from her lips.

This was when I let my Demon finally have his growl…

"Mine!"

"Well, I guess that means my work here is done… Boss, see you at the club, you can owe me a drink there." I tore my lips from my girl, knowing she needed the breath, and told Peri honestly,

"I am not sure I will fucking make it there, not with such temptation already so close to a bed." At this she walked away chuckling while my Siren gasped at the comment. But this gave her chance to pull away from me and shout after Peri,

"We will be there!" I couldn't help but laugh at this, granting her a wink when she scowled back up at me. But then I could also see the mirth dancing in her pretty eyes, so I knew her scowl lacked gravity.

"Then if that is all I am to be granted, I will still consider myself blessed and offer you my arm like a gentleman," I told her in a teasing tone, making her giggle this time. I had to admit, just like her laugh, this too was a delightful sounding tone that had me grinning like some love sick fool I didn't give a shit that it made me. She smirked up at me and put her arm in mine, telling me,

"Wow, from captive and captor to gentleman and his lady in one day… things sure do move fast around here." Now hearing this made me smirk, before telling her after a quick glance at the bed,

"Not fast enough but alas, there is still time…

Milady." At this she slapped me on the arm and reprimanded,

"Behave, you brute!" Oh, but if only she knew the truth of it, I thought, suppressing a grin as my demon concurred.

"You will soon learn that with you around, that is an impossible ask but I will lie to you and say I will try all the same."

"And I will lie back in return by telling you I expect nothing less than your gentlemanly ways," she teased back and I had to say, I was unexpectedly enjoying this easy banter between us, wondering if this was how it was to be for our future. I could barely believe I had only just met her for the first time yesterday, as it honestly felt as if I had known her most of my life.

My blinding little Halo.

CHAPTER 17
SLAVE TO MY SINS
EMMELINE

A few hours earlier…

The moment Kaiden left the room, I had deflated back onto the edge of the bed and bent forward with my head in my hands, asking myself aloud,

"What am I doing?!"

"Looks like you're having a mini meltdown to me," a lyrical girl's voice commented, and I knew it so well from my dreams that my head snapped up and before I could think too much on how weird it sounded, I was shouting her name,

"Peri!"

"Erm, yeah, you guessed right," she said smirking, as if my reaction to her was funny. But then that was Peri, she found most things funny, even the things that she most likely shouldn't. In fact, if there was one word I would say I used most when describing Peri's personality, it would be spunky. She was full of fun but mostly, she was ballsy as Hell. She took no shit from anyone, including the rest of the men on Kaiden's council.

This might have had something to do with the fact she was known as Ciguapa, a Demon more commonly known as a mythological creature of Dominican folklore. Some people believe that they were bringers of death, and others said that if a Ciguapa so desired, then to look them in the eye, a person could be at risk of being bewitched permanently. This was due to their alluring beauty, and Peri was no different as she was most definitely a head turner.

But then this could also be on account of her style, as even now, she was wearing ripped, cut off denim shorts, a pair of thick black tights underneath, chunky platform boots and a short black crop top that showed her toned belly. To this she had added a long white floor-length kimono style jacket, with wide silk sleeves.

She looked both kick ass in style and cute, with her waves of long lilac coloured hair parted at the centre. Her dark blue eyes always seemed to twinkle with mirth, as if she was thinking naughty thoughts. But as her Demon, well she had the power of persuasion over most beings, although Wrath's Demons were immune. This made it the perfect partnership for her to sit on Kaiden's council. It was also said she had the power to confuse those with the strongest of minds, making them feel lost as they would follow footsteps that weren't there.

They were also nocturnal creatures, like most Demons were, and in her Demonic form I knew her skin would appear a light blue tone than the pale white it was now. Her eyes would also glow snow white, and her feet would twist, until facing the other way.

I swear it was a little like meeting a celebrity or something, as she had featured so often in my dreams and in my writing, that I felt like I knew her… but then, also didn't. She had been such a good friend to Raina, that I was almost desperate for her to like me in the same way. It was messed up, I knew that but then again, wasn't this whole situation fucked?!

I had just been kissing Kaiden for Gods' sake! And Hell, but what a kiss! I swear I could still feel it there like a branding across my lips. Lord, but what was wrong with me? He wasn't even mine, for fuck sake!

"Now that looks like some heavy thoughts you got there, Chica," she said, making me sigh and admit,

"Ever feel like you're living a dream and you're both wishing you would wake as much as you're terrified to, because if you do, then that means none of it was real?" At this she gave me a kind look and told me,

"Then why not take control of the one you want and choose never to wake, if that is your wish." I released another sigh and told her,

"But what if what I want, is wrong?"

"Ah, so you do like the big man." I laughed once and rubbed a hand over my sniffling nose.

"In all honesty, I don't think like is ever going to be a strong enough word for how I feel about him." At this Peri gave me a warm look in return and said,

"Wow, you just jump straight into the girly talk don't you…? Hey, that's cool with me, I'm all up for the bonding shit." I grinned at this and held out my hand and said,

"Hi, I'm Halo, nice to meet you." To which she did the same in return,

"And as you already seem to know, I'm Peri and I am going to be the one who makes Kai fall on his ass in shock at how sexy I made you… nice to meet you too, Chica." I laughed again and after opening the door to Kaiden a little time later, I realized that she was right… minus the falling on the ass bit. But as for a reaction, well he had certainly made it clear he thought I looked nice. And well, thanks to Peri,

I had never felt sexier in all my life.

But getting there had taken its time, and this, Peri informed me, started with a bath. One I definitely took great pleasure in as it was luxury at its finest, with its old-fashioned, bear claw foot bathtub situated in front of an alcove of tall bay windows. A view, had it been daylight, I know would have shown beautifully manicured gardens that gave way to rolling green countryside on this private estate.

As for the rest of the room, it was classical in its style, with black and white floor tiles set in a diamond pattern and small white rectangle subway tiles on the inside of the walk-in shower. The rest was painted a soft grey with ornate wooden cabinetry for its vanity and sink.

Thankfully, Peri had also come armed to the teeth with girly stuff, which made getting ready easier and meant that by the time I had finished in the bathroom, I was shaved, scrubbed and smelling like forest fruits and sherbet. Although, it also awarded me a chance to see all the dark bruises that covered my neck thanks to Kaiden's tortured love bites. The sexual shiver that rippled through my body just thinking back to that first encounter with him in that interrogation room, was uncontrollable. Which was most likely why, by the time Peri had had enough of waiting, she walked into the bathroom finding me touching the marks as if I was feeling the ghost of his lips still there.

"Jeez Louise, forget a handbag, I'm gonna have to give you a damn steak to carry around, that way the next time he is clearly hungry for you, you can just slap him in the face with some bloody meat!" Peri said after whistling when taking in my bites for herself.

"I don't think he did this because he was hungry," I replied, making her smirk and comment dryly,

"Yeah okay, sure he wasn't." Then she chuckled to herself before handing me a garment bag and a box of shoes.

"No, really, this was his way of trying to torture information out of me." At this she burst out laughing making me frown in question.

"Now that's hilarious!"

"What is?" I asked in what was clearly a confused tone.

"The fact that you think he was torturing you, when trust me, Chica, a man like Wrath doesn't usually walk out of an interrogation room without wearing someone else's blood on him…"

"And?"

"…and if that's all he did to you, then I would say it's proof that you were the one doing the torturing, and the only thing he most likely walked out of there wearing was a great big hard on!" she told me, making my mouth drop and in response, making her laugh even more at the obvious shock.

"Besides, a little manhandling obviously didn't put you off, now did it?" she added, this time wagging her brows at me and making me blush.

"So, he is like that with all his women then?" I asked before I could stop myself, and the knowing smirk she gave me told me I had given her too much.

"All his women? Not sure if you know much about Wrath, but he fucks, he doesn't date." I winced at this and tried my best to keep the pain of hearing it from featuring across my face.

"But what he absolutely does not do, is spend time

with them unless it includes fucking. Nor does he buy them dresses and send me in here to help them get ready, and he certainly doesn't give a shit enough to feed them and care for them like he actually has a heart that's used for more than keeping his vessel working. Food's here by the way." She finished this little speech with a wink and left, walking back into the room and leaving me staring at my own shocked face in the mirror.

So yep, this was a lot more than Kaiden Wrath trying to fuck me.

A little time later and now with a gratefully full belly, I was all ready and by the time Kaiden came back to pick up his prisoner, he found me dressed to impress. Oh, and speaking of dress, it was stunning and unlike anything I had ever worn before. Wide straps of the V-neck bodice extended over my shoulders, which also formed the V shape at my back. There was a band, embellished with beads and sequins that defined my waist and added a dash of sparkle. After this, it flowed down into tiers of tulle that glided over my hips when I moved, each layer with a horsehair border to create a fantastic high-low skirt. There was also a matching wrap, like the skirt, that would do little to ward off the chill but would look beautiful all the same.

As for my hair, it had been loosely lifted into a twist,

so it overflowed with curls down my back and my make up Peri had done with two words in mind, smokey and sultry. In fact, I looked so stylish and sexy, that I doubted even Nat would have recognized me, as I barely even recognized myself!

But it had been Kaiden's response when seeing me that still had me feeling as if I were walking on air and not the four-inch, black strappy heels I had been given to wear by Peri. Because walking hand in hand with Kaiden as we navigated our way through his mansion home, most definitely had me back to feeling like this was a dream again. But then the problem with this was that every step I took, I started to feel more and more like an imposter. Like when we were walking down the gallery, with tall arched windows all along one wall. It was night beyond them, therefore acting like a mirror and I swear, the sight of myself with him had me stopping dead.

"Is something wrong?" he asked the moment he saw me staring at myself as if I was transfixed by the sight. Was there something wrong? Gods, but how was I to answer such a thing?! How was I to tell him all the things that were now wrong with what I was staring at, for I wasn't his Siren like he foolishly believed. I was the woman standing in her shoes, taking her place and going against the Gods themselves by just being here!

Oh yes, there was something wrong alright. Which was why I looked back up at him, put a hand to his cheek and told him,

"I am sorry but I…" In the end I never got to say what I wanted to say, as he told me,

"You're perfect." Then he kissed me and just like that, my will crumbled, as I became a slave to my desires…

A slave to my sins.

CHAPTER 18
THE ELEVATION OF HONESTY

A *slave to my sins.*

Because I had never wanted something so much in my entire life and that was why it tore me up inside, knowing that I wasn't being fair to the man I loved. The longer I was here, the more chance I was taking away from him in finding his real Siren. *From finding his Raina.*

Not his little Halo.

I wanted so badly to tell him this but the moment he stopped kissing me, he took my hand and walked us through the rest of his home with more purpose. After this, I soon heard the crunch of gravel under my shoes and couldn't help but look back, seeing a beautiful home that I had always loved.

A stunning mansion of Greystone, that was located only thirteen miles from Manhattan and had beautiful views of the Hudson River. But right now, it was illuminated by the warm glow of up lights that showcased its grand entrance of columns and ornate portico architecture.

The estate was over thirty acres, surrounded by a thousand acres of preserved natural beauty, and was approximately four hundred feet above sea level. Information I knew as I had written it, as well as knowing that the property started when driving through a winding tree-lined driveway that led you to what was his private compound with woodlands, parklands, a naturally flowing ravine, and even a pond. The property was also graced with beautiful rock formations that were featured in its extensive gardens, something seen by Raina when she would find Kaiden watching her walking the grounds from one of the many arched windows.

I had been so disappointed when transported here with a piece of cloth tied over my eyes. But then, they hadn't known who I was. Hell, but they still didn't and if they did, then I knew I would be treated far worse than when I was first brought here as a prisoner.

I would be quickly established as the enemy, making me shudder at the thought and no doubt the reason Kaiden lifted my wrap so it covered my shoulders, obviously believing me to be cold. He also continued to play the perfect gentleman, holding a hand to the base of my spine, with his fingers teasing just on the edge of touching my ass.

"You have such a beautiful home," I said, feeling the need to tell him this before I missed the opportunity. He grinned down at me and raised my hand up for him to kiss, before telling me,

"I am happy to hear that, for you will be spending a great deal of time here, no doubt about it." I opened my mouth ready to argue, but he purposely ignored my need to speak, instead opening the door to his Porsche 918 Spyder for me. A car I knew was one of his other favourites and reminded me of a sleek silver panther. More as a concept car, it looked years ahead of its time, with its typical Porsche style combined with that of an aerodynamic beauty. One that even made a motor novice like me look twice and swallow hard.

I knew he didn't like to be driven anywhere, so I was not surprised when he lowered me into the seat before walking around to the driver's side. As for the inside, well this looked more like a cockpit, with its glowing dials and centre console. One that rose up towards the front of the 918 Spyder and housed a touch screen for intuitive control of the car's functions. I also felt as if the car was trying to keep me contained, as its contoured sports bucket seat was something my body sank into.

After taking his own seat behind the tech covered steering wheel, he pulled away out of the grounds of his estate, and I took note of all the guards just in case I may need to escape once back here. Because I knew even in that gallery of his that he would never listen to reason now, even if I told him I wasn't his Siren. Not when he believed in his heart and in his mind who I was, both of which, were clearly made up.

No, the only option left for me was to run.

Because there was one thing he didn't know, and it was the one thing I was counting on. I knew the inside of his mansion home like the back of my hand, including all the hidden passageways. Tunnels that were like a labyrinth of ways in and out of what was essentially a stronghold in disguise.

"Which part of England were you born in?" he asked, breaking the silence. I gave him a wry look and said,

"Nice try." He shrugged his shoulders unapologetically and stated,

"But you are English."

"Obviously… I'm not that good of an actress." He gave me a sideways glance and grinned.

"Perhaps not." I tried not to react to this but then he asked me his next question, making me tense.

"So, it is not only your name you will keep from me?"

"If the answer can be used to trace back to discovering who I am then it is an answer I cannot give," I told him, being as honest as I could.

"Cannot?" he questioned, making me reiterate.

"Will not."

"Do you fear for your life?" At this I released a sigh and told him,

"No, I actually fear for yours." He was shocked by this.

"You think if you tell me who you are, it will put me in danger?" Again, I wanted to sigh but instead took a deep breath before telling him,

"Not exactly… look, I can't go into it, but just know that the reason anything I've done from the point of walking inside your club, has only ever been because I care for you." At this he raised a brow in question and told me,

"Answer me this, before the interrogation room, had I ever met you before?" At this I looked away, now deciding that watching the world pass me by was easier than facing the truth.

"You never saw me before," I said, only telling a half lie because if he didn't remember seeing me only days before, then I wasn't lying when saying he clearly never really saw me. It was still a sour spot with me, as it was said that an Enforcer would recognize his Siren at first sight, or even when they heard them…

Well, Kaiden had witnessed both that day and yet he had only the briefest reaction to me. One not profound enough for him to even remember.

That was how I knew for certain I wasn't his Siren, no matter how much I wished it was so. And from the looks of things, so did he. But it was too late to go back to our first meeting. It was too late for… *us.*

"Then tell me something you can share," he asked, making me think about it before I told him,

"I'm an orphan."

"You have no family?" he asked in a shocked tone, as if the idea of me being alone was a painful one for him.

"I didn't say that exactly. No, I was brought up by my nanna. She was my father's mother and when my parents died, she took me in and raised me as a daughter," I shared with a small smile.

"Then I am thankful for your nanna," he replied, and it was so sweet, it tugged at my heart.

"I do find it curious you have yet to ask me anything about my own past, or anything about my world at that," he commented, making me tense again before purposely choosing not to reply.

"I know you know who I am or should I say, what I am." At this I continued to remain silent.

"Who told you of us?" he asked, and again I shook my head, telling him I couldn't say. This time he scowled and with his hands tightening on the wheel, said,

"Did he hurt you or threaten to hurt you should you speak of these things with me." My head snapped around to look at him.

"Who?"

"The one you are protecting," he replied, making me gasp.

"You think someone put me up to this!?" I cried in outrage.

"Didn't they?" he pushed, granting me a stern look that promised death to anyone who dared do this.

"No! No one put me up to this… Gods, but how could you even think that!" I snapped, making him narrow his eyes at me and say,

"Then your continued silence makes no sense and therefore can only be for reasons that include another." I released a frustrated sigh and asked him,

"Did you ever wonder why I asked your brother to let me go and never to mention my involvement to you?"

"Fear," he replied surprising me, something he knew when my eyes went wide.

"I was there in that interrogation room, my Halo, it was easy to spot, even if I wasn't a Wrath Demon and could smell it a mile away," he said, confirming for the first time what he was.

"Did you ever wonder why I was so afraid?" I asked, knowing I was treading on delicate ground here.

"It is not an uncommon first reaction." I looked him up and down, still getting used to his size myself and well, I wasn't surprised by this.

"But that is not the reason you feared me… is it?" he guessed, and at this I found I couldn't lie, replying with only one whispered word needed.

"No."

"You had heard of me before we met, which is why I know you protect another. It is the only explanation for your reaction to me." Well not the only one, I thought wryly to myself.

"I don't think I want to have this conversation anymore," I commented, making him scoff.

"Tough shit, my girl, for we are having it!" he snapped, making me shout back,

"Then you will find it rather one sided as I refuse to answer any of your questions!" He rumbled a little at this, and I flinched.

"Because you know that I am right, and you fear me discovering who is behind all of this… perhaps you fear what I will do should I find this person who plays you like a puppet!?" This time his words came out as a growl and I found myself trying to put more space between us, something that was impossible inside the rocket on wheels! But despite this slight spike of fear, I still found myself with enough bravery to throw my thoughts at him.

"I don't fear that because there is no such person! What I do, I do for myself and no one else!" I argued back, and just as we arrived at his city building, he turned the engine off and turned to face me.

"And what of me?" he asked in a calmer voice this time.

"What about you?" I snapped back.

"You risked your life to save my own… is that something you did for you too, or did you do it solely for me because you had no choice? And remember, what you say next may make little sense considering we had never met before," he said, making me open my mouth to argue but nothing came out.

"That's what I thought," he said before getting out the car as I called his name.

"Kaiden, I didn't…" I jumped when I heard the door slam, and I didn't know what to do next. Stay in the car or get out and try and make him understand?

In the end, the decision was taken from me as my door opened and his hand came into view ready for me to take so he could help me get out of his car. But once I did, he shifted me to one side so he could slam it shut. Then he started to walk away without checking on whether I was following. So, I looked back up the ramp, wondering if I could just get away with walking away right now.

"You wouldn't get far, but feel free to try it and find out if you wish," he warned, now looking back at me. I ignored this and the crazy urge to test his threat, and instead walked up to him as he stood next to the elevator.

"After you," he said, nodding when the doors opened. Then after following me inside, he said,

"Should I do the honours, or would you wish to try your luck again?" He was of course referring to the code and the way he knew I had got up into his club the first time. In the end my silence was answer enough, and he tapped in the code. We remained silent the whole way up and I fidgeted for most of it just like the first time.

"You're nervous?" he questioned, making me realize he had been watching me this entire time.

"The first time was scary and quite possibly the most terrifying experience of my life so far… interrogations not withstanding of course." At this he finally grinned before taking my hand back in his.

"You were very brave."

"That or stupid, I am still undecided which," I teased, making him growl playfully. Then, just as the doors opened, he was about to walk out into the lobby area when I held him back. Because I couldn't let him think bad of me, despite knowing that he should. So, I gave him something I should have given him back in the car.

"I can't tell you how, but I… *I do know you.*" He looked surprised but I carried on regardless.

"And well, because of it, I chose to come here and save you, despite what could have happened to me. No one made me do this, Kaiden… it was all my choice, one I will never regret, no matter how this turns out… *no matter what happens to me.*" At this he growled low and before I knew it, he was at me. He was pinning me to the back of the elevator, and suddenly the start of my dream of him was becoming my very first reality.

And stranger still…

Raina wasn't the girl in his arms…

No... It was me.

CHAPTER 19
WHISKEY KISSES

Kaiden's kiss.

Good lord, it was like being injected by pure, unadulterated lust! I could barely think, let alone focus on all the reasons we shouldn't be kissing again. But then what else did I expect would happen the second the man of my dreams had me pinned against the wall with his lips on mine? A beast and man combined, who seemed starved of my touch. Even the way he growled against my lips had me near begging for more and as for his hands, Gods, but they were everywhere!

At one point I feared he would just rip my dress from me. And I felt it pulled impossibly tight against my breasts, as he had what little material there was held in a tight fist at my back.

"Fuck!" he hissed through gritted teeth before letting his head fall to my shoulder, now breathing me in. So,

seeing as he was obviously struggling here with something, I acted before I could stop myself, wanting so badly to offer him comfort. Which was why I reached up and put a hand to the back of his neck and started stroking him there. The second I touched him, I felt him shiver before that rumbling growl made me stop. But before I could remove my hand, he covered it with his own and told me,

"Don't stop, I make those sounds because my Demon and I like your touch." My eyes grew wide at hearing that his Demon responded to me… but surely, *shouldn't he be the one trying to push me away?*

"Come, my Halo, we should leave before I let those doors close and not open again until I have finally claimed you."

I swallowed hard, making him chuckle as he finally let my feet find the floor. Then he took my hand for the second time and walked me from the elevator. This time when I entered the lobby filled with guards, they bowed a head to their Lord and strangely, no one questioned the mortal he had in tow.

Did his people know of me already?

This thought was why I pulled back on his hand to get his attention, making him look down at me.

"Won't your people wonder why you have a mortal with you?" At this he smirked, and his only answer was to wink at me as he continued to walk me to his table. His brother and council members were already there waiting for him, and all stood at our approach, making me feel as this was all still nothing but a dream.

"My lord Wrath, my Lady… erm…"

"Halo. Her name is Halo," Kaiden informed Boaz, who I knew was his second in command and was trying to address me as being Kaiden's lady, making me instantly feel uncomfortable. However, I also noticed the way Hel watched me with curiosity. As if he was analysing everything I did, ready to report back to his brother. At this and my shaking hand, I couldn't catch my wrap in time before it slipped off my shoulders and floated to the floor. Hel reacted first and bent down to retrieve it for me, unknowingly recreating a moment between us from the first time I saw him.

However, I had a horrible feeling the second he passed it back to me, that it may not have gone as unnoticed as I would have liked as now something deeper played in his eyes. But then again, he was always the perceptive, cunning one and now I could see it as his eyes narrowed.

The memory was coming back to him.

"Erm… thanks."

"You're welcome, *Halo,"* he replied, making a point of saying my given name as if the hidden promise to find out my real one was there, behind those startling blue depths like some personal mission. After this, Kaiden, who was seemingly unaware of his brother's silent challenge, led me to the middle of the massive U-shaped seating area. This was one where the back part of the middle was significantly higher and clearly indicated where the master and ruler of this sector sat. The second he let my hand go, to turn ready to sit in his throne, was when I started to step away, going to find a seat more suited for my lower station. After all, I didn't want people to think of me as his. This was already getting harder by the minute, and I couldn't trust myself to think around him.

However, the second I made it a step, his hands were framing the entirety of my waist and he was growling down in my ear,

"Just where do you think you are going, my pretty girl?" I swallowed hard and told him,

"To find my seat."

"The decision of where you sit is not your own, for it is mine and I do not recall releasing you as my prisoner as of yet." I lowered my head to the floor and took a shuddered breath as I let his words flow over me like some sexual caress.

"You sit by my side, my Halo," he told me on another growl of words… Words I had no choice but to take seriously, especially when his hands tightened against my flesh before he picked me up and only let me go again when I was sitting next to his unconventional throne. Then, when he was satisfied, he himself sat down, making the rest of his men do the same. I felt my cheeks get so hot, I was so embarrassed in front of his council, who I felt were no doubt judging me and the reason I was still

here with their master. I already knew it was forbidden for a supernatural to be with a human unless they were fated, and I was trying to save him the offence he didn't seem to even realize he was committing.

A bit of kissing in private was one thing, but by having me sit by his side like this…? It was nothing short of their Lord making a statement. Which made me question what would happen to him once the King of Kings discovered his wrong doings.

Dominic Draven was said to be the most brutal Supernatural of all Kings and well, one utterly terrifying bastard, as he was basically as close to a living God on Earth as you could get!

Gods, but just thinking about what could happen to Kaiden should his King find out about me was the most terrifying thing of all, and one I should have thought of long before now. But this farse was spiralling more and more out of control by the minute, and my choices were at two. I could either tell him the truth and risk him killing me or I could simply leave.

He still didn't know who I was, so it wasn't as though I would need to change my name. I still had a shot at hiding. I still had a shot at surviving this. *That was if I didn't first die of a broken heart!*

Because how was I ever supposed to carry on after this? How was I ever to find a life to live after this, knowing that the man of my dreams existed? Knowing how wonderful it felt being in his arms and how incredible it felt when he kissed me? How was I supposed to just move on from that?

How was I to ever let go?

"I fear your little Halo is deep in thought, brother," Hel said, making me snap my head up and frown at him. But Kaiden was chuckling next to me and hit the nail on the head when he said,

"No doubt still trying to plan her escape. Well, until an impossible one that would work comes to mind, what would you like to drink?" His brother laughed at his comment and replied,

"From the looks of it, something strong no doubt."

Kaiden agreed and the whole conversation made me feel small and weak. Because these two jerks had no idea the internal struggle I suffered was all done to keep the man I loved still living. Well, I would show them! The one thing I had always prided myself on was being able to drink most people under the table, so they could bring it on… I would give them nothing!

"Whiskey on the rocks… Scotch if you have it," I said, surprising Kaiden as I knew this was also his drink of choice and the reason I had started drinking it in the first place. I had wanted to know how to describe it so had bought myself a bottle. Although, I couldn't ever have afforded anything he would drink personally, they were usually thousands of dollars a bottle, sometimes more.

"She either knows you well, brother, or her tastes

match that of your own." I rolled my eyes at this, making Hel chuckle.

"A bit of both I think," Kaiden replied, and this is when I found my limit with these two!

"Erm, you do know I am right here… right?!" I snapped, making them both laugh… *The cocky bastards.* But then Kaiden laid a big hand on the back of my neck and pulled me closer so he could growl into my cheek.

"I know exactly where you are... mine." Then he kissed me there and gave me back my space, but without removing his hand this time. It felt like being owned and under his heavy hand, I couldn't help but find it a big turn on. To be owned by this big brute of a man who could quite easily crush men to death, felt nothing short of exhilarating.

"Bring a bottle of The Balvenie," Kaiden ordered, making me near start choking knowing this was most definitely at the top end of that expensive bottle list. So, I took some time to process this, jumping when suddenly the very bottle was put down in front of Kaiden. Then I watched as he himself poured me a glass first, handing it to me. However, when I took it, I couldn't help but just stare down into the smooth amber liquor as if it was liquid gold.

"Problem?" he asked, now rubbing the bare part of my back, making me squeak out,

"It's a fifty-thousand-dollar bottle!" At this he

frowned a moment, and looked to his brother again before asking me,

"So?"

"So?!" I questioned back as if he were crazy.

"Then consider it a thousand dollars per year, as a fifty-year-old whiskey is a thing of beauty and all beauty should be savoured... isn't that right, brother?" Hel said, pointing out something it was clear his brother agreed with. But then it soon became apparent that he wasn't the only one who agreed, as this time, it was Kaiden's Demon that answered him, quickly growling down at me,

"Indeed, it is." Then he downed his glass in one and still with his hold on the back of my neck, he yanked me to him, ending this Demonic statement on a...

Whiskey kiss.

CHAPTER 20
POKER FACE

It became quite apparent after this that Kaiden had no problems with touching me, kissing me and basically branding the knowledge of who I belonged to, in front of not only his men but his entire club!

I shivered again and in response, his hand tensed at the back of my neck in an even more possessive hold, one that wasn't helping with trying to get my heart to stop racing! A few seconds later he pulled back and told me on a growly rumble of words,

"Fucking worth every penny. Whiskey never tasted so good." I blushed at this and couldn't help but bravely whisper back in return,

"Thank you... you... taste good too." His reply to this was a growl as his grip on me tightened but then my eyes lifted from his to notice we were being watched... *by*

everyone. I felt his own burning gaze stay on me for a few moments longer, watching my reactions, but when my eyes raised to see the waitress still lingering, he finally took notice of something other than me.

Kaiden spared her a glance before dismissing her with a wave of his hand, and I finally realized that the waitress was one I recognized from my book. Someone, that if my writing was correct, was also a girl who had a thing for her Lord. Hence why she was now looking at me as though she wanted to drive a spike through my mortal skull.

"Katina, you've fulfilled your duty, now go!" Hel snapped at her when he too took notice of the look she was now giving me. She flinched and had the good sense to do as she was told, as Hel was one scary Demon when he wanted to be. And right then, *he most certainly wanted to be.*

He also caught me looking at him with what I knew were silent questions showcased in my wide eyes, something he just winked at. I also ignored his chuckle the second I quickly looked away, instead now focusing on the rest of Kaiden's council, who all looked to be in attendance other than Peri.

There was of course, Tristan and his easy boy-next-door charm who had already given me a salute when we had first walked in. But as for the others, there was one called Teko, who I knew was titled as a Necromancer. Basically, he was Kaiden's sorcerer and held the term

Necromancer, not because he brought the dead back to the living. No, it was because he could use his powers to draw a Demon's soul and essence up from Hell and house it in its new mortal vessel, fusing the two as one.

Of course, he also looked like some GQ magazine cover model, with his tailored dark burgundy suit, black waistcoat, and a black silk scarf in place of a tie. One that hung either side of his lapels and matched the handkerchief tucked stylishly in his breast pocket. As for his handsome face, this compliment was given thanks to prominent cheekbones, a cut jawline and a long straight nose. He was all angular grace with a pair of dark arrogant eyes.

After him came Adjo, a name I knew meant Righteous in African. He was a huge muscular guy who was covered in raised tribal lines of a continuous tattoo, making it looked as if he had black rope buried under his skin. He wore a pair of black combat trousers, military style boots and a tanked khaki vest that showcased the contours of both his tattoos and his extensive muscles. His hair was a mass of twisted dreads, held back by a pair of steampunk style goggles that matched the mechanical glowing bands of metal around his wrists. Adjo, had a kind face, with the type of smile you couldn't help but grin back at and an infectious booming laugh you couldn't help but chuckle with. His eyes were an unusual shade of amber, verging on yellow, and they would glow when he was deep in thought or like most Demons, when he was pissed off or outright horny.

I also knew him to be the equivalent of some mad mechanic, where with Teko's help, he would combine the casting of sorcery with machine, after his own powers would scorch runes and Demonic symbols onto the objects he was working on. It was how I knew that these two would have been used to aid in Kaiden's release, as both could use their combined gifts to undo what Dagon obviously had made to confine him to that box.

And last but my no means least, came Kaiden's second in command and best friend, Boaz. And well, seeing as these guys in the Supernatural world were big on picking names for their meanings, his unsurprisingly, meant 'strength' in Hebrew. This was no doubt because out of all of them, he was the closest in size to Kaiden's immense build of muscles and height. He was also the roughest of them all, wearing jeans ripped at the knees and a motorcycle T-shirt that looked as if it had seen far better days… as in, decades ago!

He was ruggedly attractive, with his dark blonde hair that lay in a mess of waves. Loose curls that had obviously felt a touch of hair gel in an attempt at controlling them back from his face… I felt his pain of course. But this managed to give him that bad ass look, along with his tanned face half covered by a blonde and rust toned beard. One that was most definitely not as trimmed or neatly kept as Kaiden's was. And like Hel, his light brown eyes were ones of cunning and silent calculation as he seemed to watch everything…

Including me.

"Now, give me good news and tell me you have an update of Dagon's whereabouts," Kaiden asked his men after he too scowled at Katina the waitress, doing so as she walked away and obviously now understanding his brother's annoyance.

"Wish I could but he's in the fucking wind," Boaz replied in that deep voice of his, making me respond before I thought how stupid doing so was.

"Perhaps you should try Afterlife. Isn't it this time of year the King of Kings holds meetings with his Enforcers?" At this Kaiden's hand tightened at my neck for a few seconds while everyone in his council stopped and stared at me.

"And what does a mere mortal like you know about the King of Kings?" Teko asked me, in a knowing way that made Kaiden growl his name in warning for speaking to me like that.

"Teko enough!"

"I am sorry, my Lord Wrath, but I do not trust her as you do yet, for she knows too much of us, while we are left knowing nothing of her." Okay so he had a point, making me reply,

"Knowing nothing doesn't make me your enemy."

"Then what does it make you?" Adjo asked this time. I knew he was good friends with the Necromancer, and no doubt had the same mindset as his friend did, in regard to me.

"In the wrong place, at the wrong time," I answered honestly when I felt Kaiden stiffen next to me, which was why he slammed his fist down on the table in front of us, creating large cracks around the impact. Then his Demon roared,

"ENOUGH, ALL OF YOU!" Everyone tensed in sight of their Lord Wrath, as his Demon rose to the surface, making me flinch. Then he took large lungfuls of breath, trying to calm his raging beast.

"Our only enemy is the one who put me in a fucking box to rot! Now it is time for him to feel the full extent of our Wrath! Find him and bring him before me on his fucking knees, for I want no fucker to rest until this happens... *am I understood?!"* he ordered, making me tremble at the sight of his Demonic rage. However, despite my fear of him, I bravely reached out to him and took his hand in mine, using my thumb to stroke soft circles on the back of it. And as for his brother, he couldn't take his eyes off us, taking it all in and no doubt filing it away ready to use at some point. Because Hel never forgot anything and often used his incredible memory as a tool for his cunning plans.

But as for my touch, it seemed to calm their furious Lord, making me wonder what had made him angrier, the fact that his enemy was still out there or the fact his council had been questioning me? Or had it been my own comment about being in the wrong place at the wrong time?

I never found out which as I was suddenly plucked out of my seat and placed on his lap, making me squeal in shock.

"What are you doing, I can't be sitting here!" I hissed, making him growl into the back of my neck before biting it there, holding my flesh in between his teeth in warning.

"Ahh... ahh..." I moaned before he released me and told me of my offences.

"Are you trying to tell me what I can and can't do with you, my little prisoner?" I sucked in a quick breath and shook my head telling him no, I wasn't that stupid, even though, yeah... *I totally was.*

"Good, then you will sit here and be good for me," was his cocky reply, before he started soothing the hurt with his kiss, one that travelled around to the other areas he had bitten when in the interrogation room. He seemed fascinated with them and for the rest of the night, he continued to play with them in one way or another. It was the stroke of his thumb, or the backs of his fingers. It was his kisses or when he would outright start sucking on one and at the same time listening to his men speak, often making me wonder if he was listening at all. However, he would comment or answer as if he had in fact been giving his full attention, and what he was doing to me was completely normal.

Meanwhile, I had been fidgeting on his lap more and

more, because this was purely torturous for me. I had been getting more uncomfortably turned on by the minute and he fucking knew it!

"What is your name?" he asked me after about an hour of this, and four utterly deliciously smooth whiskies consumed, telling me exactly what his game had been.

"I could sing Mambo number 5 for you again if you like and give you many choices." At this, some of his men sniggered after obviously hearing of my joke played on him in the interrogation room.

"Ah, so that was what that technique was?" he hummed against my neck, and I could feel his grin when I said,

"My singing can often break most men." After this I felt his hand come to rest dangerously close up my thigh as he told me possessively,

"No, that is my job if any of those men think to come near you again." I swallowed down a shameful lump of lust at hearing that jealous side of him… *lust and fear*.

"However, lucky for me, I *innocently* know it to be said in jest," he added, emphasizing the word innocence and making me know just what he was referring to. As it was clearly my virginity, and the reason why my joke was known as just that.

"But what is this?" Kaiden asked after he took my hand in his and started entwining his fingers with mine, lifting the two combined as if he wanted to see for himself how they looked. However, this question was in reference to the cat scratches he could now see on the inside of my wrist. Long, angry red lines that he was now running the pad of his thumb over as he had both his big arms wrapped around me from behind.

"Proof that Roger hates me," I told him, making him grumble,

"Then I'm glad he goes hungry, for nothing or no one should get to mark your skin but I," he said before I felt his lips at the darkest of my bites that he had seemed most fascinated with. It was also one that I felt him grinning against the moment he made me tremble in his hold, knowing exactly what he was doing to me… *yet again!*

A little time later and after a few more whiskies, I was starting to relax a little too much as the last few days were obviously catching up with me, which meant that I was unable to help yawning.

"Tired, my little Halo?" Kaiden asked, as he seemed to notice everything when it came to me. When I was finishing my drink, he was ordering a new one, when I fidgeted, he would move me in a way to make it more comfortable for me. It was as if we were connected and what I felt, he then felt too. Which was why I wasn't surprised by the comment.

"I have never been able to sleep on a plane," I said pausing mid-stretch as my whole body froze when I realized what I had just said. Of course, neither Hel or Kaiden missed it, as he looked to his brother and stated,

"She took a flight here, check all airports and their

security footage for her face, find me which flight she was on." I almost choked as I coughed, trying to get my words ou.

"Y-y-y...you won't find me."

"No?" he asked in a knowing, smug tone.

"I was just saying that to throw you off," I said, making him chuckle along with his men. Then he turned me, so I was now facing him. He took hold of my chin and gave my face a little shake in a condescending way. This was when I realized I was completely screwed after he told me with a knowing grin...

"Don't ever play poker, sweetheart."

CHAPTER 21

BURNING ME OF MY SORROW

"I *need to get my Siren to bed."*

I started to stir when I heard this being said, making me vaguely ask,

"Am I dreaming again?" I heard Hel's chuckle before he teased,

"With my brother carrying you to bed, I would say more of a nightmare."

"Get the door, asshole," Kaiden grumbled in reply, and I opened my eyes in time to see that somehow, we were now back in the mansion. And well, with the amount of whiskies they had given me, I wasn't really surprised that I was now drunk. As yeah, I was a good drinker but good lord, I wasn't some medical marvel that was immune!

"Getting her wasted was your idea, brother," Hel replied, making him growl,

"Yes, and little good it did. Gods, but I didn't know such a little thing was capable of consuming as much!"

"Fucking Demons would get pissed before her!" Hel agreed.

"Just call me the interrogation goddess!" I decreed, making both of them laugh.

"Well, at least she is a happy drunk, if not a truthful one," Hel commented, making his brother scoff as I zipped a line across my lips with a giggle. But then I saw that he had taken me back to the room I had first begged to stay in and in my drunken state, I was glad. So, the second he put me on my feet, I started dancing around with my arms out like I was twirling, making the room sway, but I didn't care.

"Oh goodie, I like this room," I told them when stopping to catch my breath, and both were now staring at me as though they were equally captivated by the sight. My hair had long ago come free of its attempted up-do, no doubt looking wild around my head and shoulders. I knew I was red faced, as I felt hot, but I was grinning widely at them both before reaching out a hand and telling them,

"Come dance with me!"

Hel took a step forward and soon found a firm hand pressed to his chest.

"She was talking to me, brother." Hel looked as if was shaking himself out of some spell or something, before telling him,

"The call of the Siren is strong, forgive me… Go and be with her."

"And you?" Kaiden asked with a raised brow.

"To go clear my head with a stiff drink and fucking cold shower."

"And then?" Kaiden asked, this time with a pointed look as if he were trying to convey something private to him.

"Then I have a lie to reveal," Hel replied, making me pout at him.

"Spoil sport, and technically I haven't lied, so mah!" I said, sticking my tongue out at him before I started twirling again in my drunken madness.

"Yes, well I will leave you to deal with… erm… *that,"* Hel commented dryly, making Kaiden laugh.

"Inform me the moment you have anything." After this the door closed and off his brother went, no doubt trying to play detective. Then I shrieked out in a fit of giggles when Kaiden grabbed me from behind, spun me quickly and threw me over his shoulder, after saying,

"Come here, little Halo!" Then he let me drop to the bed that we had slept the day away in, and it quickly reminded me of the first time, making me say in a breathless tone,

"I think we have been here before, handsome." Then I winked at him, making him grin down at me.

"That we have, little one." His husky voice spoke of his own lust, that along with the way he scanned the length of me laid out before him like a feast. Which, in my drunken state meant I couldn't find any reason not to enjoy this, so walked my fingers up his arm and along his large, muscled shoulder, doing so in a playful way.

He held himself still at the feel of me touching him for the first time in such a teasing way. Then I let my fingers skim down his neck and the first few buttons of his shirt that were undone. After this, I looked up into his heated gaze and because what I saw there was only longing, I continued to be brave, letting the alcohol fuel me. So, I reached up with my other hand and started to undo the rest of his shirt buttons, revealing more and more of that gorgeous body of his as I went.

Then, just as I finished with his shirt, I continued further, never leaving his gaze as I hooked my fingers into the waistband of his jeans. At this, one hand shot to mine to restrain me, then he growled down a warning at me,

"You play with fire, little girl." This was when I'd had enough and my restraint around him finally snapped. Which was why I lifted my body up, and after putting my lips to his, I told him the only truth that mattered in that moment,

"Then burn me, my Demon." At this he snarled back and before I could give him an inch of space, his lips crushed to mine. Then he ripped the rest of his shirt down his arms, and I suddenly found myself being restrained to the bed with my wrists shackled in his large hands as he kissed the breath from me.

"Yesss!" I moaned the second his kiss made it to my neck, as this had seriously become a big thing for me. The teasing he had done all night had made me so hypersensitive, I felt as I if I could come undone once more. Although Kaiden had other ideas as he lowered himself down the bed, gathering up my dress as he went, without taking his dark eyes from me. It was frightening the way his eyes changed to that of his Demon but strangely, the fear only managed to turn me on more.

"This time you find your release in my arms, from a different kiss of mine," he told me on a rumble of lust-filled words. I swear, it was as if his Demon was pushing at him to break free and take me as well. And somewhere in the back of my mind, I knew this was wrong. I knew I should be stopping this. I should be trying everything in my power to save him the sin.

But I couldn't.

I wasn't strong enough against him. I wasn't strong enough to tear myself from the bliss. From my addiction. *It consumed me.* It fed the entirety of my soul, and I couldn't stop now as it honestly felt as if I would die if I did!

Then, he really did burn me!

Because the second he ripped my underwear from me, spread me wide and had his first taste of me, my will was burnt to cinders in the pits of Hell from which he was born!

"Ahhhhh! Yes, Gods yes! Don't stop... Don't ever

stop!" I cried out, making him growl against my quivering flesh that had never experience such pleasure! He sucked and bit and kissed my clit, stopping only to lick up the length of my glistening folds before sucking me back into his mouth in this brutal onslaught of sensation. I felt my hands fisting the covers beneath me, but it didn't feel strong enough to hold me to this dream. It was as if it would all just slip away, just like it usually did before he made me come, like I would wake just on the cusp of feeling it crashing into me. It was my cruel reality, and one I couldn't go back to…

Not yet.

I couldn't give this up just yet.

Surely the Gods wouldn't be so cruel.

Which is why I begged without thinking.

"Gods, please don't take this from me again… just let him be real… just this once!" I prayed, making him growl against me, stopping only long enough to snap,

"I am real, my girl, and I am going fucking nowhere!" Then he went back and this time when he did, he made me scream as I came with a ferocity that made me see fucking stars! My back bowed like I was some instrument to be played, straining against his tight hold on my legs, keeping me spread and open to him as he continued to take me somewhere I had never been.

A purely euphoric place.

His own brand of Heaven in the midst of Hell's flames.

I screamed again and again, this time begging him to have mercy on me, for I couldn't experience it again. The pleasure actually frightened me. As if it truly did have the power to tear me apart and cut me deep enough that all my secrets would come spilling out.

"I want more!" he snarled against my quivering thigh, and I whimpered,

"I... please... I can't... I am scared," I admitted, making him chuckle into my flesh before he showed me just what it was like to beg a Demon.

"Then I will feed from your fear and make a true lover's feast of you... *now give me more, my Siren!"* he said, making me cry out until tears were pushed from the corners of my eyes and my mouth remained open as if the sound just wouldn't stop. And neither would he. He lapped me up as though he was some hungry wolf devouring his meal. That's when I knew he truly had the power to take everything from me. The power to cut me wide open and leave me bare for all to see.

He held all the power over me, and I was left shaking in terror at the same time screaming out yet another orgasm, this time calling his name, like some master who owned me.

"Kaiden! Gods, Kaiden please! KAIDEN AHHHH!" I shouted one last time before I felt myself falling back to the bed, exhausted. It was then and only then that he realized I had well and truly hit my limit. Then after kissing me softly over my soaked flesh, he rose himself above me. I felt my wild hair being pushed back from my damp forehead with a large palm, before he buried his fingers in my curls.

"You came for me so beautifully, my girl… so beautiful, my blinding little Halo, for it is a gift I will treasure always," he told me, before shifting me closer and lifting me into his arms to hold me from behind.

"What is?" my sleepy voice foolishly asked.

"The way my Siren begs for me," he whispered in my ear, and I tensed in his hold, making him coo down at me,

"Ssshh now, easy little one, for we will discuss your future with me tomorrow but for now, sleep easy in my arms once more." I did as he asked, knowing that this would be the last time, even though when I finally did close my eyes…

I did so with tears of sorrow.

CHAPTER 22

IT'S ALL IN A NAME

WRATH

"Come in, Hel," I said the second I felt my brother at the door and knew my little Halo had long ago passed out. Gods in Heaven, they had sent me such a fuckable little Angel, it made my mouth water just thinking back to what I did to her. I could have eaten her for hours, if I knew that she would have been able to take it. But after thirty minutes of forcing her to come as many times as she was capable, I knew when she had hit her limit. A limit that I chose for her as she believed herself there long before I deemed it so.

"So, she passed out on you?" my brother asked, clearly amused.

"With some help, yes," I replied with a grin and a lick of my lips.

"Lucky bastard."

"I am indeed," I said when looking down at her sleeping like an Angel in my arms.

"Now, I take it you have news."

"That I do, so get your lucky ass up and come with me," Hel said, making me really grin this time. Fuck me, but I felt almost excited, more than eager to discover who my lush little Siren was.

"And is it as I hoped?" I asked after slipping my curly bundle of cuteness from the crook of my arm and onto her side. Then I grabbed a T-shirt from the bag of my things I'd had packed whilst temporally being in this room and yanked it over my head, pulling it down my abs, stopping mid motion when he told me,

"It is… for she will finally be known to you."

"You have her name then?" I asked after finishing the uncomplicated act of dressing.

"I do, brother, I do indeed," he replied with a knowing grin, and I looked back at my sleeping girl and commented before leaving the room with my brother.

"Excellent."

Shortly after this we found ourselves in my office, and one that looked vastly different to the office at my club, 53 Sins. But then that was most likely down to the rest of the classic décor of the mansion. Which meant wooden panel walls, heavy carved, antique furniture, leather Chesterfields and hand-knotted silk carpets made of cashmere that reflected the skills of Indian carpet weavers. Books filled the bespoke cabinetry and oil paintings adorned the forest green walls.

Needless to say, it was old school and miles away from the sleek lines of my club. But it also needed to be said that I felt more comfortable doing mortal business here, as my club was a place that fed the darker side of my nature. But right now, it was the perfect place for discovering secretive little Sirens and unravelling the mysteries they weave.

"Tell me!" I all but growled.

"So, you know how we both felt as if we had seen her before," Hel told me, making me lean back against my office desk, for I couldn't sit down, being too on edge to do so. And what my brother said was true, as we had both felt this way around her. As if we had seen her face somewhere before.

"And?" I snapped impatiently.

"Well, when she dropped her shawl back in the club, it came to me, making me wonder why the memory affected me."

"And why did it?" I asked, wishing he would get to the fucking point already.

"Because it had happened before," he replied surprising me.

"When was this?"

"Do you remember the girl you grabbed at the..." the second he said this, it all hit me like a fucking thunderbolt!

"Fuck... *the hotel!"* I snapped as that same memory came flooding back to me, also making him comment dryly,

"Yep, and there is it." I ignored this and started shaking my head, as if there was a piece missing, which was why I said,

"But her hair..."

"Yeah, I think that's what threw us, as she must have been wearing a wig or something because..."

I once again interrupted him. "There is no doubt it was her and fuck me, but I felt it even then!" I said, feeling as though I wanted to kick my own ass for being so blind! I had heard her speak and something in me had snapped as I found myself trying to hold on to her and fuck, how I had wished I had held on and never let go. But then I thought back to even before then, when she had first stepped into that elevator, her face had said it all as she had looked utterly struck down in her shock.

"She knew me," I muttered more to myself.

"Yes, well that's the part so far we have not figured out, but in all likelihood after her reaction to us, then I would say yes, she knew us all the second she stepped inside that elevator," Hel said, and I had to agree with him. Her beautiful face had blushed as if shamed with some secretive thoughts of hers, and her big brown eyes had widened, reminding me of some little doll haunted by the very sight of me. I had at the time just believed her reacting to the size of me, for I knew I had that effect on some mortals… *I was intimidating.*

"Did you trace her back to staying at the hotel?" I asked, shaking the thought of her shock from my mind.

"Of sorts, yes."

"What do you mean?" I asked, making him tense as if what he would tell me next, I was not going to like.

"Alright, so there is more of that day you do not know." I frowned at this.

"Like what…? Fucking spit it out, Helmer!" I said using his full name, one he hated to hear being used as it reminded him of who was the older one between us.

"That was not the only time I ran into her that day," he admitted, making me growl at him as my hands splintered the wooden edge of my desk.

"What? And you didn't think to tell me this?!"

"You mean, I didn't think to tell you about some grabby asshole who was hassling some random cute mortal girl, who I will add, had seemed terrified at the very sight of you the first time… no, why, should I have?" Hearing this, my blood started to boil, as I grabbed him and snarled dangerously,

"What asshole?!" After this threat he told me what had happened when he came across her for a second time

and at the very least, I got some pleasure from hearing what she had said to him. Yet it was not enough to save him from my Wrath as I ordered dangerously,

"I want the fucker's name!" My brother's sinister grin in return was just as dangerous as he commented in a knowing tone,

"But of course, you do."

An hour later and after a little bit more digging, I was looking at a picture of my girl on a screen with the name written below that when shortened, quite literally meant my 'Entire' world. For this was its translation. Emme, as her friends called her, Emmeline being the name that I assumed would show on her passport. A name that meant determination and dedication, two traits I believed she possessed in spades.

Emmeline Raidne.

I wondered if she knew of the true origins of her last name, for it was said to be one of the names of the Lost Sirens. But then, this hadn't surprised me either, making me briefly wonder what would start to happen if word got out. Would this be a way for other Enforcers to find their own Sirens and if so, would this not then be interfering with the Fates' plans. It was always meant to be that a Siren was the one to call out and find her Enforcer, doing so in what I now knew was not in the literal sense. For all my Halo had said to me had been scarcely a thank you and admittedly, it had barely been enough to get me to react. Gods, but the idea that I had let her go, sickened me. To know that it could have been my one and only chance at claiming her, well it was too painful a thought to even think about beyond this point.

After my brother had told me of the asshole with an unknown death wish, he then explained how she'd told him she had a room at the hotel. But this, even my brother knew was a lie, as she was obviously just trying to get out of the elevator quicker.

The biggest question had been why?

Why was it that we had terrified her enough to want to run from us? It made no sense. However, he remembered seeing guests for a wedding there and once again, I was classing my brother's eyes for detail and his memory for even more, as a blessing. He then had the guest list tracked down through the catering… and I had no fucking clue they needed this for food choices. As it turned out, she was one of the bridesmaids and after tracking the cab back to JFK airport, we discovered she had arrived only hours before turning up at the club.

After this, the discoveries just kept coming in and an hour after learning her name, I was unravelling her whole life, loving every fucking second of it! That was until Franklin uncovered something while getting closer to his screen.

"That's strange," Franklin said, pushing up his glasses.

I knew this was done out of habit still left over from his human days.

"What is it now?" I asked at the same time Hel moved closer so he could see what he was working on.

"It looks like she deleted a lot of things on her social media straight after the wedding." I frowned at this, wondering why that would mean anything. Clearly though, I was a dinosaur to these things, as social media was still new to me and not something I could see myself participating in any time soon.

"So?" I enquired.

"It's like… erm…"

"What?! Just fucking out with it, Franklin!" I barked out this order, making him flinch in sight of my Wrath breaking through.

"Well… it's like she is trying hide something," he finally replied.

"Why is that suspicious?" I asked, making Hel look at me and remind me,

"I get you are not ready to call her our enemy but remember, she still knows us and our world from somewhere and after seeing us in that hotel, you don't then find it odd she would start deleting parts of her life from social media?"

"Good point… can you discover what it is?" I asked Franklin after agreeing with my brother, feeling a little foolish not to have seen it as suspicious myself.

"Looks like about a year's worth of posts, pictures, she even shut down profiles. When you type her name, it comes up with account recently closed… okay, so let's try a google search, as she wouldn't be able to hide… oh Gods… well… shit me…" he ended, making me snap back when my brother hissed,

"Oh you've gotta be fucking shitting me!"

"What is it!?" I snapped.

"Is this… is this fucking legit?" my brother asked, ignoring my outburst and just as Franklin nodded to him, Hel then rose from his position. Then he turned to face me, purposely keeping his body in front of the screen so I couldn't see it.

"What the fuck is it!?" I barked again, now folding my arms and feeling the material tighten around my biceps.

"Well, brother… I think I know why she knows so much about us and why she fears you ever finding out her name." I closed my eyes a moment as I started to try and rein in my Demon.

"Explain… *now!*" I gritted through clenched teeth. My brother took a deep breath and told me the very last thing I ever expected to hear!

"She is an author and wrote a fucking book about you." I took an astounded step back as if I had been struck.

"Come… come again?" I whispered in a dangerous tone, making Franklin flinch again.

"She wrote a book about you," my brother stated what I hoped I hadn't heard the first time.

"How the fuck do you know that?!" was my irrational first question to ask.

"It's a bit fucking obvious, that's why," Hel replied, making me narrow my gaze at him.

"How so?!"

"Tell him the name of it," Hel ordered but before Franklin could utter a word, I snarled,

"Like that fucking matters!"

"Actually, it does," Hel told me, and just as I lost it and thundered,

"Why the fuck…?" I paused the second he moved out of the way and right there on the screen, was the front cover.

"Because, brother, *it's got your name all over it,*" my brother said, and he was right.

She had written a book and called it…

Wrath's Siren.

"Fuck!" I hissed, turning my back to the screen and rubbing the back of my neck. It felt as if my skin would catch alight and burn my vessel's flesh right off as my Demon took over completely. Because everything she had ever said started to play back to me, doing so now and having deeper meaning. Her reluctance and refusal to believe she was mine. The way she tensed whenever my Siren was mentioned or anything of the Fates. It was how she knew me…

She fucking knew everything!

"When was it written?" I gritted out.

"It says here it's a year old, but in her Author Bio, it states she started writing it six years ago after having dreams of the story," Franklin told me after pushing up his fucking glasses again.

"Fuck... six years," I muttered, making my brother release a sigh.

"It says here it's the story of how Wrath the Enforcer meets his Lost Siren, a woman called… oh dear," Franklin paused, making me growl,

"Give me the fucking name!"

"It says here that it's a woman called, Raina," Franklin told me, making me swear again!

"That's why she is freaked out just by being here, she fucking believes she isn't my Siren, but this other fucking woman, this fucking Raina is! Someone she believes I will no doubt find one day!" I snarled the retaliation to what I thought of as a cruel fucking twist of fate!

"Yeah, that's my guess," my brother agreed.

"Well, that fucking ends now!" I shouted, before turning and near breaking the fucking door in my haste to leave when the voice of Franklin stopped me in my tracks.

"Erm… boss…"

"What the fuck is it now?!" I roared when Hel was the one to answer me, after Franklin pointed to something on the screen.

"HEL!" his name came out as warning from my Demon's wrath this time.

"I am pretty sure she knows a fuck load more about us, but more importantly, Kai… Gods, but she knows about this place, like say… *how to fucking escape it!"*

"Fuck!" I said before bolting from the room, this time allowing my Demon side to aid me. Which meant that by the time I barrelled through the bedroom door, I couldn't find it in me to care if what met her was the sight of my Demon. No, it couldn't fucking be helped, despite knowing that seeing me like this for the first time would most likely terrify her!

But in the end, it didn't fucking matter.

For she was…

Gone.

I threw my head back and roared a curse up at the fucking Gods!

"NOOOO! FUCK!" My bellow of rage ended after I took a breath, just so I could start making my fucking orders!

"Find out everything about her, I want fucking everything!" My Demon growled without looking at my brother who I knew was right behind me, seeing for himself the reason I was named Wrath.

I was fucking beyond furious!

So, I tore myself away from the sight of the empty bed I had not long since tasted her in. Then I gave him one last order, roaring it out this time, so the rest of the house knew of their master's rage.

A rage that shook the whole fucking building as my power pulsated from me.

"And get me that..."

"...FUCKING BOOK!"

CHAPTER 23
WRATH OF A STORM
EMMELINE

I felt Kaiden slip his arm from beneath me, waking me enough that I became aware that we were no longer alone.

"And is it as I hoped?" The moment I heard Kaiden's voice ask this, I tried not to react. I hoped it wasn't what I dreaded it to be but when his brother replied with,

"It is... for she will finally to be known to you." This was when I knew my time was up. It was now or never for me.

I had to escape.

"You have her name then?" I heard Kaiden ask in a hopeful tone that nearly broke my heart, as I knew his excitement would be short lived when he discovered the full extent of my identity. *When he discovered what I had done.* Gods, but I couldn't bear the thought of it, knowing how he would look at me so differently. No, I couldn't think about that now, I just had to concentrate all my efforts of on leaving and lucky for me, I knew just about every way out of here there was.

"I do, brother, I do indeed," Hel replied in that cocky, self-assured way of his, and I even found myself wondering what he too would think of me. Well, I would certainly be giving his entire council enough reason to hate me, because as they suspected I would be, I was now back to being the enemy.

"Excellent," I heard Kaiden say, hating that this was it, quite possibly the very last time I was to hear that sexy deep voice of his. It was so painful that as soon as the door closed, I had to put a fist in my mouth just to stop myself from crying out in my heartbreak. But I knew my tears would have to wait, as there wasn't a moment to lose.

So, I got up, found my clothes I had come here wearing and quickly tore off my dress, doing so now like the memory of what happened when wearing it burned my skin. Because it had been so perfectly wrong that the satin now only represented sin to me. I vowed never to wear it again, as it would only remind me of the shame found in that one true, perfect moment with him. As for Kaiden, well he would soon know that he was never mine and I was never meant to be his.

He was destined for another.

Once dressed in my own clothes, I found the few hundred dollars I'd turned up with, that thankfully they had obviously seen no reason to take from me when finding it. After this, I slipped out of the room, knowing Kaiden would find no reason to have it guarded, because as far as he was concerned, there was no escape for me. Not when every exit in and out of the mansion had guards stationed there.

But then, not many knew of the secret passageways that ran like catacombs under his home… *one in particular.* Meaning I would have no choice but to face the one room I had avoided for a reason.

His bedchamber.

Which meant pulling up my big girl panties and sucking it up. So, with this firm, mental state of mind, I sneaked down the hallway and after taking a deep breath, I quickly rushed inside the second his door came into view.

"Gods," I muttered, and a whoosh of air left me as I deflated back against the closed door. I knew I didn't have time for it, but I couldn't help but take it all in again. It was like watching all my dreams projected as ghosts. I could almost see for myself all the time the two of them had spent in this room. The laughing and flirting on the sofa. The romantic drinks on the balcony, watching the sun setting as Raina listened to stories of Kaiden's past. The fights they shared with Raina trying to storm away, before being pulled back into his embrace as he kissed the argument from her mind. But most of all, it was his colossal bed and all the sex scenes I had written between

them, secretly fantasizing it was happening to me, not her.

I swallowed hard and forced my body to move, crossing over the masculine space of his living room. Then I took another breath and willed my feet to take the steps up to his bedroom, never once taking my eyes from that sacred space.

His bed seemed even bigger, being now compared to the one in the other room, making me wonder what it would have felt like waking up in this one with his arms around me. If I were honest, I don't think that would have stopped me from letting something slip, as that would have felt more like a dream than anything else before it. I had mentally slept in this bed with him for the last six years but earned just one night of reality in it. However, even I knew that would have been going too far by crossing an even greater line.

So, as much as it pained me, I walked closer to it, unable to help myself from grazing my fingertips across the sheets before reaching for the carved posts at the ends. Then I felt for what I was looking for, which was a slightly raised Demonic symbol that I knew meant Wrath.

I pressed it in, feeling it click as the boards beneath my feet shifted. I looked down and found the handle there, that before had been part of the grain when flat. I hooked my fingers under it and pulled it up with all my weight, knowing that I had made it seem easy when writing the part of Raina first finding it.

"Come on!" I complained, until finally the trap door gave enough that it revealed a spiralling staircase that I knew led deep down and into an unground tunnel system. One in particular that I knew would lead far beyond the gated grounds and into the surrounding woodland. Which meant only one thing…

It was time to run.

After forty minutes spent running through the tunnels, I finally made it to the opening at the end. Thankful at least that my dreams were true enough that I not only knew the way but that there was electricity down there. This was after some scary seconds, feeling around the walls for the switch.

However, what met me at the end was no longer the clear skies that there had been when I first woke from being rolled out of Kaiden's arms. A furious storm now raged overhead, as if it was soon to mirror the heart of the son of Wrath. Especially after he discovered his prisoner had escaped, one that I had no doubt he would want to see punished for her sins.

Punished for my sins.

So, after about five seconds of letting the rain pour down around me, soaking me to the bone, I started to run to where I knew the nearest road was. Thankfully, as secluded as the estate may have been, beyond that, it wasn't that difficult to find civilization, as the mansion was close to a place called Tarrytown. Another hour's walk, shivering in the rain, was all it took me, and from here I was able to hail down a cab. Then, after enduring comments about being out in this weather without a jacket, something that was still curled into a ball in the cell they had first put me in, I told him where I needed to go.

Once I had pulled up to the departures at JFK, it was as if I had come full circle. As not only was I back where I started, but I was also soon typing in the same code I had done when in the elevator making my way up to Kaiden's Club. It was one I knew well, only now instead of it being used as my own personal code for everything, its true origins had gone from dream to reality. But like I said, I had used this same code for everything, and over these past six years, it had become a comfort for me. As though Kaiden had the power to watch over my bank accounts, my mobile phone, even the password to my laptop.

Ironic really, considering he was now the one I was running from. And evidence of that was made even more prominent after punching that same code into the locker, before retrieving my bag and my only means of getting the hell out of this country!

So now with my meagre things back in my possession, I quickly scanned the flights, finding the first one I could get away with. Basically, anywhere back to England, not giving a damn about my car for the time being. I just needed to put distance between Kaiden and my mortal self before he figured it all out. So, with only moments to spare before the gate closed, I ran for my plane, letting my desperation fuel my body into moving faster.

"No wait! I am here… I am here!" I shouted just as they were putting the belt across the door.

"Is that all the luggage you have?" The woman asked, making me nod frantically.

"Yes… Please, I really can't miss this flight!" She looked at my ticket and passport before she released a sigh. Then after thankfully taking one look at the tears in my eyes and after speaking with someone on her radio, she let me through.

"Thank you! Thank you so much! You're a real-life saver!" I told her, knowing that she would never fully understand the true depth of that statement. But then again, not many people would as I highly doubted many would have even believed me!

Then, after running down the air gate, I made it onto the plane and purposely ignored the scowls of annoyance from the other passengers that had been made to wait. I took my seat, glad to find that the plane wasn't full and there was no one sitting next to me. Because I knew one thing for sure…

This was not going to be a happy flight.

I knew this as I could already feel the unshed tears building up inside me. Because now the realization of what I had done had really started to kick in. But more than that, it was the realization of what…

I had lost.

What I had been forced to give up. Because sure, I may have been able to convince him that I was still his Siren, but what would have happened in the end when she finally walked into his life? No, I couldn't do that to him, and I couldn't do that to her.

I may have also been able to convince him not to kill me, had I decided not to go down the runaway route. Perhaps by making a plea of helping him find her. But then I knew that the price for my life would have been a lifetime of misery. A lifetime of being forced to watch another woman love him the way I only dreamed of being allowed to. But even worse,

Watching as he loved her back.

No, that would have been a cruelty I wouldn't have survived. A cruelty I couldn't have endured. Which meant after playing every single option in my head, I realized this was my only choice. I had to forfeit my life either way. I knew just hiding out in my nanna's caravan was only going to work for so long before he was able to trace it back to me. Which meant, somehow changing my name and moving towns, perhaps even countries was the next plan from here. Maybe I could try somewhere hot, although with my pale skin and near white-blonde hair, I would burn up like a lobster in a pot in no time.

Okay, so not Spain then, and well, I wasn't even sure

my crappy little car would even make it across France. Well, wherever it was going to be, I needed to make a decision by the time I got back to my little caravan.

Because now, after meeting him, I had a feeling Kaiden wasn't the type of man to let this go.

Wasn't the type of Demon…

To let me go.

CHAPTER 24
THE STORY OF OBSESSION
WRATH

After this, things started to unravel for my little runaway pretty damn quickly, no matter how smart she thought she had been. I automatically went to the most obvious tunnel she would no doubt know about, seeing as the room had featured quite a lot in her dreams. And therefore…

In her book.

It also explained of her reluctance at first being in here, making me remember her words, telling me how it wasn't her place. It fucking made sense now, all of it, and it was infuriating to think that she believed herself to being nothing but the author of my story!

That she didn't play a bigger part.

Like being the one who was my Gods damn fated Siren!

Fuck, but I was furious at her! Furious that she hadn't

trusted me enough to tell me the truth. Trusted me enough to give me a chance to explain my feelings to her so she may fully understand what it was that she meant to me. How I cared little for what her dreams had led her to do.

But it was also clear that she must have seen her actions as a grave offence against my people. And yes, technically, she would have been right. However, as my Fated, it was little wonder her dreams had manifested her feelings into those strong enough for her to want to write about them. She would have felt compelled to act in some way and for a mortal who knew nothing of my world, then this compulsion had naturally formed into the written word. It made me then wonder that had she been an artist or a singer, would it have been expressed into some other creative medium?

Either way, once the discovery of her dreams had been proven to be true, then it was not surprising her reaction to us. Gods, but it was little wonder she had been so afraid of me and my men. After all, she had clearly known what we were all capable of. I knew that the moment I finally got my hands on her book, reading it and discovering an insight to her mind and her dreams for myself. She had known so much, which made her bravery all the more admirable when risking what she must have known would be her life to save my own.

But before I had received the gift of her words, came the painful and infuriating task of retracing her steps, telling me exactly where she would find herself at the end of this tunnel.

"Ah, so this was how she got out," Hel commented after coming to see himself, having already dispatched our men to all airports, the main one being, JFK.

"Which means she will be long gone, as this is the most direct access out of the grounds," I had rumbled in annoyance.

"And no doubt why she picked it. Fuck me, but I am starting to like this crafty little Siren of yours," my brother remarked, making me growl,

"Yes, well you can save your fucking praise until she is back by my side and shackled in chains again, for those links will be connected to one place this time, and that will be my fucking hand!"

"Well, that should look good for the wedding pictures… Joking, okay? Fuck, brother, don't bite my head off!" he said when my Demon snarled at him.

"Then you'd better be here to tell me something fucking useful, or I may release my Demon and you can tell him you jest at our fucking expense!"

"Alright, so you made your point and yes, I am here to tell you the chopper will be landing in five minutes. Also, it was as you suspected, the locker she had used at JKF was empty when our men got there."

"And flights?" I asked, storming my way back through my home knowing my brother would follow.

"She took one to Birmingham airport"

"That was not where she flew here from," I stated, making him agree.

"I believe it was the first flight she could find and not close to where she was meant to be, as we know she has a car registered to her name."

"So, it is most likely still in Manchester then," I surmised.

"I agree, as I doubt she would want to waste the hours driving when she already lived close to an international airport," Hel added, making me nod.

"Check the plates against any cars in the long stay parking, as I doubt even she knew how long she would be here and would most likely have planned for longer," I said as I re-emerged through the trap door that led back into my bedchamber, as my brother and I had made it back in a quarter of the time it would have taken my Siren. This was because she may have known these tunnels, but clearly, she didn't know them all, as her scent had taken her a longer route.

"You hope to get to the car before she does?" he asked, making me grin at him as I heard the distinct sound of helicopter blades flying through the air.

"We are not that far behind her and besides, we have a faster plane, one that will get us to the place she herself hopes to find." And wasn't that just the beauty of owning a number of private jets, as typically they travelled faster compared to commercial planes. This was because they flew at higher altitudes, meaning that the smaller the jet, then the faster it could travel and well, thankfully my Angel was currently on one big ass plane!

"There is a chance she won't have thought of that, I will see what Franklin can discover," he said, getting out his phone and already sending him a message as we waited for the bird to land. I looked at the Eurocopter EC 155 as it came into land and not for the first time during all this, I thought it was fucking good to be rich. Because despite this being labelled as a luxurious chopper, I was more thankful right now for its impressive top speed at 200 miles an hour with its range of 533 miles. It could also seat 13 passengers and right now, it was worth every cent of the ten-million-dollar price tag as my men piled in.

Heading to Manchester international airport, knowing we would land before her, meant that I was awarded the time needed to complete the next part of my plan…

Research.

So, for once, I didn't view the travel a waste of time as I had something important to do, or should I say, I had a book to read. One that literally had my name on it. Because Franklin had come through in time and had managed to have a digital copy sent to my email. He had also sent me all he had found on my little author, including the most important things, like her home address.

But as I started to read her romantic story, I couldn't help but see too many similarities between her and this character Raina. Of course, there were the obvious differences between them, like where Raina was tall and slim, my little Halo was little and full of mouth-watering curves. And clearly unbeknown to her, was far closer to my preference in a woman. Raina's hair was tamed smooth and sleek, whereas I much preferred the riot of wild curls that seemed to take on a life of their own, much to the chagrin of their adorably frustrated owner.

I remembered my utter joy and amusement when I first tugged at her chains, making her go stumbling into me and watching her having to blow the curls from her eyes when looking up at me. Fuck, but I think I must have fallen in love with her in that very moment.

Love?

Gods, was that what this was?

This burning obsession I felt, unable to spare my mind even a moment of her. This inability to get her scent from my Demon's mind, as if she had already started to immortalize herself there, deep within my vessel's skin. I wanted her like no other had even come close! As though there was none before her, I craved her body, mind and heart like the Gods were continuing to brand pieces of her to my fucking soul!

But then to read the way she felt about me. The same burning desire in her character's mind, as if she were speaking from her own experiences was fucking, delicious torture! I was even questioning if my own addiction to her could be matched, for she seemed to write of me as if I was her personal God she worshiped.

As if I had long ago already mastered that of her heart and soul.

Gods, but what had she thought of me when those elevator doors had finally opened, and she found me standing there? The man who consumed her dreams and fictionally owned her heart for the last six years. I wish I had taken her in my arms and that I had the power to rewrite our own story. That I could be the author of her life from this point on and in it, I would erase all differences there were between my Halo and this Raina.

I would remove every fucking word that spoke of Raina!

A woman she foolishly believed to be my Fated.

"That is not the look of a man who is enjoying that book," my brother commented.

"It is beyond fucking frustrating for she believes this woman to be my Siren and yet, it's like she knows everything about me but not what I would want in a woman!"

"She does not write this Siren as being like her?" he asked with genuine curiosity.

"Parts of her slip through and in all honesty, they are my favourite parts, for her talent is a gift of words to the reader, this cannot be denied," I told him, speaking without being biased, even though, all would know that I was and had every right to be.

"But the other woman…?"

"Is pissing me off!" I snarled, putting it down, having

to take a moment to get my anger under control before I destroyed the phone I was reading it from.

"What annoys you so?" he asked, which wasn't helping. Yet despite this, I found myself answering all the same.

"She is tall, athletic and just kicked me in the balls." At this my brother burst out laughing like I knew he would.

"So not a curvy little submissive, with a riot of blonde hair and comical sense of humour, then?" I growled,

"No, *most definitely not.*"

"I have to say I see why your preference is set on the Siren you've got and not the Siren she picked for you. But then again, I know my brother." He nodded his head at this last part, and I released a sigh, regaining some calm. Then I told him the truth of her words.

"That's the thing, she knows me, speaks my mind as if it is my very own, yet the only parts she gets wrong are the times that include the wrong woman… it is… *frustrating to say the least.*" Hence why I found my hand on the back of my neck trying to rub the tension from my muscles.

"Perhaps a feeling made even more so because you have already met your Siren, and know your own mind and that of your heart has already been claimed by another." At this I looked out of the window and finally saw the right part of land coming into sight.

"Yes, but the challenge now is convincing her of that," I admitted without looking at him.

"Yes, well in that, let's hope she is nothing like her female character… after all, you will need your balls if you're to claim her." At this I chuckled, thankful for my brother's distraction.

"And like I said… *I always have my chains.*"

"Then I suggest you buy some more… *this time for her feet.*" Again I chuckled, but I also had a nice thought to think of as we landed. Because I would be lying if I said that the visualization my brother painted, didn't now make me hard as fucking rock!

Chaining my Halo to my bed was now an image that wouldn't leave me, and I had to say, it was a far better one than of ball kicking Raina.

And speaking of Raina…

She was about to get written out of this story.

CHAPTER 25
DEMON STALKER

Upon landing, the first thing we did after departing the plane was make our way to the long-stay parking lot that her car had been traced to. Again, I had Franklin to thank for this, as he hacked whatever systems were needed to gain whichever information I asked for, doing so as and when I required it.

Which was why I was now staring at a piece of shit Volkswagen Golf that had a cracked mirror, a large scratch down one side and a broken bumper. This naturally made me wonder if she bought it like this, or if she was in fact a danger on the road and would therefore soon find herself being driven everywhere.

I shook my head at the thought as I took in the damage again before moving on to more important things. Like instantly violating her space by making the lock open. I had ordered my men to go straight to her home and wait for me there, just in case she managed to make it before us, as the journey had taken slightly longer than expected due to the weather.

I also didn't know if she had a friend who would pick her up or if she would try and make her own way back to her car. Either way, I wanted to be prepared for both scenarios. I also didn't know enough about her life to know of her friends, only knowing of one called Natalie. An obvious choice considering she had been her bridesmaid not long ago. But this too seemed like an unlikely source of aid as she was currently on her honeymoon with her new husband, and Jamaica was a long way away.

I did discover though, that she hadn't lied to me about her tragic up-bringing, for she had been orphaned as a small child and therefore was brought up by her grandmother. A woman who, it was discovered, was now in a home for the elderly and was therefore also unlikely to offer her any help in this.

No, it seemed that my little Siren was all alone in the world, and I had to say, as much as this benefitted me, it also pained me to know that she had no one to help her. She seemed so full of life, so exuberant and often chatty. It didn't seem right that she should have so few people in her life, despite how much easier this would make things for me. As I knew now that I could quite literally snatch her away with little needed on my side to conceal the kidnapping. She even worked from home, so there were no colleagues to question where one of their own was.

It almost seemed too easy.

As for her car, well it was obvious to see that she had packed in a hurry, making me wonder why she would bring all of this stuff to an airport, only to leave it all behind? And was she really hoping to get a box of books on a flight and wait… *was that a kettle?* I shifted some things around and then my heart broke a little as I saw a box of canned food, realizing exactly what this was.

Her whole world packed up in a little car.

After this I closed her door and relocked it, before walking away to the car I had waiting for me, telling one of my men,

"Wait here and inform me the moment she arrives to retrieve her car." That way, if we didn't discover where she was headed, at the very least, she could be followed.

"Yes, my Lord Wrath, it will be done." I nodded and then folded myself into the next car waiting. A luxury Maybach, that for once, I allowed someone else to drive as I seated myself next to my brother who was waiting.

"Find anything of interest? A giant cut out of you perhaps?" he asked, making me grumble,

"Tell me, am I looking at decades of jest here or more like, centuries?"

"That depends," he replied with an ominous grin.

"On what?"

"Whether your little Siren ends up being more like this

Raina than you think, and I also have my own balls to look out for." I laughed at this and remarked,

"Ha, but you are clearly losing that famous memory of yours if you fear my little Halo but not what I can do to you in the ring, little brother."

"But of course..." he paused, making me raise a brow at him before he continued, this time making me laugh. "After all, *you don't hit below the belt.*"

A short time later, I found myself standing in my Siren's private little world. Or should I say, what was left of it before her whirlwind packing had clearly taken its toll on the space. One which I assumed had once upon a time been tidy and organized. But then the scent of her back in my Demon's mind at least had the power to calm us both.

"Each of you take a room, I want every piece of her space gone through and looked at."

"And what are we looking for exactly?" Tristan asked, and Hel answered,

"Any clue as to where she was planning on taking that car full of possessions, as she must have had a destination in mind." Boaz nodded after hearing this and took charge of our men, being that he was their commander. So, I let my men do their work, feeling torn that things had taken me to this point, knowing that my orders would not be received well when discovered. But it wasn't to be helped. The girl was mine now and seeing as it was clear she was not to be trusted to make the right decisions, I would have no choice but to make them for her.

Starting with my next order.

"Once finished here, I want all of her belongings packed and ready to be boarded onto the plane." At this my brother looked at me and then with a silent look at my own balls, he didn't need to say anything. Besides, I wasn't worried, *for I still have my chains.*

"I think I found something," Tristan said, making me walk through her small home, finding myself from her bedroom and inside her kitchen in mere footsteps I could quickly count.

"Her grandmother," I commented, recognizing the older woman from the information Franklin had sent me.

"We checked her records, they had to sell her house to pay for her care," Hel said, knowing practically as much as I did about my Siren, being as he was the one I had charged with her discovery.

"Yes, but did you know she had a holiday home… A static trailer in this, Sunshine Holiday Park," Tristan said, after reading what looked like some forgotten mail that had her grandmother's name on it.

"Is that the only clue of the place, you found?" I asked, now folding my arms and giving this information deeper thought.

"Yes, and it wasn't obvious, my Lord Wrath."

"Excellent, find out where it is," I told him with a satisfied grin.

"Why is that excellent?" Hel asked.

"Because she would have not left it had it been obvious. I doubt she even knew about it, seeing as it was left unopened until we came along," I replied, now holding up the envelope for him to see. Then, to prove my point, one of my men came back through the door after he had been charged with speaking with her neighbours.

"Report!" Boaz demanded.

"They all say that she left only a few hours after the wedding."

"And they are sure of this?" Hel asked.

"Yes, they remember because none of them would, and I quote, 'Look after that fucking cat again!'" I smirked at this, knowing that she had obviously not been exaggerating about the little furry fiend.

"There, even more proof," I commented as my grin grew, for my plan was about to come to fruition, and that net I was ensnarling her in was getting pulled tighter.

"How is that proof?" Boaz asked this time.

"She came back here after seeing us at the hotel and panicked. Quickly packed as much as she could fit in her car and, believing we may come here and go through her things, she chose a place she believed we would not find," I reminded him.

"And how do you know she wasn't just planning on

going to some hotel somewhere?" Hel asked, making me point out,

"Three reasons, the first being she couldn't get anyone to look after her cat, the second, you don't take a box of canned food to a hotel, nor a kettle."

"Ah, the contents of her car, I presume," Hel commented before Tristan asked,

"And the third?"

"How much were her airfares?" I asked Hel, who told me,

"In total, she spent over two thousand pounds… okay, so I am seeing your point here."

"Exactly, for we know how much she had in her bank account," I said reminding him, as he had been the one to have Franklin dig into her finances.

"Yes, and it was only a little over what the cost of the flights were," my brother added, making me grin.

"Exactly, which means she has little left and what little that is, she can't afford to waste, say on the likes of a hotel," I told all of them, however, it was Hel that commented first.

"But a free trailer owned by her grandmother… alright, I have to agree with you. Question is, what do you want to do now?" I allowed myself the satisfaction of a smirk, knowing that the trap was tightening even more around my little Siren, and she didn't even know it.

"Pack it all up, I want it ready and on the plane before we leave. Contact the pilot and have it ready to leave within the next few hours, for she can't be that far behind us now." I moved to walk out of the meagre apartment she rented, knowing she wouldn't be seeing it again, for it was nothing but luxury for my girl from here on out.

"Hel and Tristan, you are both with me," I told them, knowing they would follow, and I swear that my palms started to burn in anticipation for getting my girl back and once more in my possession. My Demon also growled at the thought of sweet, seductive punishment we would administer, but all in good time I told him. First, we needed to have a little chat…

My Siren and I.

Which was why we were quickly in the car and on our way to what I was soon to discover was even more proof of my little Halo's lack of funds. I suppose I should have been glad, as it had made my life easier. But then to know that she had spent even one night here, and I was curling my lip up in anger. To begin with, it would have only taken barely a kick to get the door to open, knowing now how little it would have taken a mortal.

I wanted my girl safe.

I wanted her protected.

I wanted her locked in my home.

"I can tell you're thinking possessive thoughts again," Hel commented after hearing me growl at the room.

"But then I have to agree with you, this is a shithole and not worthy of our girl." I would have killed anyone else for saying 'our girl' knowing she was no one else's to be claimed. But this had come from my brother's lips, and therefore I knew what he meant was more in a familial sense, no doubt already classing her as a sister and therefore blood.

"No. It. Is. Not," I gritted out, feeling my temper rise knowing she had run back to this! Just then my phone rang, and I swear my heart almost skipped a fucking beat!

"Speak!"

"She's just arrived, my Lord Wrath."

"And what of her state?" I asked, for I cared deeply for her and wanted to know she was unharmed and most of all, safe.

"She looks fucking cold and depressed," he told me, making me grit my teeth again.

"Follow her from a distance, but whatever you do, do not let yourself be known."

"Affirmative," he replied before cutting the call.

"She is on her way?" Hel asked, making me grin.

"That she is and unbeknown to her…

"Straight into my trap."

CHAPTER 26
FUCKING CAT
EMMELINE

Gods, I was dog tired!

I was also cold and couldn't seem to warm up for the life of me. But then it didn't help that I had been without a jacket this whole time, and the crappy little heater in my car had been playing up for months now. Although, these weren't the worst things. As I swear the moment I finally did make it back to my car, I broke down and this was because I could still smell him. As if his presence lingered around me or something. I was half convinced that if I looked to my passenger side I would have seen him there. It that was that strong.

I had even wanted to call him and leave a message for him at the club, just so I could tell him that I was sorry. Perhaps I still would, when it was safe for me to do so. But then what could be the worst thing if I did so now? After all, I had charged my phone on the plane and now there it was, just in my bag, teasing me like some fucking beacon of guilt.

"Oh, fuck it!" I snapped, digging it out of my bag at the same time trying to reach for a thick knitted cardigan out of the back seat. Then, while tugging my arm through one side, I rang the number for his club with the other. I had already discovered all the details in case I had needed it, back when I had been trying to speak to Hel about his brother.

But of course, I had saved it as a contact on my phone.

"Hello, my name is…" I paused, thinking for a moment before giving them something he would know without a doubt. "…Halo. I just wanted to leave a message for…"

"Wait just a moment while I connect you," a voice said quickly, making me panic as the phone started ringing again and before I could hang up, his voice was suddenly on the other end of the phone.

"This better be important!" he snapped, and I gasped, making him take pause.

"Who is this?" I released a held breath and told him with my eyes closed,

"Erm… hey… it's… *it's me.*"

"Little Halo?" he asked in disbelief, making me sigh.

"Yeah. I just needed to hear… I mean, to say…"

"Where are you now?!" he shouted quickly, making me flinch at the authoritative tone of his voice. Gods, but had he always sounded so masterful?

"It doesn't matter now," I told him in what I knew was a despondent tone.

"The fuck it doesn't!" he argued, making me realize what I went on to tell him.

"I shouldn't have called… this was a mistake."

"Then tell me, pretty girl, why did you?" he asked more calmly this time, as if he really wanted to know.

"I guess I just wanted to say I am sorry, you know for…"

"Running from me?!" I released another painful sigh and told him,

"You know what I am sorry for, as you no doubt know my secret by now." This made me flinch when he growled in response.

"I know everything," he told me as though it was some secret promise and this time, my whole body tensed all over.

"Then you know why I am sorry and I… well, I just wanted you to know that I would never have written any of it… had I known… you were… well, I guess it doesn't matter now, as what's done is done," I told him with so much emotion that it was making it difficult to speak. As if I was trying to force the words though the depth of my sins against him. Which was why I was now wiping away my tears that had started to fall, making him sigh this time.

"And now, what comes next for you, little Siren?" I tensed and closed my eyes tight as I grimaced. Because this question only made even more tears fall, forcing me to bite my lip to stop myself from crying out in my anguish.

"It... it doesn't matter... what comes next... for me," I forced out, making him growl,

"Bullshit! You have your plans, my girl, and I have mine, so make no mistake they will cross, *for I will find you!"* I shuddered at the threat, knowing that I was wrong in calling. *I had been so wrong.*

"You're angry right now, I get that..." I tried, making him snarl this time,

"Too fucking right, I am! *You fucking ran from me!"* He roared this last part at me, and I could hear his brother in the background urging him to calm down making me wonder if he was still at the mansion?

"And if I ask you not to come looking for me, what then? What would you say?" I braved asking.

"I would tell you to wake up, for you are clearly dreaming again," he retorted, making me feel it like a lash against my heavy heart.

"I saved your life," I reminded him, hoping this was enough.

"Yes, you did," he agreed instantly.

"Does that really mean nothing?" I asked in a pained voice.

"It means everything to me!" he replied sounding just as hurt as I did, making me cry openly, not giving a damn whether he could hear this time.

"Everything...? But just not enough... to save myself from *your Wrath?"* I forced myself to ask despite my tears, making him take a deep breath before telling me,

"My wrath is not what you should ever fear." I sucked back a startled gasp at this.

"No? Then what is it I should fear from you, Kaiden?" I asked, getting angry this time, which was when he rocked me to my core with his answer.

"You should fear for every minute you keep yourself from me, for I will be claiming every single one of them back, this I promise you, girl!" I drew in a quick breath and not knowing what to say to that terrifying threat, I told him,

"Then you should expect them to keep mounting... goodbye, Kaiden." Then I hung up, threw my phone to the dash and folded my arms on the steering wheel so I could really let myself cry. I cried for the beautifully perfect memories I had gained and for the dreams of reality I had lost.

But mainly, I cried for the man I loved more today than I did all the days before this heartbreak. Because love wasn't clean cut and understandable enough to simply speak of. The words I love you rolled far too easily off the tongue but when the emotion was truly felt, they were words that sounded more as if they had been ripped from your very soul. Like you were handing over a piece of yourself other than just giving someone the gift of your words. It was not just a throwaway sentiment that you could take back at a moment's notice or deny the second you felt it all going wrong. It was terrifying, and scary and the hardest thing you had ever experienced all because you fear every second of the day it will be taken from you!

It's about trusting someone with that power over you. Trusting them to take your love and protect it, nurture it and love it in return. For them not to abuse it, tear it apart or warp it into something that fits them better. It was not something for them to use as a weapon against you, one that felt as if Kaiden was using against me right now.

That's the power he held over me.

And as for me.

I felt powerless in return.

In the end, I don't know how long I sat there and cried for, but it was long enough that my eyes were red and sore. I looked at the time and realized that I needed to go pick up my damn cat before I put the next part of my plan into motion. Because it was clear from that phone call that Kaiden wasn't going to let this go like I had hoped I could have convinced him to do. No, now he just seemed even more determined. So I knew I couldn't stay at the caravan park, as eventually something would lead him there.

I tried to figure out how much money I had left and what was due to come into my account from jobs I was owed money for. It might get me across the channel tunnel and into France, but I knew I would have to wait at least a few days for that. Then I would have to risk it and hope that my car would make it that far. But of course, I was going nowhere without the money to buy fuel. So, for now, I had no choice but to go with the only plan I had.

It was back to the caravan park.

But first, I had a Hellcat to pick up. So I pulled into the cattery, and I swear the woman looked beyond relieved to see me. However, she wisely left me with the task of getting Roger back in his carrier. Which meant I left twenty minutes later with half a bag of cat food, a plaster on my bleeding hand and a 'nice doing business with you but please don't bring that devil cat back here again'. Well, if she had known where I had just come from, she might have looked differently on Roger being the Devil.

This all meant that by the time I pulled in next to the caravan, I was so tired, I felt as though I could sleep for a week! I hadn't been lying to Kaiden when I let slip that I had never been able to sleep on planes. Which meant that I barely knew which day it was anymore, let alone what time zone I was in. I just needed to lay my head down and sleep this new nightmare away.

I just needed my dreams of Kaiden back.

My safe little dreams.

However, what I got was the very last thing I ever expected to see, and I was left wishing that it was a dream! That I could have woken up and escaped them. Or should I say… *Him.*

This was because the second I opened the door, who

did I find sitting there with his forearms rested on his knees, but one…

Kaiden Wrath.

His head rose at the same time I dropped my cat, making Roger cry out angrily. Then I quickly turned around ready to run when Hel stepped out from beside the door, blocking my exit.

"Hello, little Siren," Hel said with a bad boy grin, reminding me of that first night at the club. It was one that spoke of so many things, but mainly the trouble I was now in. Which was why I quickly turned back to face Kaiden, to find that he was watching me like some kind of predator would do with his prey. He looked so powerful, dressed once more in his black combat gear, as if this was some mission he was on.

And I guess that it was.

Then he slapped his hands to his knees and rose to his full height, making my nanna's pokey little caravan look like it was only ever meant for dolls. I swear, I wished I hadn't swapped my boots for flat comfy converse, as I was now as small as I was ever going to get. Something that had us both realizing that I had never looked so tiny next to him previously. He seemed to notice it too, as he had never seen me without heels.

Gods, but if he thought I was little before, now he was going to think of me as being miniature and even more breakable! Which was why I started to back away as fear began to make me panic internally. Oh, but who was I kidding, I was shaking on the outside just as much.

"You made me wait, pretty girl," he stated, and I shuddered at the slight bite of anger in his voice. I looked down at my cat and said irrationally,

"Roger didn't want to go in his carrier." At this his lips twitched as if he were fighting a grin. Then he looked down to my hand and said,

"So, I can see… another Roger inflicted war wound?" I nodded quickly before backing up some more the second he took another intimidating step towards me. However, I felt his brother's chest hit my back, telling me silently, that I was going nowhere.

"W-w-what are you... doing here?" I asked on a whisper and now with him being so close, I couldn't help but look at my feet. However, he didn't allow this for long, as I felt him hook my chin and raise my head up and up and up some more.

"I told you… *I came to claim back all my stolen minutes.*" I sucked in a quick breath and held it as he lowered his face, having to bend his neck further due to discovering an even greater height difference between us, now I was minus my four inches.

"Now, do I bring Roger or leave him here to starve for the offence of making my girl bleed?" he asked, making let go of my breath on a whoosh of air.

"Please don't make him starve." At this he smirked and ran the back of a thick finger down my cheek.

"And what about you… are you going to run from me again?" he asked, making me answer honestly,

"First chance I get." His grin got bigger this time and I swear it was all his Demon.

"I thought so." He then nodded to his brother behind me, who must have been waiting as I suddenly felt a pinch in my neck, making me cry out in shock. My hand went to the spot but I felt sluggish by the time it got there. Then suddenly I was falling forward and quickly caught in Kaiden's arms. I felt my head fall back over his arm as he looked down at me,

"It's nice to finally meet you… *my Emmeline."* At this I started to close my eyes, telling him,

"Now I know I am definitely dreaming again."

"Then from now on… *we dream together,*" he told me just before I felt myself being lifted fully in his arms. Then, as he was walking me from my not-so-secret hideout, the last thing I heard was him issuing an order…

"Bring the fucking cat!"

CHAPTER 27

MAKE IT A GOOD LIE

WRATH

Speaking her true name for the first time had strangely felt a bit like coming home. As if the name had felt as right coming from my lips, as did the one I had given her, for she would forever be my little Halo. And Gods, but little was right as I had never noticed before with her always wearing heels, for she was tiny compared to me.

Fuck, but strangely it made my love for her stronger, for the need to protect her clawed at me and my Demon, making her all the more precious. It made me want to throw her over my shoulder again and carry her around with me like some fucking caveman!

Even now just watching her sleep, I found myself on edge waiting for her to wake. Now worrying if the drugs used were too much for her smaller frame, something we hadn't accounted for, as it would make her lighter.

"I told you, she is fine. Stop worrying, she will wake soon," Hel assured me, knowing where my mind had wandered to, *yet again.*

"You're sure of this?" I asked, no doubt making him resist the urge to roll his eyes at me.

"You can hear her pulse, brother, you can hear her heart and her even, steady breathing, does anything sound like its struggling to you?" he pointed out once more. I didn't answer, but instead let my head fall back to the headrest and looked out the window, wondering how long it was until we landed, for I was anxious to get her back within my own domain again. There, I could control every situation and now I knew what she knew of my homes, I could control that as well. Because in truth, her honest words were now plaguing me knowing that, given the opportunity, she would run from me. Something I wouldn't be foolish enough to allow to happen again, for she was going nowhere.

"And what of her cat?" I found myself asking irrationally.

"You mean the little hellraising fucker? Sleeping last time I looked, I didn't fucking care enough to check." I scoffed at this as most of my men were the scariest fucking Demons in existence, but neither of them had braved going near the little clawed furball either.

"Should have left the thing to starve," he muttered, making me grin. But then I looked to her hand, one that I had checked to be assured she had cleaned it properly. After that I re-bandaged it, so it was covered by something a little more substantial than a fucking sticker that didn't even cover half of it. Like I said, my girl needed to be cared for.

Hence why she was currently sleeping on the sofa, with a blanket covering her, a pillow under her head and a belt around her waist so if there was turbulence she wouldn't fall. She had looked so small and fragile the moment she finally walked inside that shitty trailer. Her eyes were red and sore from her tears, and she was shivering even with the thick woolly jacket thing she wore, one that looked as though it belonged to someone twice her size.

But then I knew after our phone call how upset she had been, for my phone had rung straight after it with an update on why she had not yet moved from the parking space.

She had been crying.

At this I had nearly fucking lost it and with it, my plan to be here waiting for her. Had it not been for my brother, I would have released my Demonic wings and flown to her, scaring the shit out of her when she found my Demon form at her car door.

To be honest, I had been astounded that she had felt compelled to call at all. But then the second I heard her voice, I knew why…

Guilt.

She cared enough for me that she needed to hear my voice. I knew this despite her asking me not to try and find her. Her reason for calling was not to try and convince me of anything, it was only ever for her to have a chance at saying goodbye. To hear my voice one more time. I knew this like I knew my own heart. The one that had refused to allow me to let her go. However, her actions in calling me had meant something to me and managed to at least douse the flames of my anger at her.

As for now, well I was just angry at my decision to drug her, for I only wanted her to wake so I could find comfort in those pretty brown eyes of hers. Speaking of wishes…

"Umm… what am I…?" she murmured in that sleepy voice of hers I had heard before.

"You slept on a plane," I told her, making her suck in a quick breath, which I was quickly learning was a habit of hers.

"Not the same thing when you get drugged," she commented dryly, making me suppress a grin at her quick wit and instead I shrugged my shoulders. Then I nodded to the seat opposite me, wishing now there wasn't a table between us so I might easily touch her if I wished. Which knowing of my growing need for her, then yes, I fucking would.

"Come sit down, Emmeline," I said, speaking her

name for only the second time and again, I felt it to my core, for it felt right. However, the second she heard it, she froze.

"So, you know everything then, it wasn't a dream?" she asked in small voice, and it pained me to see how she struggled so. However, I knew not to make this easy for her, as I needed her to know the seriousness of her crimes… *she should never have run from me.*

"I do," I stated firmly, watching as she sat up and pushed the blanket back. Then I watched as she struggled with the belt, and I itched to go help her, forcing myself to stay seated. Then she swung her legs round and after first leaning forward, she pushed all her hair back with both hands. Only then did she ask,

"Why am I still breathing then?" I swear the question felt as if she had punched me with a fucking hammer in the gut!

I was fucking furious!

"Is that why you never told me, because you thought I was nothing more than a cold-blooded killer only too eager to end your life!" I snapped, growling out my words and making her flinch because of it. But then she let her shoulders sag and told me quietly,

"I…I wouldn't have blamed you, not after what I did." After this I took a calming breath, losing some of my anger in sight of how she still struggled with her guilt.

"No Emmeline, I wouldn't have fucking killed you!" I

bit back, again, unable to force that sentence out any other way.

"Why not?" she asked, and I swear I was going to start breaking things off this fucking plane, if she carried on.

"Is that a fucking joke!?" I snarled again, making her recoil back.

"Brother, a word," Hel said having heard our whole conversation.

"Not now!" I barked.

"It's important, Kai," Hel said, trying to communicate something with me. So, with a frustrated growl, I got up and followed him to the back of the plane out of earshot.

"What the fuck is it!?"

"Look, I know you are gonna want to rip my head off, but if you will just give me the benefit of the doubt 'til I finish before tearing out my tongue for the offence," Hel said, making me groan, knowing this was going to be yet again something I wouldn't want to fucking hear.

"Just spit it out for fuck sake!" I demanded with zero fucking patience.

"Fine, you want it, then here it is… You're being a royal ass!" Hel said coming right out with it.

"You're closer to losing that tongue, Hel," I warned.

"Okay look, she clearly has no fucking clue who she is to you and you knowing is not making it any fucking easier." I frowned at this and snarled,

"Get to your fucking point!"

"Use it to your advantage," my brother said surprising me.

"How?"

"She wrote this book years ago, Kai. Franklin hacked her computer remotely as soon as we got it and there are dozens of books on there and guess what, they are all about you and this Raina." I sucked air through my clenched teeth…

Fucking Raina!

She was a thorn in my side and the bitch wasn't even fucking real!

"It was only a year ago that she had the guts to get the first published, but she started writing six years ago."

"I know this," I reminded him, making him go on,

"Yes, but just because we have dealt with the fallout, erasing everything that she could not, it doesn't mean she knows that. As far as she is concerned, she wrote about our world, *about you* with another fucking girl. Not her. *But someone fated to you.*"

"Again Hel, get to the fucking point, for I know this!" I snapped, looking back and seeing the way she rubbed her head now as if she felt pain there. *Fuck, but I never should have drugged her!*

"Gods, Kai, fucking think about it!"

"Well, I would get to thinking about it a lot fucking quicker if *you fucking got there quicker!*" I snarled, making him roll his eyes at me and I swear, I couldn't wait to get my cocky little brother in the fucking ring again! I was going to kick his ass so fucking bad!

"What I am saying is that she believes she is still out there, because the second she saw you, she knew it was all real. She took down the book and was terrified she would get caught. She pulled all social media and fucking moved to a shitty trailer in the middle of nowhere! She even googled how to change her name. She was terrified because in her mind, what she unknowingly did was expose our kind and what is the biggest offence…?" He let that question linger and I tore my gaze away.

"Fuck!" I hissed, understanding more of her reasons for running. She really did believe she was here now to be punished.

"Yeah, there it is," he said, making me growl.

"I know it's hard, but try and look at it from her point of view. She thought you would class her as your enemy if you found out her name. That she had committed some personal crime against you, a fucking crime punishable by death. She wrote a fucking book about it, for fuck sake!" Hel said getting frustrated himself.

"Right fine, you made your point, now get to the solution part of this conversation," I told him, as it was clear where and why her mindset was where it was.

"Instead of telling her that she is your fated and spending all this time trying to convince her of something she will always doubt…"

"She will not fucking doubt it! Not when I…" Hel quickly interrupted me just as I had done with him.

"Oh, so you don't think she will always be waiting… worrying that one day when who she considers is the real fated girl, comes along and snatches you away from her."

"That wouldn't fucking happen!" I growled low, feeling myself quickly losing it.

"Yes, we know that, because we know without a fucking shadow of doubt who she is to you but try convincing her of that. Emmeline has only ever seen you in her dreams with another girl… Your relationship with her will be built on fucking doubt, brother!" Hel snarled back this time, and it was yet another fucking point I couldn't do anything with but take seriously!

"Fine, I get it! Now what the fuck do I do to fix this? It isn't like I can get rid of this fictional fucking girl!" It was at this point that Hel started grinning, and I felt another 'oh fuck' moment as I usually did when my brother got an idea in that fucked up head of his.

"Oh no, what are you planning, Helmer?" I asked, exercising the use of his full name to get across the importance of the situation we now faced.

"Let her prove that she doesn't exist," he said, making me frown.

"What do you mean?"

"Tell her instead of punishment she now has to forfeit her life to you and as payment for her crime, she must help you find your fated girl." At this I couldn't help but grab him, curling my fist in his shirt instead of the neck I wanted to strangle.

"Are you mad! *She is my fated girl!"* I snarled venomously.

"Yes, but *she doesn't believe that!"* he pointed out yet again. This time through the grit of his teeth.

"Then I will just have to make her believe it!" I countered again, quickly trying to find any way in my mind to be able to accomplish this.

"And if you can't, what then? Start a life together trying to convince her daily not to run away from you because she believes she will never make you happy or that what she is doing is a sin against the Gods... *against the Fates."*

I growled at the thought.

"We don't know that would happen," I gritted out.

"No? Then why when we had her computer checked, we found that she has been searching for the girl."

"Fuck!" I hissed, and I swear it was another kick in the gut!

"Yeah, like I said, she is convinced that if you and our world is real then so must this Raina be, and she has no fucking clue it's actually her... *that she is the Siren."*

"So, what, your advice is that I should pretend it's not her too, that this Raina is?" I asked in a tone that said it all... *there was no fucking way it was happening!*

"No, that is not what I am saying," he admitted, making me narrow my gaze.

"Then get to the part of this plan that I will be fucking okay with, because I've got to be honest here, brother… I am seconds away from saying fuck it and tying the girl to me and claiming her, whether she believes it or not!" I responded with nothing but a dark promise in my tone.

"My advice is simple." I raised a brow in wait.

"Play the facts to your advantage, not as the disadvantage you feel it is."

"And how the fuck do I do that exactly?" I asked in what I knew was a disbelieving, sarcastic tone.

"Tell her that if she believes Raina is real, then this is her chance to pay off her debt for the crimes committed to our people, that she is charged with finding her." I narrowed my gaze even further.

"I am not loving this plan, brother," I warned dangerously.

"Yes, but this is the part you will start to like, for tell her she is to prove Raina is real and if not, then she will have to accept who she is to you." Now at this my gaze widened in surprise as I had to admit, this was getting closer to the outcome I hoped for. However, I did still have to remind him,

"That is all easier said than done, I am sure."

"I am sure patience is going to be needed on your side."

"I will fucking remind you of that if and when you are lucky enough to meet your fated, for then you can speak to me of patience when your Demon is riding you hard to fucking claim your woman," I snarled, making him shrug his shoulders.

"Noted." He released a sigh then and added,

"Look, make her your personal assistant so she never leaves your side. Spend every fucking second with her and cloud every thought she has about not being your Siren. Consume her every thought if you have to! But I am telling you, that trying to bombard her with the truth right now will only backfire if you don't first allow her the time to discover for herself that this girl Raina doesn't exist." Damn it but I fucking hated it when he was right and about this, well I hated it even more so!

"When did you get so wise, asshole?" I asked, making him grin,

"When I realized I had a dumbass for a brother and knew I had to step up if we were to succeed," Hel joked, making me growl now he knew my temper had cooled enough to save his head and that of his tongue.

"Oh, you will pay for that one in the ring, little brother."

"So, does this mean I will have to protect my balls?" My Demon's growl was my only answer to this before I admitted,

"Fine, I will do as you suggest and hope, in time, it is enough to make her see the truth, for I cannot promise lasting long without claiming her fully."

"Restraint, brother, practice restraint… after all, if monks can do it…"

"Fuck off!" I retorted, making him laugh before patting me on the back and offering me a,

"Good luck and don't forget, if you get desperate, there is always the fisting shuffle."

"Funny fucker," I commented, making him laugh as I walked back to my terrified girl.

At least now I knew why.

She thought I was to become…

Her Demon Jailor.

CHAPTER 28
PUNISHMENT
EMMELINE

I couldn't believe I was back on a plane already!

I had sworn to myself I wouldn't be on a plane again for as long as I could help it, well clearly, this couldn't be helped. Not considering I had just been drugged, kidnapped and was currently being held prisoner… *again.*

But then, one look at Kaiden and I would say that he was less than pleased to be back here playing this game of jailor again. Or was I wrong? This question came when I saw him speaking with his brother, and at the end of what had mostly looked like a heated conversation, something had just made him grin. Of course, seeing him smile was what I would have normally considered a gift, for he was incredibly handsome when he did. But as for this time, well I just knew with the way he looked back at me while doing it, that it most likely didn't mean good things for me. No, in fact, he looked as if it promised nothing but wicked things.

Which was most likely why, the second I saw him storming down the aisle with purpose, I stood quickly, wishing for my heels back once again. Gods, but he looked more intimidating than he had done back in that interrogation room when I had been chained to the floor. The sheer size of him had me swallowing hard and near choking on it!

But even when I took a fearful step back, he didn't stop. No, he just watched it happen and carried on. Now only stopping when I had no choice but to arch my neck back just so I could keep his face in my sight. His lips twitched as he fought a grin, as my small height obviously amused him.

"Am I under arrest or something?" I asked stupidly, making him smirk this time.

"Do I look like a cop to you?" was his cocky reply, and my own came shortly after,

"No, but you look like the badass who just kidnapped me."

"Then I am you captor once more, now sit," he stated, nodding to the sofa I had not long ago been sleeping on.

"What, no chains this time?" I teased, making his eyes dance with mirth before he asked,

"Do I need to put you in chains again?"

"No, definitely not," I blurted out quickly, making him full on grin this time without holding it back.

"Then it might be best not to give me ideas, little Halo... *for I remember how well you looked in them the first time,"* he said, adding this last part as a wicked and lustful whisper. Then he nodded again making me wisely sit, so as not to piss him off.

"Besides, it is not like you can go far at the moment," he added, motioning to the plane with a look.

"No and I don't fancy becoming an Emme pancake." At this he chuckled before sitting next to me, and after a moment of silence had passed, he asked,

"Emme?"

"It's what people usually call me... Emmeline can be a little long winded."

"I like Emmeline, it is a beautiful name," he told me, making me blush and shyly push a curl behind my ear. He watched the motion and smiled when it soon sprang free again. Then he reached out and did the same thing I had done, watching in what seemed like fascination, waiting for it to do the same as before.

"I have to say I am surprised," I admitted truthfully, as with him being so nice to me was messing with my head a little.

"Surprised at what?"

"That you're being so gentle with me," I admitted again. At this he finally broke away from watching my curls and gave me an intense look that made his green eyes turn darker.

"What did you expect?" he asked in what I knew could be a dangerous tone.

"I don't know, chains," I joked, making him scoff.

"They might yet still be in your future but as for being gentle with you, I am clearly not the ruthless bastard you thought me to be." At this I sucked back a quick breath and before I knew what I was doing, I reached for his hand. He looked down at me touching him and before he could say anything, I let my mouth do the talking.

"I never once thought you were a ruthless bastard to me, I just meant that after what I did… after what I didn't know I was doing… I mean, you can't imagine what I thought after seeing you… I was so scared you were going to hate me!" At this his hard gaze softened before he covered my hand with his own, capturing it and keeping it caged, dwarfing it in his massive paw.

He made me feel so tiny.

"I doubt there are many who could hate such an adorable beauty, even in my position," he told me, making me blush again.

"Thank you," I whispered in return, needing to escape his intense gaze by looking instead at our entwined hands.

"So, what will happen now?" I asked after another silent moment had passed between us. At this he released a sigh and started playing with my hand, turning it over so he could run a fingertip around in circles on my palm. Then he surprised me.

"You believe you are not my Siren, correct?" he asked,

making me wince, and I know he didn't miss the way I closed my eyes as I tried to hold back the pain for my answer.

"Yes."

"And you believe this other woman…" I quickly corrected him, knowing she deserved better than the way he made out she wasn't even real.

"Raina"

"Yes, Raina… you believe her to be my Siren, yes?" he asked, and I swallowed hard before pulling my hand free of his before uncomfortably agreeing again.

"Yes." At this his jaw hardened for a few seconds before he continued on.

"And the crimes committed against my people, our near exposure… you believe you need to be punished?" I cringed at this but was at least brave enough to accept it, so conceded again.

"I do." He nodded once as if he respected me for my honesty.

"Then your punishment will be of my choosing." I definitely gulped at that and pushed forward with my bravery, asking,

"W-w…which is?" At this he actually smirked, before telling me,

"You will spend your time proving that I am wrong and your claims that Raina is my Fated are true." I gasped at this.

"You…*you want me to prove that I'm not your*

Siren?" I whispered incredulously to which again, he grinned.

"If that is what you believe then you will have to try and make me believe it too," he told me, shocking me to my core. Was he for real?!

"I...I... don't know what to say," I admitted, making him simply shrug his shoulders and tell me,

"Unless you wish to give up this notion and trust that I do know who my Siren is." I braved looking at him then, only to find that he was serious.

"No, I can't let you do that... *I can't do that to you,"* I told him in what I knew was nothing but a sad tone, one that compelled him to give me a tender look in return.

"Then you will prove it and find her," he stated, making me take a deep breath before letting it go again.

"And to do this, will I erm... be given my own space?" I asked, knowing that being forced to be around him while doing this was going to be damn near impossible. For one, the more time I spent around him, the less inclined I would feel about actually wanting to find her! Especially as it was clear now that he still believed me to be his Siren!

"No," he stated firmly.

"No?" I questioned hoping for more... like a bloody good reason.

"You will do all of this by my side... *and in my bed,"* he added after leaning in and taking my hand back in his so he could pull me closer.

"No! I can't! To ask that is too cruel," I cried out after yanking my hand from his and shifting back away from him.

"It is a cruelty we both suffer if you do not," he informed me, and my mouth dropped open in shock. This made him continue further and by the end of it, I was wishing that he hadn't as it was also a cruelty considering how I felt about him.

"Try to understand, that to me, you are my Siren and until you prove otherwise, I will continue to act as such."

"But that's… you can't…" I tried to argue against him, but he reached for me, this time taking me by the tops of my arms, making it impossible to pull away this time.

"Do you know what would happen to deny me and my Demon your touch…? He believes, as I do, that you are our Fated and now that we have found you, neither of us will let go of what we feel so easily… he will crawl out of my skin without you close." I swallowed hard at the thought as I tried to see the dishonesty in his eyes where there was none.

"Trust me on this, just this day apart has proven as much," he told me, making me flinch. Finally, he let me go and gave me some much-needed space now that he had convinced me.

"So, you want me to find her and if I do, what then…?" I asked. And the whole sentence felt like trying to speak through acid in my throat… *painful.*

"Then you will be allowed to go free," he told me simply and again, it was anything but easy seeing as I loved him. But I couldn't tell him that. No, it would just give him more power over me and besides, I had a feeling that he already knew. Which was why this was most likely the worst punishment there was for someone in love.

I was to find my replacement.

"I would ask for your word but if it's anything like your brother's..." I let that sentence trail off, allowing him to make his own vow,

"I give you my word, if she is found and it is not you, then I will let you go," he told me, and I had to say I couldn't help but trust him in that.

"And as for sleeping in your bed, how can that possibly work?" I asked, knowing this was going to be a hard limit for me, seeing as I was already too close as it was.

"Simple, we continue as we have been," he told me as if this was the most natural thing in the world.

"But we can't..." I tried to say when he interrupted,

"I can promise that I will not claim you." I wished I hadn't winced at the disappointment I found in that, but I did, and fuck, but he didn't miss it.

"So, no sex?" I reaffirmed.

"No, pretty girl, no sex," he told me again, smirking this time, and I got the feeling in that moment that he was playing a game with me... *a very cruel game.*

"But that doesn't mean I will not get to touch you," he added quickly, making me shout,

"You can't do that!"

"I think you will find it is impossible to ask me not to, for it's like I said, in my mind I have already found my Siren, meaning you cannot be so foolish as to ask me not to touch her." I sucked in a harsh ragged breath, now feeling as if I couldn't breathe and close to having a fucking panic attack again. However, I took a few deep breaths and shivered at the intensity of his words. It was as though I was asking him not to breathe or something equally as impossible.

"So, I will what?" I asked on a quiet voice.

"I told you, we will live as we have been, with you at my side during the day and in my bed at night, it is that simple." Ha, but it was anything but bloody simple! Hence why I told him,

"It is anything but and you know it." Again, he shrugged his shoulders and said,

"Punishment is never easy to endure and is named such for a reason, little Halo." I shook my head and almost told him that punishment didn't also mean getting your heart ripped out right in front of you. But then again, pain was a big part of it, so maybe it was. Either way, this was going to be the hardest fucking thing I had ever done!

"Why are you doing this to me, Kaiden?" I asked, unable to stop myself. At this his jaw hardened and he told me firmly,

"You are my Siren." I shook my head and told him,

"I am not a selfish person." He frowned at this, making me go on to tell him,

"If I find her…"

"If?" He quickly picked up on my slip up. So, I closed my eyes and gritted out,

"*When I find her*… I will do right by you and walk away. Of that I can promise you."

"And as promised, *I will let you.*" At this I stood up and just before I walked away, needing to put space between us, I told him the truth of my heart…

"And that there is what makes it a punishment…"

"Of the worst kind."

CHAPTER 29

THE GAMES WE PLAY

Thankfully, after saying this, he gave me the time he knew I needed and only came to inform me when we would be landing soon. However, he still did so by placing a heavy hand on my shoulder as if he had the need to touch me riding him hard. But then again, I had written this reaction once before. And well, if he truly did still believe me to be his Siren as he said he did, then I knew he wasn't exaggerating when he told me his Demon would be urging him to claim me.

Which meant I was torn, as I knew when he spoke of his need to have me close it hadn't been done as a cruelty as I had originally accused him of doing. It was as he said it was, a necessity, or who knew what his Demon would do. Half of me, the wrong and dangerous half, wanted to push it and see what happened. But then the good girl in me was too terrified to. Because when I told him I wasn't a selfish person, I hadn't been lying. For no matter how hard this was going to be for me, I knew in the end, I would do right by him.

I would give him up if she came to claim him.

Gods, but I think I was even starting to hate this Raina!

But then that was the bitter green-eyed snake talking and I could only hope that when the time came, I had the strength to keep my word. I would walk away and Kaiden would have no other choice but to let me. But one look at him now and that day seemed a long way off as he seemed more like a man obsessed. His intense gaze never strayed from me for long. I could feel him watching me even when I was purposely trying not to look. It made me shiver and I held myself around the belly as if this would help in delaying my own need for him.

"Come, little one, it is time to situate you in my home once more, for your journey of discovery starts now," he told me, giving me his hand to take, and half of me wondered what would happen if I didn't take it. What would my punishment be then? Because I knew now that he wouldn't dare have hurt me, not when he clearly still believed me to be his Siren.

"And on this path of discovery, will I be given any help?" I asked as he walked with me from the plane and down the steps to where there was a line of blacked out SUVs parked waiting.

"You may have your laptop but that is it." I frowned and snapped,

"Oh, jeez thanks, why not take that from me and make me go real old school and just put me in a library?"

"I could take it all and just give you a phone book if you want to push it," he threatened as he opened the door for me, making me throw back,

"Wow, you really don't want me to find her, do you?" At this he grinned, then he placed a hand to my belly and pulled me back hard against him. Again, I was made to feel so small tucked against his massive frame and by being so close, he felt my arousal for himself as I shuddered in his hold. I knew that when I felt him grin against my neck before he told me,

"Ah, now she's getting it. After you, *my Siren.*" He added this last part to make his point, making me roll my eyes at him. Whereas secretly I loved how sure he seemed to be and was silently relishing in it, despite beating myself up over it in guilt. But instead of saying anything more, I looked to Hel who was currently making his way to his own car. He grinned at us and gave me a cocky salute when he saw me staring at him. That's when I looked back up at Kaiden over my shoulder and upon seeing his face, I knew I had no choice on the matter. Especially when he nodded for me to get in and warned,

"I will have no problem picking you up and putting you in myself. I see your defiance as nothing but a challenge, and little tip for you, pretty girl… us Wrath

Demons… *oh but how we do love a challenge.*" At this I quickly got inside the car, making him chuckle behind me before it was cut off when he shut me in. I then watched as he took long, determined strides round the front of the car towards the driver's side. After this he slid in behind the wheel. But as I glanced back at the plane, I narrowed my eyes when I saw boxes being unloaded from it, quickly prompting me to ask,

"What's in those boxes?" At this he started the engine and after donning a pair of dark aviators against the glaring sunlight, said,

"You shall soon see."

It was in that moment that I really started to panic, as I had a bad feeling I really didn't want to know.

A little time later, we were pulling up to the familiar sight of his home, stopping at the guard house, so he could make a point of saying,

"Bishop, this here is Emmeline Raidne, also known as my Siren. She is not to leave under any circumstances unless I am with her. Am I understood?" I visibly gulped at this, coming to understand that it was clear that Kaiden was taking no chances with my escaping again.

"Yes, my Lord Wrath," he replied with a bow of his head, obviously taking this order as seriously as they came.

"Good, now make sure my orders have been obeyed as Boaz assured me that he'd doubled the guard around the perimeter." Bishop nodded like a good little solider boy and the second Kaiden seemed satisfied, we pulled away, meaning I was now free to snap,

"Was that really all necessary?!"

"You ask me that after I finally discover your name only to find you gone before I am given the chance to speak it aloud in your presence?" I swallowed hard and didn't comment, making him scoff a sound in the back of his throat.

"Don't think by being back in my home you will be given a second chance at escaping me, for I tell you now, it will not happen again... *I have certainly seen to that,*" he warned, making me wonder what he had done. Besides, where did he think I would go if I did manage to miraculously escape? Because clearly, I wasn't very good at this 'being on the run' game. Which made me ask,

"How did you know about the caravan?" At this he raised a brow at me before he parked the car in front of the house. Then he stated simply,

"You should really open all your mail in future." At this he got out the car, leaving me to wonder what he had found exactly that led him to my nanna's holiday home, which was when it hit me.

"You went through my nanna's old mail, didn't you?" This was asked the moment he opened my door and instead of answering me, he reached across and undid my seatbelt.

"It matters little, for even if I found nothing in that little home of yours, we found your car and had you followed the moment you pulled off the parking lot." I slid from my seat to the floor and gasped when he said this, feeling shame the second I did as I knew what must have been witnessed. I again looked down, hoping to hide the shame in my gaze but like usual, he didn't allow this for longer than a few seconds.

"I am sorry I made you cry, little one," he told me after forcing me to look up at him, and I could see the sincerity in his alluring green eyes. Eyes that I could feel myself getting lost in. He could be so tender that it near broke my heart to know that I wouldn't have this for all time like I would have dreamed.

"You didn't make me cry… I did that… *I did all of this,*" I said, walking away from his tenderness before he snagged back my hand to stop me, making my arm stretch behind as he grumbled my name,

"Emmeline." So, I looked back at him and said,

"Now it's time I pay to fix it." Then I pulled my hand from his and continued walking until I reached his grand entrance, leaving Kaiden to curse behind me. After this he didn't say a word, but simply held the door open for me, waiting for me to precede him. And just like that, I was back and about to find myself a prisoner once more within its walls. Which was when I stopped abruptly before stepping inside and finally realized something.

"Oh wait, what about my cat?!" I shouted, feeling like the worst pet owner ever! At this Kaiden chuckled and told me,

"You mean, did I leave the little bugger to starve?" At this he picked up my hand and rubbed a gentle thumb over the bandage I now found there instead of the plaster. Now knowing that he must have been the one to care for it while I was unconscious.

"He was on the plane, although I cannot be certain that he will ever leave it." I laughed at this and when I tried to pull my hand back, he merely tightened his grip and silently refused to give it back to me.

"That sounds like, Roger," I commented in a quiet way, as what he was doing to my hand felt far too intimate for this conversation.

"I will have him brought to you, but any more scratches like this one and I will have his claws removed, understand?" I gave him wide eyes, trying to figure out if he was being serious or not… of course, *he was.*

"Or we could release him into the wild to become an overlord, ruling over all other wildlife, where he will then create an uprising against all mankind and make us his underlings." At this he threw his head back and laughed before hooking me behind the neck and pulling me in for a hug. Then he pulled my hair slightly, enough to get me to do as he wished and look up at him so he could reply,

"Then lucky for you, your man is already a Demon overlord." Then he winked at me, making me chuckle but more in a nervous way this time. As this was most definitely too intimate, especially when his brother walked past and said,

"Don't mind me, or all the men for that matter… however, I wouldn't recommend fucking on the gravel… it gets in all manner of places." Then Hel winked at me, making his brother groan.

"Although I might put him on cat duty, just for shits and giggles," Kaiden threatened, one aimed at the back of his brother's head as he walked inside.

"I heard that! Ain't fucking doing it!" I couldn't help but burst out laughing at this, a sight he seemed to enjoy seeing.

"Come on, my little runaway, let's get you settled once more," he said, before taking my hand and not letting it go again until we were back in the same bedchamber we had seemingly claimed as our own.

A dangerous thought indeed.

CHAPTER 30
POWERLESS

'*Then lucky for you, your man is already a Demon overlord.*'

These words played over and over in my mind and no matter how much I tried, I couldn't get them out of there or stop the incessant loop it seemed to be on.

'*Your man...*' this was what he had named himself, as though he was mine. Which meant doing research into trying to find another woman to claim him felt, as though I was going against some secret grain from some Gods be damn fated tree! It felt as if our souls were already entwined there for all eternity to do nothing but grow and grow together, becoming stronger with the gift of time.

Which was why, every time I wrote her name into yet another search engine, I was starting to loath the fucking name! I was starting to grit my teeth and tap on the keys as if they were foe, when once they had been a friend.

"Fuck it!" I snapped and slapped by laptop screen down, so it slammed shut. Then I heard Roger meow and I gave him my evil scowl.

"And you can be quiet on the matter." He looked at me from his new favourite sleeping spot, after claiming the plumpest cushion within seconds of being let out in here. Then he did that thing that baffled most people when their furry pets rose, turned around a few times and then flopped down in the exact same place they'd started off with, making us wonder what the hell was the point.

"And as for I… do I also have to be quiet on the matter?" Kaiden's amused voice filled the space, making me realize I was no longer alone. I swung my head around from where I lay on my belly on the bed and said,

"That depends, are you going to tell me I am wasting my time again?"

"Most likely, but then again, I'm a Demon and often like to walk that dangerous line." I couldn't help but laugh at this, reminding him,

"I threw a pillow at you the last time you said it, so I would hardly call that walking a dangerous line." He grinned at me in that playful way I had come to adore, making me often realize there were things about Kaiden I hadn't known and therefore hadn't written about.

He had never been playful with Raina.

"Yes, but add your cat to the mix and one of these days that pillow might come with claws." I giggled at this and again, it was a sight I knew he liked as his eyes always darkened when I did it.

"Then you will just have to keep me on your good side," I teased back, making him respond,

"As long as you're kept at my side, then you will find me obliging you in most things, along with being good... well, as much as can be expected," he added, making me smirk.

"Yeah, yeah, Demon... I remember," I said, getting there before he said it and making him shrug his shoulders in a nonchalant way. I got off the bed and was walking up to him when I started to say,

"You know you can't use that excuse for..."

"You look delicious tonight," he told me, interrupting my argument and making me blush like he knew he would.

"I... erm... I am just... erm..." I stuttered my words as I looked down at my clothes. I was wearing a pair of worn blue jeans that yes, admittedly, I kept around because they made my ass look way better than it did out of them. But to this I had just added a plain black top that had cute ruffle cap sleeves and a lower U-shaped neckline that allowed my black lace bra to play peek-a-boo over the edge.

It also had to be said at this point that I had undoubtably been dressing on the sexier side of the comfy casual scale, as well... I was only human. Which granted, also gave me just another thing to feel guilty about. As I may have continued to do my job in trying to research for his Fated Siren, but it didn't mean that I hadn't wanted to look as nice as possibly when doing it.

So, I found myself making more effort with my hair, or should I say, trying to tame it. I also exchanged my usual baggy writing attire for tighter, more form fitting outfits that showcased the fact I had curves instead of hiding them under layers. Something that didn't go unnoticed, as Kaiden never failed to mention how good he thought I looked. Something that I shamefully blushed at and secretly adored, despite knowing it was just adding to the list of 'Wrong thoughts' that was growing by the day. Just like every time I relished his attention, as every touch I received kept adding to my addiction and I became fearful that I would never have the strength to give it up.

But despite this internal battle, I still found myself pushing at it more and more before I would then mentally torture myself with guilt. Like the evening I 'got too deep in research' and he found me laying like I had been tonight. So, there I had been, laid out on the bed and on my belly, wearing the cutest PJs I owned. A pair of little black shorts that were most definitely showing off more of my bum than they should, but were cute as they had little honey pots all over them. Added to this was a yellow cami-top, one that *I knew without a doubt was definitely showing off more than it should*... but was even cuter as it had a flirty cartoon bee on the front with words that said, 'I can BEE your honey pot' underneath.

As for my mad hair, I had tied this up in a big bouncy ponytail, leaving some curls down to frame my face. A swipe of clear lip gloss had finished the look. Gloss that I had been in the process of licking off as it was strawberry flavour, when I heard the door open. However, being as I was totally engrossed in my work, I didn't look at him, just told him,

"Sorry I got a bit distracted but won't be long getting ready, I just need to finish… Ohh." This ended with me releasing a slight moan as I felt his fingers running along the back of my bare leg, tensing the moment I heard his rumble of words,

"You aren't playing fair, pretty girl." At this I bit my lip and instantly felt bad, as he was right… I had known I would get a reaction out of him for wearing this. Which was why my guilt made me react and I started pulling my leg up ready to move, telling him,

"I'm sorry… I should just leave…" I was cut off the second my ankle was shackled by his big hand, ceasing my escape. A growl followed as I was roughly tugged further down the bed, away from my laptop. Then, before I could make a move to try and get up again, I felt him leaning down over me. A heartbeat after this and I found myself quickly caged in with his fists either side of me, with his powerful build held suspended above my body.

"I think it's time to talk about the rules, Emmeline," he rumbled above me, making me shudder under him. Then I felt him run his nose up the part of my back that was exposed, before making his way across my shoulder blade towards my bare neck.

"First, you don't ever apologize for how fucking sexy you are, *do you understand?"* I sucked in a breath and held it prisoner in my lungs when he said this, one I only released again when I felt his teeth at my flesh.

"Ahh... ohhaaah." I felt him grin sadistically at my reaction, doing so still with my flesh held in his teeth before he let me go.

"Secondly, I like your voice, my Halo... especially seeing as along with the fucking gorgeous sight of you, it makes me hard. Therefore, if I ask a question, I expect to hear you gifting me with your words," he told me in that commanding voice of his, before showing me a tenderness by kissing me where he had bitten. But when I forgot to reply, he growled my name against my abused skin in warning.

"Emmeline."

"I'm sorry, what was the question again?" I asked in a breathy and clearly aroused way, one that made him chuckle.

"Too fucking cute," he muttered before saying,

"Tell me you understand my needs and demands of you." I nodded, making him bite me and growl,

"Make me hard with your words, girl."

"Yes! I understand, holy shit, but I really do!" I said when his bite got harder, making him release me on another knowing chuckle.

"Good girl," he rumbled in a pleased tone, now licking and sucking on my bite, soothing the slight sting he had ruthlessly made.

"Now, as for the third…" he said, taking a purposeful pause and making me tense beneath him. Then, before I had chance to question him, I was suddenly flipped around so I was on my back, and the intimidating bulk of him was looming over me, making me want to squirm like some frightened animal. He shifted so one forearm was to the bed holding the most of his weight, so he was free to fist a hand in my hair. It was only when captured like this that his Demon growled down at me. and it was a rule I would have been foolish to deny,

"You're going fucking nowhere!" After this he kissed me and I swear it felt powerful enough to burn me, scorch my insides and consume me in the flames of his desire. I was lost. A slave to both our sins combined. I wanted him as if my very life depended on it. For when his lips were on mine, I felt like the Hell I could be damned to was worth the crime a hundred times over.

That's how powerful his kiss was.

Hence why I was powerless against it...

Powerless against loving him.

CHAPTER 31
SILENT TREATMENT

That passionate, heart soaring kiss had been last night, and the second I felt it getting too close to reaching beyond that deliciously tempting point of no return, I pulled back. This naturally made his Demon growl but the moment I whispered,

"I'm sorry, but you know we can't," he rumbled his reply against my neck,

"Not yet but soon... very fucking soon, Emmeline." I shuddered at this, feeling the promise clinging to every word said and branded against my skin.

But that had been only one of many moments like this, as I swear, he was on some not-so-secret mission to tear down all my walls of doubt and guilt. Although saying this, I hadn't made it too easy for him, especially not when I soon discovered that I had my pick of outfits, considering all my possessions were now in his home!

Something I had totally freaked out about the second I was informed of this. Oh, and something he had just waved off as though it was nothing to have someone totally invade your space, box up your entire life and ship it to where you didn't want it to be!

This was also hence the reason I spent that night being a moody bitch… something he seemed to find extremely amusing.

Three nights ago…

"So, it is still the silent treatment I am to receive then?" he commented on the way to his club, which was the first time he had visited it since he had brought me back to his home yesterday. The only occasion he had given me time alone to think was just after we had arrived back at the house, although it was something I could tell he was not eager to do. It was also why I got the impression that this was something he had been advised to do by his brother, who seemed to be guiding him in all of this. Something that had become obvious after witnessing their heated conversation on the plane.

Yet, despite all of this, I still found myself waking up in his arms this morning, knowing that he had obviously hit his limit providing the time I'd asked for. I had just needed some space between us. Some alone time to think about everything and admittedly, this had also included having a bit of a cry in the bath.

Of course, it had done little to clear my head but hey, at least I smelled nice. But then beauty products hadn't been the only thing I found Kaiden had his people buy for me. No, now I had a whole new wardrobe to add to my own pathetic one and with more dresses in it that I was sure one person could even own. I think this was a not-so-subtle way of Kaiden telling me that he expected me to be sat by his side every night at the club. Not something I relished the idea of, considering I knew how hard it was spending the whole night with him constantly touching me in some way.

It was sweet, seductive torture.

But back to my freak out at finding all my stuff, as after that bath it was something I'd discovered when stepping inside the walk-in closet. Box after box, all labelled with my name and the room in which it had been packed from. It was my entire life wrapped up in cardboard and the second I saw it I let my head fall back and started to ask the Gods why this was happening to me?

Naturally, I had demanded to know what the meaning of it all was. Doing so when he had walked into the room, after the five seconds it had taken him to first inform me that we would be leaving for the club in an hour. Hence why my reply to that was,

"I am not going anywhere with you!" He chuckled

before snagging me around the waist, pulling me close and telling me in a condescending way,

"It's cute you think that, pretty girl"

"Don't you *pretty girl* me! I want to know what in Hell you think you were doing by having all my stuff packed up and brought here!"

"I knew exactly what I was doing, as it is now where it is meant to be," he told me without shame.

"But what about my flat?!" I asked with what sounded like some high-pitched wail even to my own ears.

"Condemned, if I had my wish," he muttered sarcastically.

"Oi! I heard that!" I snapped, making him grin.

"It's not funny, that place was my home, Kaiden!" I complained, still outraged. At this his jaw hardened and before I knew it, he was commanding my personal space by walking me backwards until my ass fell on the sofa and he was looming over me.

"No, Emmeline, that place was *not your home…*"

"But it…"

"It was an overpriced, five hundred square foot shithole, that had leaking plumbing, no security and barely enough room to store your shoes, let alone your clothes. It was also a place you had rented for a little over a year and picked solely for the reason it was cheaper than the place you last rented, to allow you more time to focus on your writing and self-publish your books." At this my mouth dropped open in shock that he knew all of this

about me. I also felt the heat of embarrassment invade my cheeks before I started to try and argue against all of this, starting with,

"How dare you! You can't…"

"Oh, you better fucking bet that I would dare to do anything when it comes to you, as I will not have my woman living another Gods be damned minute in such a place! Now you can be pissed with me all you want, for it will not change my mindset or my law."

"Your law?!" I shrieked, making him get even closer as his hands fisted the armrest and the back of the sofa, caging me in and making me sink back against the cushions.

"Yes… *My. Law*… The one that was made the moment I first walked in that interrogation room and met my Siren staring back at me. The one that states that, *you*... will be protected, *you*… will be safe and above all, *you will be cared for*… That, Emmeline is… *My. Law.*" He said this last part as a growl of words only inches from my face. Then he kissed me, making me cry out in surprise. Something he took as an invitation to sweep his tongue inside and taste both the shock and infuriation from me.

I don't know long it was before my mind started to catch up with what my body was doing, which was of course, letting him kiss me, but it was long enough to shamefully feel my arousal dampen between my legs. However, before I could come to my senses and slap him, he pulled back from my lips. Then, with his knowing grin firmly set in place, he gripped my chin and gave it a little shake before telling me in an arrogant, bossy tone,

"Now, you have forty-six minutes to get dressed." Then he kissed me once more, this time lasting only a few seconds before he was gone, making me mutter,

"That cocky bastard!"

His reaction to my complaints, and the demanding and forceful way he had dealt with it only managed to add to my foul mood. Which meant that to make a point, I spent this time scowling at the door and refusing to get dressed out of the PJs I had put on after my bath. Something he took one look at when walking back inside and when finding my obvious defiance, he simply smirked and shook his head to himself. Then, after making a show of looking me up and down in a slow and predatory way and obviously finding me still wearing my PJs, he informed me,

"If you think being dressed like that will prevent you from being by my side tonight you underestimate my position as leader here, for I am rather used to getting what I want, *Emmeline,"* he said, and I swear, why did he have to make saying my name like that sound like some sexual promise?

"Now, you have ten more minutes to get dressed or I will be walking you out of here wearing that and into my club... *pink fluffy kittens or not...* am I understood?" At this I turned my face away and didn't answer him, instead feeling him walk over to me, kiss the top of my head and said,

"My girl understands me." Then he left, making me want to throw something at the door. However, instead, I chose to run back into the walk-in closet and quickly get ready, throwing on an A-Line, red chiffon cocktail dress. One that swooped down into a plunging V-neck that I had picked to try and punish him. It was also knee length and crossed over under my breasts and tied at the back in a big ruffle bow.

Then I pinned my hair up in a twist of curls and set the record for quickest makeup application in history. I walked out just as he was walking back in, and this time there wasn't a fluffy kitten in sight.

Instead, what there was, was a heated gaze of lust from a man who looked as if all he wanted to do now was tear this dress off me and set the record for getting someone naked the quickest.

However, because I was still pissed at him, I grabbed a pointless bag that held nothing but a lipstick and some eyeliner in it. Then I stormed right past him, snapping,

"That was nine minutes, asshole!" I then ignored his booming laughter and kept walking, not stopping until I was at his front door. But this wasn't all I was forced to ignore, like how amazing he looked in his dark jeans and dark navy shirt, or the way it clung to his abundance of muscles. Or the amazing scent of his aftershave, and how I just wanted to bury my nose in his neck and breathe in deep. I also ignored the way he opened the front door for me or how he purposely placed a hand to my lower back, as if he needed the excuse to touch me.

Which then brought us to being halfway there, and again finding our means of travel another super expensive sleek car that just remined me of how rich he was. This was also the time he finally spoke, asking me if the silent treatment was his punishment. I made a humph sound and ignored the way his lips twitched as if he found this all very entertaining.

"Mm, I can already foresee tonight being interesting," he commented in an amused tone.

"In what way? Did you finally get your yearly supply of Viagra delivered?" I joked with a sneer, making him growl playfully,

"Behave, little Halo, or I will show you exactly why I don't need a fucking blue pill to aid me in putting you in your place."

"My place!" I shouted outraged!

"In my fucking bed beneath me, once and for all… yes, your place!" he snapped, making me back down from this conversation as I swallowed hard at how hot that statement made me.

"Interesting because like I said, I do enjoy a challenge and as always… *I rise to it.*" He added this last part with a grin looking down at his crotch making me do the same, seeing for myself the very obvious erection there half way down his fucking thigh!

"Fuck me! What the hell is wrong with you?! Christ, it's like a bloody weapon, what's your aim, to split me in two!" At this he chuckled before reaching across the centre console and taking my hand in his. Then while kissing it, he told me,

"Fear not, sweetheart, it will fit… trust me, you're perfect for me… *every inch of you,"* he said, making me blush at the compliment.

"Well, as nice as that is to hear, you messed up."

"And how is that?" he asked with a sexy raise of his brow.

"You just gave me something else to be terrified of," I told him, and I honestly didn't think I was teasing him this time.

"Emmeline…" My name came out as a purred rumble that I felt down to my strappy silk-covered toes.

"I would never do anything to hurt you," he told me softly, making me say,

"I know you wouldn't mean to but I…" He squeezed my hand again and interrupted me.

"I know it would be your first time and trust me when I say that I do not take such an honour lightly, which is why I would treasure your trust in me to do right by you," he told me in a tender tone, and I swear it was so sweet. It was also such polar opposite to how I had been treated in the past, or at least how I would have been treated had I been foolish enough to go through with it.

"Is there a reason you…?"

"Waited?" I finished off for him.

"I know, twenty-seven-year-old virgin, pretty pathetic, eh?" I said, making him growl.

"It is anything but pathetic! Do me a favour, Emmeline, *never say those words to me again,"* he all but snarled at me, making me flinch. I would have said something else, but I was too upset about being snapped at like that, so opted for the silent treatment again. Then about fifteen minutes later, we arrived, and Kaiden still looked beyond angry that I had said what I had about my virginity. I also had to say that we couldn't have arrived quick enough for me, as I had been wondering if the steering wheel was going to survive the rest of the journey.

Needless to say, it did, and soon I was having my door opened again, just like he had the first time he had brought me here. However, this time I ignored his hand, unfolded myself from the seat, and got out by myself, letting him know that I was back to being pissed off. He growled at me when I purposely bent over to retrieve my bag, telling me,

"It's not wise to push me or my Demon's limits, little Halo." Which was when I told him,

"Yes, well didn't anyone ever tell you, it's not wise to piss off a woman you're dating either!" Then I walked away, wanting to smack myself on the head when realizing my slip up. Which was why when we were in the elevator, I tried to cover it up, at the same time losing the heat out of my argument.

"I mean… not that we are dating or anything… I just mean for your future erm… endeavours." Okay, so this was the wrong thing to say, as suddenly I was in his arms and he was snarling down at me,

"Fuck future endeavours! You're the only one I want!" Then he was kissing me, and I swear everything in my crazy fucked up life felt complete! I was in his arms, being hoisted up to his height, despite my heels, and being held in place so he could have easier access to my mouth. And Gods, but didn't he just know how to kiss! Jesus Christ, it felt like he was taking my virginity without even touching me down there! He made it feel as if I was being owned. As though I was being claimed, breaking down my barriers against him, against every reason why this was so wrong.

I hadn't even realised we were on the right floor and the doors had opened, as we were both panting hard. He placed his forehead to mine and we continued to breathe as one, both of us fighting for restraint.

"I am sorry I shouted at you, little one," he told me after a moment, making me put my arms around his neck, hugging him while I could at the height he still held me at.

"I'm sorry, I was insensitive. I'm just embarrassed about it is all." I told him being honest and making him growl a little. Then he lowered me to my feet and cupped my cheek with his big hand.

"There should be no shame in the gift you will soon grant me," he said, making me suck in a deep breath before letting it go again on a sigh.

"Kaiden... I can't..."

"Hush now, no more talk of it. Let's go," he said, cutting me off and stopping me from saying what I knew he didn't want to hear…

I wasn't his gift to take.

CHAPTER 32
WHISKEY FLAVOURED GIRL

Naturally, after a kiss like this, my silent treatment didn't last. I did however continue to try and to pull my hand from his, only stopping after he tugged me into his body and growled, *"Behave, little Halo."*

"I just don't think we should act like a couple in public… What if Raina was to show up here… you know people could get the wrong…?"

"That is another sentence I recommend you not finish for I don't give a damn what people think. If they think of you as anything less than being mine, then they are foolish and risk encountering their master's Wrath!" he snapped as he tightened his hold on me as if to prove a point.

"Kaiden, please, we made a…"

"No, Emmeline, we will talk of this no more! Now

you will walk into my club by my side, with your hand in mine, or I will throw you over my shoulder and carry you in, the choice is yours, but I can guarantee more will talk if you choose the second… either way, I get what I want." I released a frustrated sigh and told him,

"You know you're not making this very easy on me." At this his eyes glinted with mischief and before I could try and make a move back, he stepped into me.

"I never said I would," he whispered dangerously. A statement that ended on a cry of shock as he picked me up and put me bodily over his shoulder.

"What are you doing!? Put me down, you bloody big Neanderthal!" I shouted, making me shake over his shoulder when he started laughing. Then, without an ounce of shame, he walked us both straight through the doors to his club, making even more of an entrance than what I had been concerned with just by holding his hand. There were some cheers and even some comments of encouragement from his loyal subjects who were known as regulars in his VIP, all of which made Kaiden reply in the same way.

"Mine!" I felt free to roll my eyes at this, considering the top half of me was hanging upside down and my only view was of Kaiden's muscular back. Which also meant that my only indication we were finally at his council table came when he had stopped long enough and I heard his brother's smug tone.

"I would ask where you picked this little mortal morsel up from but then she may try and kill me in my sleep," Hel remarked with a grin I couldn't see but knew was there all the same.

"Put me down right now or so help me, you will both die in your sleep!" I growled myself, making both Kaiden and his brother chuckle. Then I was gripped at the hips and purposely pulled slowly from his shoulder, and he made sure I slid teasingly down the length of his body. This meant that by the time I was back with my feet on the ground, I was left gazing up at him. No doubt granting him a look that was shamefully sexually frustrated, with my hair in what felt like a chaotic mess around me.

"I…I… you can't just… erm, you know… like that and stuff…" I tried to reprimand him, just needing something to say in reaction to the way he was looking down at me. Because he was seriously making me feel like a fish on the end of his hook just waiting for him to release me back into my natural environment. I almost felt the need to start gasping for air or something, as I swear he had the ability to just suck it all out the room!

He smirked down at me, clearly amused by my scrambling for words, and making it harder when he raised a hand to my hair and started playing with the escaping curls.

"Then I suggest giving me what I ask for the first time or you may not like my idea of an alternative." I gulped and he watched the motion of me swallowing hard with rapt attention, grinning when I did. Because everything about his expression told me that he knew what it was he could do to me.

"Which is why you have no doubt learned your lesson and will therefore not make a fuss when indulging me and my need for you… especially, *when I want your ass in my lap,"* he told me, getting closer and whispering this last part in my ear, at the same time pushing my curls back.

"I, erm…" was my uncool response.

"That's what I thought… now come, my good girl, for any longer with you staring up at me with those beseeching eyes of yours and I may be tempted to start the night off with the feel of your ass squirming against my dick." At this my eyes widened, and I instantly took his hand and made a point of pulling him to his seat quickly.

"And we are sitting down now… *in our own seats."* This made him boom with laughter, especially when he let me push him down into his own seat before I purposely made a show of taking my own. But then I also didn't miss the way the waitress named Katina glared at me as it was clear to everyone around, I was the one who had made Kaiden laugh.

"Katina, get a whiskey for our girl here," Hel demanded, and I couldn't be sure but it kind of looked as though he was making a point, as he seemed to notice her animosity towards me.

"Oh, I don't know if that's such a good idea, maybe

just a water for me," I said, remembering the last time these two got me drunk.

"Bring both, for if *my girl*, has a taste for whiskey, then she can drink it from my glass," Kaiden said, making a point of calling me his and being the cause of his brother's laughter. Katina gave him a fake smile at this before scowling at me, again something Hel didn't care for, as clearly, she was careful enough when Kaiden was looking but not his brother.

"Is there a problem?" Hel remarked, making her bow and say,

"No, my Lord, no problem."

"Then be on your way, girl," he replied with a nod, telling her basically to piss off, which thankfully she did.

"I think it's time to pick a new waitress for our table," Hel said as he watched her leave with an untrusting glare. Kaiden looked over his shoulder to glance her way before saying,

"It is harmless, I am sure." I looked at Hel who didn't say anything to this, but then again, he didn't have to, as his face said it all.

"Speaking of waitresses, if the rumours are to be believed, then the King of Kings has broken one of his own rules and allowed a mortal to work upstairs in his own VIP," the one named Teko said, who tonight was wearing an extravagant blue suit that had velvet black lapels and cuffs, with embroidered black flowers on the pockets. My eyes widened at this news, making me wonder if this meant he had found his own Chosen One.

Of course, this Fated girl wasn't one of the Lost Sirens, but she was in fact the one rumoured to kick start the chain of events with all other Kings finding their own Fated. Along with the Enforcers finding their own of course.

Well, one thing was for sure, she would have to be one hell of a brave girl. She faced a lifetime of being claimed by that ruthless, hard ass and brutal King, and he made Kaiden seem easy going compared to him. But then, this was also all just speculation from my point of view as I had only heard about Dominic Draven's existence through listening to Kaiden talk about his King through my dreams. So I had no real evidence to base this on. Which was why I found myself asking,

"Is he really like… erm…"

"How you have written him in your book?" Kaiden finished off for me.

"Yeah."

"He is a good King, fair but as brutal as a powerful being in his position needs to be. And if the rumours are true, then I am happy to hear that he will soon know the same joy that is felt when finally meeting one's fated Chosen One." This was such a tender admission and I couldn't help but say his name in an equally tender way.

"*Kaiden, I…* Argh!" I never got to finish as Katina had just heard this part when coming with our drinks, a tray she accidently… but I actually believe to be on purpose… spilt all over me. Thankfully, Hel's quick reactions meant he saved me from being smashed with the full bottle on my head, but couldn't also save me from the water or whiskey filled glass going all down me.

"Oh dear, how unfortunate," she said, sneering at me, making the two Wrath brothers get to their feet the second I did the same, now soaked to my skin. Kaiden took a furious step towards her, making her whimper back when his Demon growled angrily. His body had also started to change into his Demonic side, as one moment I was looking at smooth skin and the next, sharp jagged rock-like horns were bursting out up his neck. I tried not to react, already knowing this about Kaiden and his brother, seeing as they were the same Wrath Demons. But even I had to admit that no amount of dreaming about it had prepared me for the sight.

The rest of his skin also took on a darkness that surrounded the crimson horns, reminding me of cooling, blood lava. His skin mottled in patches as his Demon's form continued to ripple its way up his neck and to the side of his face, where smaller spiked horns pushed their way through. His eyes turned completely black with no white to speak of, making it look frighteningly like you were staring into two pools of oblivion. Crimson veins branched out like tiny bolts of red lightening, framing the edge of his face and around his eyes. His hands also changed, with spikes replacing the knuckles and dark, red talons pushing their way through his now blackened skin, over human nails.

Hence why I could see this escalating quickly, especially when Hel grabbed Katina roughly by the arm, after first slamming down the bottle on the table in his own anger.

"It was an accident! She flung her arm out and made me drop it!" she shouted, trying to defend herself by blaming me. I mean seriously, did this Demon chick have no brains? At this, Kaiden was seconds from losing himself completely to his own Demon and before I let that happen I decided to act, doing so in the last way people would have expected.

I started laughing.

Hel looked around in a slow, comical way as if asking himself if he was really hearing this right. Then I made a show of stepping up to Kaiden and after walking my fingers up his chest, I spoke to him in what I hoped was my most sultry voice.

"Hey baby, let's go to your office…" I paused, raising up on tiptoes and cupped the side of his face in a careful way so as not to cut myself. This was so I could get all his Demon's attention, something that was achieved quickly as the second he felt my touch, his intense gaze found my beseeching eyes. They started to glow almost immediately, and I swear, I didn't know whether to run in fear or jump on him and beg him to claim me in this terrifying form. In the end, I chickened out doing either of those things, and instead went with what I hoped was the more seductive route. Which was why I whispered up at him in a suggestive tone,

"I am all wet, after all." I finished this tempting offer by winking up at him, and biting my lip when I saw the sheer shock in his Demonic eyes at my brazen behaviour. Then, without waiting for an answer, I entwined my fingers with his, being careful of his claws, and squeezed his solid hand a little before leading him from the seating area.

And amazingly…

His Demon let me.

So, seeing as I knew the way, I continued to lead Kaiden out of the VIP but couldn't help glance back towards his brother. I hadn't known what to expect but what I saw was obvious shock from everyone, as all of Kaiden's council watched us leave in utter astonishment.

I continued to lead him to the lobby area, amazed that he still let me guide him to where I wanted him to go. It was as if he was locked in some kind of trance and in that I felt kind of powerful, knowing that I was capable of taming this terrifying Demon.

After turning around a corner, we made our way up the few steps it took to get us to get to the level of his office. Then I let myself in, continuing to pull him with me and as the doorway was about to close, he snapped a hand out and held it. This was so it didn't have the chance to split us up but as I looked back, I now noticed the wood had given away and splintered under his Demonic grip. Deadly talons had left long thick gouges in the panel, and I gulped at what they had the power to do to flesh.

I looked up into his intense dark gaze, one with no green left in sight. But instead of recoiling back in fear, I reached out and grabbed his shirt, using this to aid me in getting him inside quicker.

"Come on, gorgeous, let's close that door, should we?" I said, making him look to his hold on the door as if he had only just realized that's where his hand was and why it hadn't yet closed after us. But my voice was obviously continuing to have this strange effect on him, and he let the door go before allowing me to pull him all the way inside his office. Then, as soon as I had accomplished this, I blew out a breath of relief knowing the hardest part was over… *or was it?*

Because now with the way he was looking at me, well damn, but I was starting to feel like a giant cooked chicken did to Wile E Coyote. Of course, it most likely didn't help that my dress was wet through, clinging to each curve. It was completely plastered to my body and my skin still dripped with whiskey… *his favourite drink.*

Which was most likely why, when I tried to pull my hand free of his, he refused to let it go. So, my gaze snapped back to his, and I muttered under my breath the moment I saw the burning lust there making his eyes glow,

"Oh shit… okay, Kai… just take a few deep bre…

Whoa!" I shouted the second he growled at me, which became my only warning before he yanked me to him and kissed me senseless. But the sharp press of his horns against my skin became less and less as his Demon side started to seep back beneath his handsome host. However, his hold on me wasn't any less brutal. His embrace quickly escalated to him kissing his way down my neck and licking the skin on my heaving breasts, making a meal of his whiskey flavoured girl.

"Oh, Gods..." I moaned, letting my head fall back at how good that felt but then he was pulling down hard at the strap of my dress, clearly intent on freeing more of me. However, just before I could stop him, he tore down the cup of my bra, at the same time banding an arm around my waist. Then he lifted me up so he could easily latch his lips onto my nipple, which had me quickly crying out his name.

"Kaiden, ahhh!" After this he started walking us towards his desk, still lifting up my breast so he didn't need to leave his bounty as he obviously knew where he was going. Seconds later, and my ass came into contact with wood before he was using his big hands to urge my legs open.

"Kaiden we... we can't... ahhh fuck!" I ended this plea on another cry, when he growled over my nipple before rolling it around in his teeth.

"You're all mine! *Every last fucking inch of you!"* he snarled, after soothing the sting with his tongue and nipping his way back up to my neck where he sucked on one of the marks he had made, doing so in a possessive way that drove me crazy! He then lifted up my skirt and the second I felt his fingers bite into the lace of my knickers, I put a hand down there to stop him, ignoring his forceful growl.

"But we can't... *you... you promised,"* I told him, making him relax his fingers from tearing the material of my underwear. Then I felt him release a sigh before telling me,

"Yes, but I didn't promise I would not crave to touch you and this here, my Halo, this is time for me to sate that craving and... *time for you to scream for me.*" Then he went back to my breast and dipping his fingers under the lace of my knickers, before he gathered my arousal and used it to coat his fingers and the folds of my sex. However, the second he started to rub that wonderfully, sensitive bundle of nerves, I only lasted little over a minute before I was crying out my orgasm.

"KAIDEN!" I screamed his name as I came, quickly soaking his hand. But then the sexiest, hottest, dirtiest thing happened when he pulled his wet hand from under my knickers. After letting my nipple go, he used his hand to coat that same, abused breast with the release of my orgasm, now adding a new flavour to my skin. Yet, before I could shy away from this dirty act, he gripped my hips and yanked me hard to the edge, into his hard but covered cock. He then lapped up my wet release off my breast like some starved wild beast, biting, sucking, licking and nipping at my flesh and as before, paying special but brutal attention to my nipple.

By the end of it, I was shamefully rubbing myself against the bulge in his jeans so much, I ended up bringing about my second orgasm and amazingly this time, I wasn't the only one!

Kaiden threw his head back after letting my breast go so he could find his own release from having me rubbing myself against him, practically trying to ride him through the denim. The sound of his roar was deafening but worth every second it lasted as it was the hottest damn sound I'd ever heard!

I felt the wetness seeping through the material and once the euphoria had died down, I couldn't help but wonder what we would do now. Because I was still soaked through, and now in more ways than one as Kaiden had a big wet patch on his jeans from both of us. Meaning it would have made it more than obvious as to what we had been doing in here. Now, he may not have had a problem with this, but I did, because the second emotion was starting to hit me as usual and that was…

Guilt.

But despite this, I still released a contented sigh. Especially now with Kaiden's forehead held to my bare shoulder as he continued to breathe me in deep, as he too came down from his sexual high. I naturally let my hand go to his neck so I could rub soothing circles there, needing him to know what this time had meant to me. Because I didn't want to sully it by telling him how wrong it had been, when in reality, it had felt nothing but right. But then, knowing how much I loved Kaiden, it wasn't surprising that I felt this way, as it was just a shame that it also came tainted with the guilt it was coated in.

"Soon, Emmeline... soon I will have you, for you must know this." I shivered in his arms at the obvious vow in his words, making him tense his muscles in response.

"You must be cold, come on, I have something you can wear," he told me, making me pull back and unable to stop myself from snapping,

"If this is the leftover spoils of some past lover's conquests, then I think I will pass." At this he pulled back, and after first seeing that I was serious, he burst out laughing before cupping the back of my head and pulling me into him for a hug. Then he told me,

"I don't fuck in my club." I swallowed hard and braved pointing out,

"But you wanted to fuck me."

"Yes, I want to fuck you... but I want to fuck you anywhere and everywhere I can," he replied, making me draw in a quick breath in reaction to how much these words affected me.

"So, it's not exactly a strict rule then," I commented in a slightly high-pitched tone, just needing something to say. At this he laughed again and told me with another squeeze,

"When it comes to fucking and you, my Fated, there is only one rule."

"And that is?" I dared to ask, making him reply beautifully,

"...There is only you."

CHAPTER 33

LEATHER PROMISES

"There is only you."

Admittedly, these were four more words for me to obsess over. As shortly after that, I discovered the extra clothes he was talking about, were in case he accidentally hulked out in his Demon form and ripped his shirt. Hence the need for spares.

However, he didn't just change his jeans, he also took off his shirt and handed it over for me to wear. I naturally questioned this, especially after he opened the door to a built-in closet, and I saw a line of shirts hung there. Which was when he snagged the front of my damp dress and pulled me into him, making me near stumble a step. Then he tipped my chin up and told me with a deep rumble of words,

"I want my girl smelling of whiskey, sex… *and me.*" I

swear the guy was trying to make me melt to the floor in a puddle of lust!

"*Okay,*" I replied with a shy whisper, as I pushed my hair behind my ear. But this made him react in a strange way, as he fisted my hair, put his nose to my cheek and growled,

"*Fuckable and adorable... you kill me, woman.*" Then he let me go and turned his back, so he could concentrate on getting changed. I was left a little dazed by his reaction, and had to shake myself from the exhilaration and sexual thrill he kept giving me with every compliment he bestowed. I also wisely took this opportunity to change out of my dress and into his shirt, doing so with my back to him.

I did this quickly but couldn't help but take in a deep breath of the shirt before putting it on, finding that he was right, it smelled of sex and him. It also admittedly looked more like a dress on me. However, the second he turned around to look at me, I held my arms out to the sides to show him how big it was. He smirked down at me now looking lost in the tent of his shirt before a full grin was on the verge of making an appearance. It was clear he was trying not to laugh, but at the same time, he seemed to enjoy seeing me like this, especially when he decided I was to become his little doll.

This started when I tried to roll up his sleeves that were well past my hands, something he took over from me. Then he reached back inside his closet and pulled free a leather belt.

"If your shirt doesn't fit, I don't see that... oh..." I ended this complaint when he held up a finger and his Demon side aided us in providing the means of making an extra hole. After this he wrapped it around my waist. Then he purposely pulled the end through the loop with enough force that I felt lassoed enough to go stumbling again into his body.

"Well, look at that, *it fits,*" he teased, making me giggle. A sound I could tell he liked... well, if the tender, warm look he gave me in return was anything to go by.

"So it does, now if the scent is to your liking, shall we go back in there and try to order the whole 'drink thing' again?" I said, trying to take a step back but seeing as he still had the long end of my belt in his fist, I didn't get far.

"I won't be letting that bitch anywhere near you again... but as for the scent of you, you are most definitely good enough to eat." He said the first part with venom, and the second as a heated growl that was spoken in my neck after pulling me the last few inches that had been between us.

"I think you practically did that already," I replied when he gave me enough space after first kissing my love bite. Then, to make my point, I rubbed over my tender bitten breast causing him to grin.

"But you were right, it was no doubt harmless," I said, referring back to the waitress. Because despite her obvious jealously, the worst that had happened was me getting wet, and that wasn't something I thought she should lose her job over. Clearly, Kaiden felt differently about this.

"No, I was wrong and once again my brother's powers of perception were not to be ignored."

"Kaiden, I don't think..."

"But I do think, Emmeline, and as master and ruler of this sector, I will be the one who makes decisions on how those who try and harm what is mine will be punished."

"Punished?!" I screeched, making his jaw tense as clearly he was not happy with my interfering. I knew that when he snapped,

"Yes, *punished!"*

"But for what offence, spilling a drink on me?!" I asked incredulously. At this I watched as his hand fisted harder around the leather, making it groan this time as if this was helping in keeping his temper in check.

"No, but for the bottle that was aimed at your head and the real reason that accident happened, one that thankfully my brother was ready for and therefore it saved you the injury... *or worse.*" He added this last part with a grit of his teeth, making me sigh.

"So, you do think it was on purpose?" I asked, now letting my frustration deflate somewhat, as even I had suspected the same thing. But then, I guess I never thought much about the bottle or it smashing over my head as being the real reason for it to happen.

"Absolutely," he replied with a growl.

"Well, I guess that is reason enough for someone to lose their job then," I admitted, making him groan my name,

"Emmeline."

"What? Oh wait, this is something I don't want to know, isn't it?" I said in response, knowing that Kaiden wasn't the type of ruler to let something like this go with just a warning.

"Well, ignorance is bliss for a reason," was his reply, making me shout,

"Yeah, no shit… I still remember your prison!" To this he smirked and finally let go of my belt, now offering me his arm instead. Hence why we walked out of there with me wearing a shirt as a dress and him now in a dark green shirt and black jeans. Oh, and both of us smelling of whiskey, sex and a hot-blooded Demon named Kaiden Wrath.

Although, this was not before he lifted up my dress from the desk where I had left it and said,

"Now I have the first in what I am hoping will become my collection of conquest spoils from the only girl I want to fuck." I blushed at this and as a way to mask my embarrassment, I slapped a hand to his chest and said in an overly dramatic voice,

"Oh baby, but you do say the most romantic things!" At this he laughed, tagged me at the back of the neck and warned,

"Keep calling me baby in that sexy fucking voice of yours and we will be right back in there on my desk for round two." At this, it was my turn to smirk, and I kissed him on the nose before walking away with a sway of my hips, muttering to myself loud enough for him to hear,

"Promises, promises."

His booming laughter was heard long before we finally reached the VIP.

That had been three nights ago, and each night I had ended up in bed with him after we had driven back from the club. As for Katina, she had naturally disappeared and had been quickly replaced by another. A girl called Sally, who let's just say, was overly friendly with me and well, after what the Demonic grapevine must have said happened to her predecessor, then I couldn't say that I really blamed her.

Which meant there were no more 'whiskey' incidents to happen at the club, nor were there anymore dresses to add to his 'conquests collection'. But this wasn't to say that there weren't any more moments of heated, sexual tension between us. In fact, there were a lot of these, as it was clear the more time I spent with Kaiden, the more his desire for me grew. Growing to the point, in fact, that he could barely keep his hands off me. Which for me was like the sweetest torture, as I both craved these times and feared them. Because I knew that at some point, I would be forced to give them up and the thought was becoming more painful by the day.

But these nights at the club seemed to be the routine of things, making me realize why he spent so much time at the penthouse apartment that had featured so much in my book. But this did then make me wonder why I hadn't yet seen it. Often asking myself if the reason was because it had appeared so much, and he was trying to draw some invisible line between it and me? Did he not want me to think of it as being a place him and Raina spent most of their time?

I had braved asking him one night if he had ever read the book and his answer was a short, clipped,

"Yes Emmeline, I read it."

After this he hadn't said anything more and I hadn't had the guts to ask. But this wasn't the only thing he didn't want to talk about, as whenever I brought up Raina, he shut it down quickly. It was always, 'not now' or 'we will talk about it later', something we never did. In fact, I felt as if I was doing all this research for no good reason at all. As though it was just something to keep me busy, while he himself was doing the opposite, by trying to prove every theory I had wrong.

In truth, I had thought I was really on to something one day, finding her initials combined with her last name at some logo design company. But the moment I had handed over the information when we were at the club,

Kaiden had tensed his jaw, and looked to his brother. Then Hel had rang their 'tech guy' Franklin, and within seconds, he shook his head at his brother.

"It isn't her," Kaiden had told me before downing his drink and that was that. No explanation. No questions asked. It was just a simple, nope, you're wrong. So, naturally, I found this extremely frustrating, despite finding solace in the fact that if she hadn't been found, then it didn't yet mean it was time for me to say goodbye. But like I said, I was constantly in a state of being torn between right and wrong. Yet one look at Kaiden and it was clear I was the only one left feeling this way.

But then he was a Demon prince and well…

Sin was basically in his DNA.

CHAPTER 34

TOASTING FOOLS

Back to present day...

Good Lord, but would I ever get used to seeing him and resisting the urge to drool? Like tonight, wearing a black shirt that did little to hide the delicious contours of so many muscles, it was hard to focus on just one at a time! A pair of grey jeans, shit kicker boots and sleeves rolled up the forearms completed the look, as his Viking style hair remained as it usually did. In fact, to date, I hadn't yet seen it down, making me wonder if I ever would?

It was the fourth night since I had been back and yet again, I was ready for him. I was also understanding the need for so many dresses now. Although, I wasn't sure how much longer I could keep up with the pace, as I was sleeping later and later these days. Which also meant that my days were all merging into one, as I would wake surrounded by everything that was Kaiden. Then I would spend time trying to convince myself I wasn't getting even more obsessively in love with him, even though I clearly was. Then, when he would tell me he had work to do, I would be left to do my own thing, which was up until now, seemingly utterly pointless.

But then, it wasn't as if this was all I did, as I too continued to work and therefore unbeknown to Kaiden, earn a living. As let's just say, that I had a feeling I would need it. Besides, I no longer had any rent or bills to pay, so thought it was a good time to try and recoup some of my losses from the two expensive flights that took a massive hit to my savings… as in, *destroyed most of them.* Because, as much as it seemed like Kaiden was in no rush to be rid of me, I knew that the possibility loomed around the corner like some dark Demon hiding the truth.

Ready to spring on us a Devil in heels.

Raina.

I pushed this thought from my mind and concentrated on the evening ahead, which, as usual, came in the form of me standing in front of Kaiden wearing yet another dress. Tonight's choice was a peacock blue satin dress that had an asymmetrical skirt. One that reached the floor at the back but was shorter at the front, reaching inches above the knee. It also flared out around my newly shaved legs, and the sweetheart neckline with thicker straps allowed me to wear a bra.

There was also a thick band under my bust that was filled with clusters of beaded crystals that were all in peacock colours. This matched the shoes and bag that I had forgotten to pick up, hence why I told him,

"I will just get my bag." I turned around and was just about to walk in and retrieve it, when he suddenly took my hand, stopping me,

"You won't need it," he told me, making me frown in question.

"Aren't we going to the club?" I asked.

"I have other plans for us tonight," he replied while brushing back some of my loose curls behind my ear, as was quickly becoming a habit of his. It was one of the reasons that I had only pinned back one side, as I knew he liked it down. He liked it free to play with, he told me one night as he rid me of my pins.

But he would do this in bed some nights, as we lay facing each other. Usually with me telling him some silly story and making him laugh or chuckle, while he would play with my hair as though it was something he adored doing.

Consequently, this was yet another reason why each day was getting harder and harder to be around him. It was becoming impossible not to just want to lose myself in all that was Kaiden Wrath. He was like my Achilles heel, kryptonite, and Pandora's box all rolled into one. And I actually think he knew this, as I swear his aim was to try and tempt me as much as humanly possible. Like when he would purposely take off his shirt before getting into bed. I didn't know if this was just so he could see my flushed cheeks as I struggled to keep my eyes off him. He had certainly looked amused by my reaction to him every time. But I also wondered whether it was done so he could feel me next to his bare skin at night, as he would often comment on this as being his favourite part of the night… *being skin to skin.*

It was also why sometimes I would feel my pyjama top being lifted enough so he could feel my bare back to his chest, doing so when he thought I was asleep. However, despite this, he remained true to his word and kept his boxer briefs on and hadn't touched me again sexually since the last time in his office.

But like I said, that didn't mean that he had kept his hands off me, or his lips for that matter, as he seemed to be on a mission to kill me from sexual frustration. And this coming from the one who didn't even know what I was missing out on. Of course, I hadn't exactly needed an imagination to know that what I was missing out on was something big. Quite literally, if the massive outline of his cock against his jeans was anything to go by!

Gods, but no wonder I was scared of it. Yet, despite this, that totally irrational side of me also wanted it like I had never wanted anything in all my life. Because I knew that he was right, somehow, we would just fit, and it would have been perfect… *I knew this.* But I also knew that's what made it a line I could not cross. Because if I did… if I ever gave in to that temptation, then there would be no coming back from that.

That would have been the point of no return.

He would have had every last piece of me and that kind of power, well, it would have been strong enough to utterly destroy me when his true Siren finally did come around.

I wouldn't survive it.

"Come, it will be ready," he told me, making me pout and say,

"Well, as long as it comes with food, as you haven't fed me yet." He chuckled at this and said,

"You make it sound as if you are some pet of mine." I laughed and countered,

"Yes, and you make it sound as if you like the idea." To which he just winked at me before whispering in my ear,

"Well, I do still have my chains."

"Then I suggest you take up gardening and make some hanging baskets out of those bad boys," I replied, making him again throw his head back and laugh heartedly, as he led me from our room and through his home.

"I will use them to decorate my walls if you carry on," he told me making me grin.

"Well, if you like that type of dungeon décor, each to their own," I replied in a teasing way.

"And just what do you think I will put in them to decorate my wall, Emmeline? For it won't be fucking flowers, I can promise you that," he growled playfully before nipping at my neck and making me turn around and swat him on the arm.

"Behave, you brute!"

"With you in my life, not fucking possible, woman!" he replied making me grin. Our good-humoured banter continued on like this as he led me to the back of the house and this time, out onto a covered patio area where there was a feast laid out for us. There was also plush, comfortable seating around a little fire pit that just invited you to want to stay the night.

It was all lit up, giving the night a warm glow but not too much that you couldn't still appreciate the glowing flicker of the flames from the centre of the large marble table that was big enough around its edges for food and drinks. The rest of the space was an arc of sofa style seating, facing out onto the view. One that was dark right now, with only a line of tall iron lanterns lighting the pathways beyond. However, having already explored this mansion and its now well-guarded grounds, I knew that under the sunlight, this was a blanket of lush green grass framed by thick woodland and manicured gardens towards the house.

"Oh, wow, this is so romantic!" I couldn't help but cry out in excitement, taking his hand and now pulling him over there quicker, making him chuckle at my eagerness.

"I am happy you are pleased, little one."

"This is perfect! Look how cosy it looks and oooh

pizza, my favourite!" I shouted, clapping to myself, as well… clearly, *I was easily pleased.*

"I know," he said, giving me a tender look and I couldn't help but give him one of my own. Then I asked him,

"You did all of this for me?" This was referring not only to the food but to what I knew were the vases of white flowers, candles and fairy lit trees that created a canopy of twinkling lights above.

"Well, I…" he started to say when another voice interrupted him,

"No, he had all his people do this for you. But it's the same thing in my book, or should that be, in yours, Emmeline?" Hel teased after coming around the corner, making me grin before saying,

"Well, I don't care who did it, the thought of it is what is perfect!" I said, making Kaiden grip my hips and pull me back against his chest. This was before he wrapped his arms around me and nuzzled my neck, now telling me softly,

"You're welcome, pretty girl."

"And that right there is my cue to leave, brother, enjoy your night off, won't you." Then he winked at us both, making me chuckle with a shake of my head.

"Why do I get the impression this doesn't happen very often?" I commented.

"You mean trying to impress curly little blondes that hiccup when they laugh." I grinned and argued in vain,

"I don't do that!" Because yeah, *I totally did that.*

"And I suppose you would wish me to believe you also don't talk in your sleep or make a meal out of licking your fingers clean after you eat," he replied, making me jerk and tell him,

"Well, I most certainly don't do those things." He chuckled at this, kissing the top of my head and said,

"Yeah alright, little Halo, if you say so." I then bit my lip to try and stop myself from smiling as I loved that he was always picking up on these little things I did or habits I had.

"Come and sit with me… please, eat before your pizza gets cold."

"Well, I don't need telling twice," I said, patting my belly and making him shake his head as if he didn't know what to do with me. Well, I had my ideas but all of them were forbidden, so eating pizza it was.

"Extra cheese, no garlic?" I asked.

"But of course," he replied making me grin.

"Champagne?" he asked, pulling a chilled bottle from an ice bucket and making me say,

"Oh, but you are good."

"I do try," he replied with a cocky grin, and I felt like telling him that he didn't need to try at anything, I was already his in my heart. *I just wasn't allowed to be.*

The sound of the cork popping jerked me from my thoughts, making me quickly wish that this night would never end… or should I say, *would end the way I wanted it to.* The way I knew he wished it could end. Gods, but how I wanted to give him that. Give him what I knew was only ever going to be his to claim. Because after all of this, even when I was forced to walk away, I knew there was no moving on from this. There was never going to be some, 'and they lived happily ever after' with my name written in the book.

There was just…

The End.

"Emmeline? Is something wrong?" Kaiden asked, jerking me from my sad ending.

"Oh no, nothing, I just… this, it's just… it's all so perfect and well, no one has ever done anything like this for me before," I admitted, making him scoff.

"Then another fool's mistakes are for me to gain, as my victories for your smiles are worth all the effort and are therefore gift enough," he said, handing me my glass and making me lean into him.

"Thank you, that is also one of the nicest things I ever had said to me." He grinned down at me, making me chink my glass to his so I could toast him.

"Then here is to all the fools and not taking away this perfect first for me." He gave me an affectionate look in return, and told me,

"Now that, I know, is the sweetest thing I've ever had said to me and most definitely something worthy to toast to, indeed."

After this we enjoyed our meal together and soon the

evening was lost to stories told and chuckle-filled banter. It was without a doubt, by far, the most romantic night I had ever experienced and the very best of dates. But it was more than that, as it also made me wonder if this was what it would be like living here and spending our nights together? Would we often find ourselves sitting out here by the fire, snuggled up together, me nestled against his big body with his arm curled protectively around me? Would our nights be as they have been, spent in each other's arms, feeling like we were the luckiest people alive just because we were blessed with finding each other?

Because it felt fated.

Gods, could I be wrong, or did I just want to be?

"Come, it grows cold, and I don't want you catching a chill," he said, caring for me and making me tell him,

"You know, I think that's an old wives' tale."

"Yes, but I will not take that chance with my mortal pet," he teased, making me fake being insulted, something he laughed at when I stuck my tongue out at him.

"I also have very firm ideas on what you can do with that tongue, so careful when showing it to me, for I might think of it as an invitation." He winked before more laughter followed when I sucked it back in, popping my lips closed. He then pulled me up and before I could take a step, he suddenly swept my feet from under me and started carrying me into the house.

"You know, last I checked, my feet worked just fine, and well, even my legs aren't that bad at walking too."

"But they are so little," he teased back.

"Yeah, and oh what would you know, they kick just fine too, want to put me down so I can show you?" I joked, making him chuckle.

"And they call me a Wrath Demon to be feared," he said wryly, making me giggle this time, something that didn't last long when I realized we weren't headed back to our room.

"Hey, where are we…?" I ended this question the second I saw him heading towards the one place I knew I couldn't go.

The line he wanted to cross…

And the point of no return I knew we couldn't pass…

His bedchamber.

CHAPTER 35
FEARING CRUEL FATE

"K*aiden, please... I can't...*" I started to say when he let my legs slip from his grasp, putting me down and making me wonder if they had the strength to work like I had convinced myself they could. But he took my hand and led me into the room, making me struggle against him, pulling all my weight back. But he continued on, making sure I had no choice, telling me,

"No, Emmeline, your time is up, and I am done waiting." At this I pulled my hand from his and ran to the door, just as it closed without him even touching it.

"Really, we are going to do this again?" I asked with my forehead held to the door.

"You cannot fear this room anymore," he told me, making me whisper,

"Why not?"

"Because it is where you are meant to be," he replied, making me close my eyes and sigh, still refusing to move from the spot.

"Kaiden, please… *you know that's not true,"* I tried again.

"No, all I know is that you're afraid." At this I turned around and faced him, doing it this time with my anger, flinging my arms out and shouting at him,

"Of course, I am! I am fucking terrified!" At this he folded his arms and asked,

"I told you I would not hurt you, why don't you believe that?" I started to shake my head at this, as he just didn't understand. Which is why I decided to educate him.

"Because pain isn't always physical… don't you get that?"

"Oh, I get that, Emmeline, I am fucking living it!" I gasped at that and put a hand to my chest as if he had inflicted some internal wound.

"But you don't want to hear that, do you? You only want to focus on what this is doing to you, when you know nothing of my own pain!" he snapped, making me throw some cruelty back his way.

"So, it's all about sex, that's what this is about? The fact that I haven't let you fuck me yet… that I am just a fucking conquest to be won!?" At this his Demon growled low and in warning.

"Careful, little Halo, for your words are putting you on

dangerous ground," he threatened, making me lose my shit!

"Yeah, and just what are you going to do about it, Kai? Lock me up in one of your cells?!" He narrowed his eyes at me when I said this, before throwing back,

"If it would work in making you see sense, then I would be fucking tempted!"

"Oh yeah, and just what sense is it you think I need to find Kaiden?" I asked in a sarcastic tone he tensed his jaw at.

"A sense of truth, for you have lost your curly little mind if you think all I want from you is sex!" he replied, and I sneered at him.

"Then why are we in this room, huh?" I pointed out, making him groan in frustration before he snapped,

"Because claiming you has nothing to do with just fucking you, and everything to do with making love to the woman who owns my heart and my soul, doing so for the first time in my bed." I gasped at hearing this, letting the tears finally find their way to my eyes, because I knew the mistake he was making. The mistake I had let him make in thinking it was me.

"I can't listen to this," I muttered, but he wouldn't stop.

"Making love to my woman for the first time and claiming her in the same bed and all nights after it." This made me start shaking my head, telling him firmly,

"I don't want to hear this!"

"No, of course you don't, no what you want to do is run from it. Because it's safer that way, isn't it… isn't it…? *Answer me!"* he shouted and I caved. Making all my defences come crashing down, cracking my heart wide open, so that all that was left was the core of me, free to come pouring out.

"YES! Are you happy now! Yes, it is fucking easier… easier than the possibility I could wake up one day and find out that it's not me! That it's not me that should be living this perfect dream! This perfect life that I am so beyond fucking desperate to hold on to, because in it is you… you are at the core of it all and I have never wanted anything so badly in all my life, Kaiden… *never wanted anything... but you.*" I whispered this last part on a broken cry as I poured my heart out. Something that made him close his eyes, as if he were absorbing every single fucking word of it, as if he was feeding from some kind of elixir of life. As though my words had been some soothing balm for his ragged, tortured soul.

Then he opened his eyes and told me,

"Then all you have to do is take it… fucking take it, Emmeline, it is all yours… I am yours! *Don't you get that!?* Please, just take what I offer you, pretty girl and give yourself to me, I just want it all… *can't you see that?"* This time, the honesty in his words made me cry harder and I had no choice but to talk my way through my tears.

"I can't… oh Gods, Kaiden, please, you're killing me here…" I said, trying then to get away from him when he closed the distance between us. But he wouldn't let me. Instead, he took my face in his hands and said with a growl of words,

"Then we die together and let the sins of loving one another be our only undoing!" Then he was kissing me and before I knew what was happening, he picked me up and carried me over to his bed. I pulled away and started to panic again, but he was right there, telling me,

"No, Emmeline, no fear… just look at me and have no fear… don't fear our destiny… *don't fear our fate, my Siren,*" he whispered, putting his forehead to mine as he continued to walk us both to his bed. I nodded against him, letting my tears fall and soak droplets into his shirt, knowing that I had to trust him.

I had to finally trust him with my heart.

"Gods, but you are so beautiful, it makes my heart ache, for you have no idea what it is you do to me, do you?" he asked the second he placed me down. I blushed and squirmed under the heat of his gaze. So, I told him,

"Come kiss me and I might find out." At this he grinned and lowered himself over me, making me wonder if this was it… if this was finally going to be our time. I wanted to, more than anything, but I knew there was no coming back from this.

And he was right, I couldn't fear it.

I couldn't fear my fate any longer.

So, this time as he started to kiss me, I let him continue until we were both burning up inside. And suddenly I was the one trying to tear his shirt off over his head, doing so to help him get naked as quickly as humanly possible. Naturally, this made him chuckle.

"Calm for me now, there is no rush."

"Seriously, you tell me this now." He laughed and told me,

"I want to savour you, every fucking second of you, I want it to last a lifetime, starting now." I swear but this man was going to kill me with his tenderness.

"Okay, so you do make that sound better." At this he winked at me, before he sat back, so he could take the time to look down at me. I couldn't help my heart from pounding, making me breathe heavy ,and his eyes drank it all in. But I wanted more, so I pinched on the front of his shirt, tugging it a little this time, telling him in a shy tone,

"Take it off." At this he smirked down at me before obliging my whispered demand. And once again, this man was awarding me the sight of that incredible body, this time inch by delicious inch as he undid his buttons one by one. Then he parted the material and I swear it was as if he was opening the curtains for the Gods, as he was breath-taking. I couldn't help but lick my lips, making him chuckle as he pulled the rest of his shirt from his shoulders.

"You know not how it pleases me to know you like what you see," he told me, and I answered honestly,

"I doubt many wouldn't like what they see, Kaiden, you're gorgeous." His eyes heated at this, glowing with an even greater intensity.

"I care little for the thoughts of others, especially when there is only one mind I want my image to consume… *my image and my heart,*" he said, making me melt again as I bit my lip to stop it from trembling. But just as soon as I had captured it between my teeth, I let it go again, this time on a moan of pleasure. This was because his hands had started to skim along my thighs, taking with it my skirt, lifting it higher and higher.

"Gods, but how long I have waited, yearned and craved for this moment," he said with his eyes darkening as each creamy inch of me was revealed, until I had no choice but to lift up my arms as he removed the rest of my dress.

"Fuck me, Emmeline, you're stunning… just… *utter perfection,*" he whispered, making me blush and it was one I knew he saw spread out over my breasts this time. He skimmed the backs of his fingers along the heaving mounds of my heated flesh, as now I was left in nothing but my black lacy underwear set. But soon his touch turned from a gentle caress to his full palm stroking over the quivering flesh of my breasts, a pair that were straining against the material due to my heavy breathing.

"Gods in Heaven, but I am going to fucking worship you, girl!" he told me on a growl before lowering himself down and kissing me senseless! I could barely think of anything but the way he made me feel as he was right, it was not only his image that consumed my mind.

It was everything that was Kaiden Wrath.

After he had finished overwhelming me with his kiss, he moved quickly on to my neck and down to my breasts, making me cry out in an awakened euphoric gasp, now pressing myself up to his touch.

"Yes, Gods, Kaiden… yes…!" I said before grabbing his hair and pulling it from its leather tie, letting it spill around him and finally awarding me with the sight for the first time. Gods, he was beautiful!

A wave of silky-smooth strands combined with the few rough twists of dreads filled my hands as I fisted it, making him growl the second I forced his lips back to my own. He growled again as I fought him for what I wanted, making me say between kisses,

"I can't wait… I want you… want you… so badly…"

"Then you shall fucking have me… every fucking day, every fucking night… I will be yours, Emmeline… as you are already mine!" he told me, and I was crying out the moment I felt my underwear ripped from me, knowing that this was it. I was finally going to be his.

I was to be claimed.

I felt his jeans open and just as I was about to feel that

steely length held at my core, the door was ripped open, and our beautifully raw moment was stolen.

"Oh shit!" Hel said, whereas it made his brother roar and snarl at him like a wild beast…

Like a Wrath Demon,

"GETTTT OUTTTT!" I shook beneath him, but he covered me like I was some possession of his he would fight to the death over.

"I am sorry, brother, fuck, you don't know how sorry I am, but it can't wait!" Hel said, looking pained before turning away from his brother. However, Kaiden looked like a man possessed, so I reached up and touched my hand to his cheek.

"Hey, it's okay, I am not going anywhere, baby," I cooed making him growl down at me, before suddenly he was kissing me, this time more as a way to say sorry, because it ended with his forehead to mine.

"I will kill whoever is responsible for ruining this," he vowed.

"Please don't because then you would get all bloody and that's a turn off," I teased, making him scoff,

"There are many ways to kill a man without getting blood on you."

"Okay, now that, there, is definitely a mood killer." At this he finally chuckled which ended on a sigh.

"I will be back for you." I nodded but it wasn't enough for him.

"Tell me you will wait for me."

"I will," I agreed with words this time but still he wanted more.

"In this bed, Emmeline, I want you to remain in my bed." I nodded again.

"Because this is happening. There is nothing in our way, which means there will be no turning back from this now, do you understand?" I put a hand to his cheek again and gave him not only what he needed to hear but also, what I needed to accept.

"Yes, Kaiden, I understand, which is why... *I will wait for you.*" He released another sigh and finally seemed to let my words sink in. Then he kissed me once more and got off the bed, telling his brother,

"You'd better stay facing that fucking wall!"

"Yeah, last time I checked, I didn't have a death wish, Kai," Hel replied dryly. I quickly grabbed the sheets and covered myself up, before Kaiden came to me and slipped his shirt over my head. I mouthed a thank you up at him, making him run the backs of his fingers down my cheek.

"Now you can tell me, what the fuck is the meaning of this?!" Kaiden snapped when he left me, making his brother finally turn around to face him. And I had to say, I had never seen Hel looking so... well, *so distraught.* His brother looked totally shaken and whatever it was, I knew it was serious.

"Not here, brother, Non est in oculis eius," *(Translated: It is not for her eyes,)* Hel said, ending this in what sounded like Latin. Naturally, I didn't understand it but whatever it was, it caused Kaiden to look back.

"I won't be long, my Siren," he told me as if this was the last thing he wanted me to hear before he left. As if he needed me to accept the claim finally.

"I will be here," I replied, making him nod once in return. Then, after grabbing another shirt, and doing up his jeans, he followed his brother out the door. I shifted to the edge of the bed and pushed all my hair back from my face, feeling my hands shaking as I tried to get past the fear that something major was wrong. What if the King of Kings had heard about me and Wrath was in some kind of trouble for it?

Gods, but I would never forgive myself!

I had to force myself to stay there, as he had asked me to but after about two minutes of worry, instinct took over all else. Because the moment I heard an almighty roar of anger, I could no longer do as I had been told. No, instead, I bolted for the door, knowing something must have happened.

This was confirmed when I saw both Kaiden and his brother standing in the hallway with their backs to me. But even without seeing his face, I knew something was really wrong. I could tell with the way his muscles were straining against the material of his shirt, as Kaiden looked to be barely holding in his Demon. But I was more concerned with the person they hid in front of them, someone who stood a little further down the hallway with their back to us all.

"How did this happen?" Kaiden gritted out in anger.

"She came to the club asking for you, told me some girl reached out and was trying to find her. She told me she has been dreaming of you and when Emmeline reached out, she knew then that it was all real." The second I heard this I gasped, and my hands flew to my mouth, making Kaiden's snap back to me.

"Fuck!" he hissed before raising his hands towards me, as if he didn't want to frighten me. But this only ended up making it worse because as he turned my way, there was no chance to save me from the sight beyond him.

Not when she too turned to face me.

"Oh shit," Hel muttered, at the same time Kaiden growled my name in warning as he could see what was coming next.

"Emmeline… no… no… *don't you dare fucking run!"* I started shaking my head, walking backwards as only one name came from my trembling lips. And it was in that moment the very last name I ever wanted to hear spoken from my own mouth came out as a whispered nightmare.

The very last name I wanted spoken in my new living dream.

Because that would mean one thing… *one devastating thing.*

This was now my painful reality.

This was my cruel fate.

This was…

"Raina..."

To Be Continued In…

Emme's Enforcer
Lost Siren Series
Book 4

ACKNOWLEDGEMENTS

Well first and foremost my love goes out to all the people who deserve the most thanks which is you the FANS!

Without you wonderful people in my life, I would most likely still be serving burgers and writing in my spare time like some dirty little secret, with no chance to share my stories with the world.

You enable me to continue living out my dreams every day and for that I will be eternally grateful to each and every one of you!

Your support is never ending. Your trust in me and the story is never failing. But more than that, your love for me and all who you consider your 'Afterlife family' is to be commended, treasured and admired. Thank you just doesn't seem enough, so one day I hope to meet you all and buy you all a drink! ;)

To my family…

To my crazy mother, who had believed in me since the beginning and doesn't think that something great should be hidden from the world. I would like to thank you for all the hard work you put into my books and the endless hours spent caring about my words and making sure it is the best it can be for everyone to enjoy. You, along with the Hudson Indie Ink team make Afterlife shine.

To my crazy father who is and always has been my hero in life.Your strength astonishes me, even to this day! The love and care you hold for your family is a gift you give to the Hudson name.

To my lovely sister,

If Peter Pan had a female version, it would be you and Wendy combined. You have always been my big, little sister and another person in my life that has always believed me capable of doing great things. You were the one who gave Afterlife its first identity and I am honored to say that you continue to do so even today. We always dreamed of being able to work together and I am thrilled that we made it happened when you agreed to work as a designer at Hudson Indie Ink.

And last but not least, to the man that I consider my soul mate. The man who taught me about real love and makes me not only want to be a better person but makes me feel I am too. The amount of support you have given me since we met has been incredible and the greatest feeling was finding out you wanted to spend the rest of your life with me when you asked me to marry you.

All my love to my dear husband and my own personal Draven… Mr Blake Hudson.

To My Team…

I am so fortunate enough to rightly state the claim that I have the best team in the world!

It is a rare thing indeed to say that not a single person that works for Hudson Indie Ink doesn't feel like family, but there you have it. We Are a Family.

Sarah your editing is a stroke of genius and you, like others in my team, work incredibly hard to make the Afterlife world what it was always meant to be. But your personality is an utter joy to experience and getting to be a part of your crazy feels like a gift.

Sloane, it is an honor to call you friend and have you not only working for Hudson Indie Ink but also to have such a talented Author represented by us. Your formatting is flawless and makes my books look more polished than ever before.

Xen, your artwork is always a masterpiece that blows me away and again, I am lucky to have you not only a valued member of my team but also as another talented Author represented by Hudson Indie Ink.

Lisa, my social media butterfly and count down Queen! I was so happy when you accepted to work with us, as I knew you would fit in perfectly with our family! Please know you are a dear friend to me and are a such an asset to the team. Plus, your backward dancing is the stuff of legends!

Libby, as our newest member of the team but someone

I consider one of my oldest and dearest friends, you came in like a whirlwind of ideas and totally blew me away with your level of energy! You fit in instantly and I honestly don't know what Hudson Indie Ink would do without you. What you have achieved in such a short time is utterly incredible and want you to know you are such an asset to the team!

And last but by certainly not least is the wonderful Claire, my right-hand woman! I honestly have nightmares about waking one day and finding you not working for Hudson Indie Ink. You are the backbone of the company and without you and all your dedicated, hard work, there would honestly be no Hudson Indie Ink!

You have stuck by me for years, starting as a fan and quickly becoming one of my best friends. You have supported me for years and without fail have had my back through thick and thin, the ups and the downs. I could quite honestly write a book on how much you do and how lost I would be without you in my life!

I love you honey x

Thanks to all of my team for the hard work and devotion to the saga and myself. And always going that extra mile, pushing Afterlife into the spotlight you think it deserves. Basically helping me achieve my secret goal of world domination one day…evil laugh time… Mwahaha! Joking of course ;)

Another personal thank you goes to my dear friend

Caroline Fairbairn and her wonderful family that have embraced my brand of crazy into their lives and given it a hug when most needed.

For their friendship I will forever be eternally grateful.

As before, a big shout has to go to all my wonderful fans who make it their mission to spread the Afterlife word and always go the extra mile. Those that have remained my fans all these years and supported me, my Afterlife family, you also meant the world to me.

All my eternal love and gratitude,
Stephanie x

ABOUT THE AUTHOR

Stephanie Hudson has dreamed of being a writer ever since her obsession with reading books at an early age. What first became a quest to overcome the boundaries set against her in the form of dyslexia has turned into a life's dream. She first started writing in the form of poetry and soon found a taste for horror and romance. Afterlife is her first book in the series of twelve, with the story of Keira and Draven becoming ever more complicated in a world that sets them miles apart.

When not writing, Stephanie enjoys spending time with her loving family and friends, chatting for hours with her biggest fan, her sister Cathy who is utterly obsessed with one gorgeous Dominic Draven. And of course, spending as much time with her supportive partner and personal muse, Blake who is there for her no matter what.

Author's words.

My love and devotion is to all my wonderful fans that keep me going into the wee hours of the night but foremost to my wonderful daughter Ava...who yes, is named after a cool, kick-ass, Demonic bird and my sons, Jack, who is a little hero and Baby Halen, who yes, keeps me up at night but it's okay because he is named after a Guitar legend!

Keep updated with all new release news & more on my website

www.afterlifesaga.com

Never miss out, sign up to the mailing list at the website.

Also, please feel free to join myself and other Dravenites on my Facebook group

Afterlife Saga Official Fan

Interact with me and other fans. Can't wait to see you there!

facebook.com/AfterlifeSaga
twitter.com/afterlifesaga
instagram.com/theafterlifesaga

Also by Stephanie Hudson

Afterlife Saga

Afterlife

The Two Kings

The Triple Goddess

The Quarter Moon

The Pentagram Child - Part 1

The Pentagram Child - Part 2

The Cult of the Hexad

Sacrifice of the Septimus - Part 1

Sacrifice of the Septimus - Part 2

Blood of the Infinity War

Happy Ever Afterlife - Part 1

Happy Ever Afterlife - Part 2

The Forbidden Chapters

*

Transfusion Saga

Transfusion

Venom of God

Blood of Kings

Rise of Ashes

Map of Sorrows

Tree of Souls

Kingdoms of Hell

Eyes of Crimson

Roots of Rage

Heart of Darkness

Wraith of Fire

Queen of Sins

*

King of Kings

Dravens Afterlife

Dravens Electus

*

Kings of Afterlife

Vincent's Immortal Curse

The Hellbeast King

The Hellbeast's Fight

The Hellbeast's Mistake

*

The Shadow Imp Series

Imp and the Beast

Beast and the Imp

*

The Lost Siren Series

Ward's Siren

Eden's Enforcer

Wrath's Siren

Emme's Enforcer

*

Afterlife Academy: (Young Adult Series)

The Glass Dagger

The Hells Ring

The Reapers

*

Stephanie Hudson and Blake Hudson

The Devil in Me

OTHER AUTHORS AT HUDSON INDIE INK

Paranormal Romance/Urban Fantasy

Sloane Murphy

Xen Randell

C. L. Monaghan

Sorcha Dawn

Kia Carrington-Russell

Sci-fi/Fantasy

Devin Hanson

Crime/Action

Blake Hudson

Mike Gomes

Contemporary Romance

Gemma Weir